Praise for the novels of Jan Coffey

"This book's timely subject matter, explosive action and
quirky characters make it a splendid read.... Coffey weaves
a swift, absorbing tale, complete with fully formed
characters and playful romantic banter."
—*Publishers Weekly* on *Triple Threat*

"With enough twists and turns to keep you guessing from
beginning to end, Jan Coffey will delight."
—*Romantic Times BOOKclub* on *Trust Me Once*

"Jan Coffey...skillfully balances small-town scandal and sexual
intrigue with lively plotting and vivid characterizations in
this engrossing romantic thriller."
—*Publishers Weekly* on *Twice Burned*

"Fantastic...a nail-biting, page-turning thriller with the most
charming romance thrown in! Definitely a keeper!"
—*Philadelphia Inquirer* on *Trust Me Once*

"An all-consuming, passionate, and gripping story!...
Make a note to yourself to pick this one up.
You'll really be sorry if you miss it."
—*Romance Reviews Today* on *Twice Burned*

"Coffey skillfully combines chilling realism with genuine
humor and a terrific romance. *Fourth Victim* is an
excellent read, guaranteed to keep readers guessing—
and staying up really late."
—*Romantic Times BOOKclub*

"Well paced, suspenseful, and sometimes startling,
Coffey's latest unexpectedly pairs a mystery filled
with graphic violence and explicit sex with a sensitive love
story...An intense, compelling story that will keep most
readers guessing until the very end."
—*Library Journal* on *Twice Burned*

"For a tense, edgy, wholly convincing story combined with a
heartwarming romance, I highly recommend *Fourth Victim*."
—*Romance Reviews Today*

JAN COFFEY
SILENT WATERS

MIRA

ISBN 0-7783-2319-6

SILENT WATERS

To our Taft '05 Sons—
Arrin Alexander, Spencer Clark,
Ryan Cleary, Patrick Coleman, Bruno Daniel,
Matthew Davis, Camden Flath, Javier Garcia,
Freddy Gonzalez, Jake Hammer, Wesley Hung,
Minkailu Jalloh, Patrick Joseph, Will Karnasiewicz,
Cory Keeling, Christopher Lacaria, Jason Lam,
Seth Lentz, Mike Negron, Sean O'Mealia,
Cameron Picton, Will Sealy, Jeremy Tretiak,
Thomas Wopat-Moreau, Joel Yu
and
Cyrus McGoldrick

May your day be filled with blessings
Like the sun that lights the sky,
And may you always have the courage
To spread your wings and fly!

One

Electric Boat Shipyard
Groton, Connecticut
Monday, November 3
3:50 a.m.

They emerged from the black water of the river thirty feet from where the rain swept the shore. Like primordial beasts rising from the deep, the divers turned their heads to take in the surroundings.

The wind whipped across the dark waters, the swells rising up to meet the rain and the night. The leader looked at the huge steel doors of the shipyard's North Yard Ways. Then, silently, they moved as one behind him toward the building.

Close to the doors, the leader's feet touched the sloping concrete on the river's bottom. To his right, he could see the submarine tied to the far side of the wide, flat concrete pier. USS *Hartford* glistened in the floodlights and the icy rain. A single crewman stood on top of the curved hull, huddled against the black sail.

Together, the group waded without making a sound beneath the huge doors overhanging the water. The rain beat against the steel walls, pellets of water ricocheting off hollow tin.

Inside, the shipyard's cavernous building was dark and empty. The metal skids coming out of the water disappeared up the incline into the darkness, re-emerging a hundred yards up, beneath dim amber floodlights.

Before the intruders had a chance to leave the black water, though, a door opened halfway up the Ways. Two security guards entered, silhouetted by the amber light in the distance.

"Jeez, do you think it could rain any fucking harder?" one of them said as he unsnapped his orange rain gear and shook the water off.

The other guard muttered something and reached inside his coat for a smoke.

The group standing in the shallows halted. When the two men turned their backs, the leader slowly lowered himself back into the water. The rest followed suit. He looked at his watch—3:53.

"I'm really hoping it'll be a landslide," the guard said as he took a cigarette from his friend. "I hate that last-minute shit with Florida and Ohio deciding the future for everybody else in the country."

"I never thought there'd be a day when I'd agree with you about friggin' politics." He lit a match and held it out for his buddy. Their faces glowed in the light of it. "But, for chrissake, these last four years of Hawkins in the White House has been a waste of jobs, lives and every other goddamn thing this country stands for."

The intruders were thirty-five yards away.

"I warned you at the last election that Hawkins would screw the pooch before he was done."

"Look, I wasn't the only one fooled. The guy was elected legally, wasn't he?"

"Not by the popular vote."

"You're not going to get on that soapbox about electoral and popular votes again, are you?"

"You bet I am. I'm telling you, in spite of all our big talk about democracy in this country, not you or me or any other individual has a fucking word to say about who gets elected president."

"No. You're talking out of your ass...."

As the two argued, the leader of the intruders motioned to the two men on his right. Silently, the pair stripped off their tanks and moved through the water until they reached the concrete wall. Using the darkness behind them, they emerged from the water and edged along the wall toward the guards, whose argument was rising in intensity and volume.

"...don't have to reinvent the friggin' wheel just because the past four years was a mistake."

"Hawkins isn't the only president who's wormed his way into office."

Six feet away, they drew their knives.

Two

Electric Boat Shipyard
4:01 a.m.

Cutting like a razor, the wind tore up the Thames River from Long Island Sound, driving the freezing rain into the submarine commander's face.

Standing for a moment by his car, Darius McCann looked down at the mist-enshrouded shipyard as he adjusted his hat and buttoned up his raincoat. The smell of the changing tide bore into his senses. There had been a time not so long ago when this scene and the anticipation of the upcoming patrol would have excited him, energized him. But not today. At least, not at this godforsaken hour.

He shook his head. It was the day. It was his age. He was forty today. Another milestone. Another step closer to the grave.

He'd achieved every goal in his five-year, ten-year, twenty-year career plans. For what? His personal life sucked. He was forty years old and alone. No wife, no kids. Nothing of the everyday routines and the closeness that was the very essence of the way he'd been raised. That all traced back to his job. Six months away at sea at a time, sometimes longer. Coming ashore only to start all over again. This time, he had just a few weeks ashore.

And here he was looking at some dark shipyard at four o'clock in the morning on his birthday.

His own sourness was in itself sobering—a slap of reality regarding what a miserable bastard he'd become. McCann ran a hand down his face, trying to brush away the rain, along with the feeling of gloom and doom.

He reached inside the car and grabbed his coffee and briefcase before locking up. He took a deep breath and shifted his attention from inside to outside, to the job that he'd signed on to do. The job that had to come first.

There were only a dozen cars scattered around the parking lot. Floodlights positioned on tops of tall poles and on adjacent buildings cast an amber glow over the cars. The security cameras were plainly visible. Since 9/11, even the defense contractors had smartened up. They were watching everything a little better now.

A squall of rain blasted McCann as he wove his way through the restricted navy personnel lot and descended to the road that ran along the front of Electric Boat. Across Eastern Point Road, just inside the high chainlink fence, a neat line of administration and engineering buildings formed the public face of the shipyard.

You couldn't see it from the street, but beyond them, down the side of the steep hill to the river, a jumbled mix of buildings—brick, cement, wood and steel—

formed an entire city. A rabbit warren of lanes and alleys threaded between machine shops and warehouses. Various trade huts and fabrication shops huddled against the huge steel buildings that housed the Ways, where subs in the earliest stages of construction were built. All along the riverfront, shops crowded the ends of piers and docks, and even barges held three-story work spaces—all for the thousands of tradesmen who had been building the navy's subs since the days of Teddy Roosevelt.

This was his life, McCann reminded himself. With each step, he buried deeper his discontent and focused more on what was required of him.

There were few sounds of work coming up through the wide chain-link gates tonight. Since the end of the Cold War, the need for new subs had dramatically decreased. Electric Boat's third shift was now merely a formality, and as McCann approached the main gate, the smell of burnt steel on the cold wind and the sound of heavy HVAC units running on the buildings were the only signs of anything going on below.

A solitary coffee-and-sandwich truck was parked on the side of the road, and McCann glanced at the driver who'd dozed off inside the cab. Gusts of wind continued to blow against his back as he headed down the hill toward EB's main gate.

Across the street, the windows of the bars were empty and dark. Open to a steady stream of business until two o'clock in the morning each night, they'd be open again at 8:00 a.m. sharp. One day, out of curiosity, McCann had gone into one of them, a place popularly known as the Sink. A half hour before the shipyard whistle blew the signal for the noon "dinner," the bartenders were busily lining up mugs of beer six deep on the heavily marked bar. It was a constant source of surprise to the commander that *any* work got done after the yardbirds had finished drinking their dinner.

Not that submariners were exactly teetotalers, he thought. In fact, he could have used a shot of something strong himself right now. Anything to jolt his system back into gear. He entered the covered passageway that all pedestrians entering the shipyard had to pass through.

Behind the plate-glass windows of the security station, five armed security guards were visible, and one of them stood by an open door waiting to check badges. Another stood behind him.

As one of the guards came out of the booth and stood on the first step, McCann transferred the coffee into his briefcase hand, unbuttoned his raincoat and pulled it open to show his badge. "Commander McCann, USS *Hartford.* You're doing some work on her."

The guard glanced at the gold dolphins pinned to his chest, at the identification badge, and then at McCann's face before looking down at the clipboard. "Can you spell your last name for me, sir?"

He did, and the guard scanned a list.

"It might be at the top," McCann said dryly.

"One moment, sir." He backed up into the booth and said something in a low voice to an older security guard who was sitting behind a desk. The older man looked at McCann through the glass and picked up a telephone.

McCann felt the first prickles of annoyance beginning to rise under his collar. The second annoyance of the morning, he quickly corrected himself. The first had happened when his X.O. had called an hour ago asking McCann to go in for him.

The entrance passageway was acting like a wind tunnel. McCann took a sip of his coffee, but it was already cold. He dumped the entire thing in a trash can next to the door.

"Is there a problem?" he asked shortly.

The younger guard looked through the door. "No, sir. Just give us a second."

Another damp gust of wind blew through him. His pant legs were already soaked, and feeling cold, he buttoned up his coat. The hill running down to the docks was deserted, with the exception of a few security guards walking up toward the gate. The work being done on his ship was considered an emergency, though, and the yard management had promised to bring in a special crew for it. McCann hoped they were already here.

The older guard in the booth was still waiting to talk to someone on the phone. Another level of management. More bureaucracy than the navy.

Another guard, bulked up in his winter rain gear, appeared at the other end of the passageway.

"Commander McCann?"

The voice came from the doorway, and McCann turned to look into the round, ruddy face of an older man wearing a tie under a gray cardigan.

He read the man's badge. Hale. He was the director of security. In early, McCann thought.

"What's the problem, Commander?"

"You tell me, Mr. Hale."

"No problem at all, sir. It's just that we weren't expecting you. My men have one of your officers on the list for this morning," the director said pleasantly. "They're pushing through the paperwork for you right now. Something happen to Lieutenant Commander Parker?"

"A last-minute emergency. He couldn't make it." McCann flipped the collar of his coat up against the breeze. "I only got the call an hour ago."

"Sorry to hear that," Hale said amiably. "Couldn't start this job at a civilized hour, could they?"

"I was promised it would be finished by noon. That's all I care about."

"We have it down here that the rest of the crew is due back this afternoon. Getting under way tonight?"

"We'll see how it goes," McCann answered. He wasn't about to discuss sailing orders.

"Sounds like you've got a long day ahead."

A long, wet day.

"But I guess it makes no difference if it's night or day once you dive."

McCann didn't bother to answer as he looked down onto the shipyard. He could just see the stern of his sub tied to a dock near the North Yard Ways. A support building at the head of the dock blocked his view of the rest of it.

"So, how long will you be going out for?"

McCann had no interest in the man's chitchat. "We won't be going anywhere if I don't get down to my ship," he said impatiently.

"Right. Right." Hale flushed bright red and turned in the doorway. Pointing to a form that was printing out on a machine in the corner, he told the younger guard to bring it over. He quickly slipped it onto a clipboard and handed it to the officer. "Please fill in this form, Commander, and you can be on your way."

As McCann looked at the clipboard, a drop of rain fell from the peak of his hat onto the paper. His temper snapped.

"What the hell is this?" he said, shoving the paperwork back into Hale's hands. "I'm not applying for a goddamn job, and I'm not trying to get security clearance. None of this applies. I'm the captain of a U.S. naval vessel that docked in this shipyard eight hours ago. I have a job to do here, and—"

"Commander, we're only following standard security procedures."

"Bullshit. *Hartford* is here for a twenty-four-hour stay. This is no different from any goddamn SRA. That ship is under my command, and no shipyard personnel are allowed on board without my permission. And if you think I'm going to stand here while precious time is wasted, you've got another thing coming."

Nuclear submarines based in the Atlantic regularly returned to Electric Boat or Newport News shipyard for SRAs—Ship Restrictive Availability work. That was the equivalent of tune-ups or other related work that had to be done on cars. During the work, the crew generally stayed with the ship and shipyard security was well versed on how to handle the navy personnel. There was no reason for this confusion.

"Commander, you're getting upset over—"

"I've wasted enough time here," McCann snapped at him. "Where's your office? I'm calling the DOD security coordinator from your phone. And I want the third-shift yard superintendent here *now.*"

Hale glanced down at the form and looked as if he'd been hit with a bat.

"Christ. This is the wrong form." He whirled around and started shouting at the younger guard. "What the hell is going on?"

If it weren't for the fact that these morons were armed, McCann might have bulled his way through and let them straighten things out on their own. But he wouldn't put it past them to shoot him in the back and explain later. Of course, that was assuming they could even hit him.

McCann stepped into the security booth.

"All right. I'm giving you exactly two minutes," he warned. "Then I'm calling the director of NAVSEA and EB's general manager…at home."

"That won't be necessary, Commander. I have the right form here," the older man mumbled. He held another clipboard out for McCann. "This only requires your signature. Nothing else."

He looked down at the list of his crew members on the piece of paper. "This is the same form I sent over to Security yesterday."

"Correct. We need your signature to allow them to come back this afternoon."

"I signed this form last night," he said, moving down the list, double-checking the names.

Hale looked at him in embarrassment. "Just a signature, sir."

McCann signed the paperwork and shoved it back into the security director's hands.

"I can have one of the men drive you down to the dock, sir."

McCann looked out through the glass. He didn't see any of the shipyard security vehicles. He could only imagine how long he'd have to wait for them to bring one of those around. The rain seemed to have eased a little for the moment.

"No," he said as he walked out the door and started down the hill to the shipyard.

There was certainly a different face on the yard at this hour. McCann took a deep breath as he walked down the steep hill, being careful not to slip on the wet pavement. The little dispute at the security station had let him release some steam, but he didn't feel much better.

He had one stop to make at the barge that housed the NAVSEA offices before boarding *Hartford.* That was what he needed, familiar territory. At the bottom of the hill, he turned down an alley that led to an area called the Wet Docks, where subs sat tied to piers during the final stages of construction before finally being commissioned by the navy. Because of some repairs Electric Boat was making to a number of those piers, there had been no open berths in the Wet Docks for his ship yesterday, so he'd been directed to tie up at the dock nearest the North Yard Ways. Since there was no new construction going on up there now, it actually made sense to use one of those docks.

McCann strode past the old brick Pipe Shop that was located at the head of a cluster of piers, then walked down a dimly lit alley that wove between other production shops to the gray navy barge. Most of the smaller shops were dark, but the few that had lights on inside seemed devoid of personnel. He tried to remember whose idea it was to get this job started at such a god-forsaken hour. Definitely not his.

McCann finally crossed a small catwalk onto the navy barge. In the NAVSEA inspection office, a clerk had a file folder ready for him, and in just a few minutes the submarine commander was working his way back through the Wet Docks.

During the handful of times he'd been involved with different production issues in the shipyard, he'd heard a few stories about these alleys. About vendettas being paid with the flash of a blade and bodies reappearing only at the turn of the next tide. It was true, he thought; anyone could commit murder in one of these alleys and get away unseen. Like every shipyard, this one had its own unwritten code of conduct, its own methods of meting out justice.

The alleys were protected from the wind, but Mc-Cann could feel the rain coming down harder. He picked up his pace.

Out of the corner of his eye, he saw the shadowy form of a rat the size of a small cat scurrying along the base of the brick wall of a shop not ten feet from him. He watched it disappear into a corner behind some rusting metal barrels. As it did, a door slammed inside the building, rattling one of the smoke-blackened windows.

Intent on watching the rodent, McCann wasn't aware of the figure emerging from the shadows and blocking his path until he nearly collided with him. He stopped short.

In the darkness, the white hard hat was the first thing

that caught his eye. He was a member of the shipyard management.

"Lieutenant Commander Parker?" the voice asked.

McCann stood corrected. *She* was a member of shipyard management.

"No. Commander McCann. Can I help you?"

"I'm sorry for the confusion, sir. I'm Amy Russell, the ship superintendent assigned to the *Hartford* for this job. I was told I could meet with the executive officer before I brought my crew on board."

"*Hartford* is my ship," he said pointedly. "There was an emergency that my X.O. needed to take care of this morning. I'm in charge."

"An emergency?"

"That's right."

"Good thing for him you guys didn't sail, after all."

"I guess that's one way to look at it."

"Plus, we get the top dog." She tucked the clipboard she was carrying under one arm and held out her hand. "Sorry, I shouldn't have said that. Not out loud, anyway. My mouth tends to run sometimes."

He shook her hand. She had a firm, confident grip. Because of the hard hat and the poorly lit alley, he couldn't make out her face. And with the layers of clothes and the steel-toed boots the yardbirds wore, men and women all looked the same. From her voice, though, he guessed she was young.

"What can I do for you, Ms. Russell?"

"It's Amy," she said. "I'm in charge of the repair on your boat's electrostatic gyro navigator."

"Were you also in charge of the initial installation?" he asked sharply.

"Not on the *Hartford*, I wasn't," she said, not missing a beat. "And yes, I know this specific system went through an overhaul only four months ago. And no, there's no excuse for it to fail."

He was glad she'd done some of her homework. "I was told you have a replacement system on hand."

"We do. The supplier of the ESGN on your boat is the marine navigation division of SPAWAR, the Space and Naval Warfare Systems Center in San Diego. As it happens, we have three systems, refurbished with fiber optics and ready for installation. They were scheduled for other jobs, but we can switch any of them to the *Hartford*, so long as we're sure what revision level your system was installed at."

"Don't you have drawings and spec levels that tell you that?"

"We do. But the call for this job came at 6:00 p.m. last night. Our engineering department in charge of these systems closes up shop way before that. And I didn't get in until after ten, too late to even get the San Diego people on the line. And since then I've been running around trying to put together crew, material and testing equipment for your job. And that's not the easiest thing to do these days on third shift. Especially when you're talking about a system as major as this one. I wasn't even counting on the possibility of having three different rev levels of it on the shelf."

The rain was pounding sideways again. McCann wanted to get out of it. "From my experience working with Electric Boat and Newport News, this all sounds routine, Ms....Ms...."

"Russell. Amy."

"What I'm trying to tell you is that nothing you've said is relevant, from my perspective," he said curtly. "Your shipyard management agreed to turn this job around in less than twenty-four hours. Not even having started this installation, though, you appear overwhelmed. My recommendation is that you bow out, Ms. Russell, and let someone with more experience take charge here."

She turned her head and mumbled something that suspiciously sounded like "arrogant bastard."

"Did you say something?"

"Faster," she said brusquely. "This job will get done much faster if I'm left to do it. Unless you want your sub tied up to our dock for a couple of extra days, my suggestion is that you cooperate a little and let me get the job done."

McCann momentarily considered making a call to move her off of the assignment. He didn't have anything against her age or gender. Experience, though, mattered a hell of a lot.

"How familiar are you with the system?" he asked.

"Very. I managed three installations on 688-class upgrades, and one for an SRA, Selected Restricted Availability, on the Seawolf."

The cold rain was starting to trickle down his neck. "What do you need from me?"

"I want to see and test the system and determine the revision level before I bring the crew and material on board."

"Sea trials are over. We're not going for any spin around Long Island Sound so you can test the system."

"I'm not asking you to take me on any spin. I can

test the system at the dock. I just need access to the control room to get everything I need."

"Have you read the rejection report?" he asked.

"Of course I did," she responded, obviously growing impatient. "But 'it ain't working' wasn't much of a help."

He glowered down at her. "I was the final signature on that report, Ms. Russell. I don't recall that phrasing in it."

"Really?" She pushed the brim of her hard hat back. "I'm kidding."

"At four o'clock in the morning?"

"You were being pretty condescending, Commander."

"Ms. Russell—"

"From the moment I stepped into your path, you've been treating me like a moron, sir." She put a hand up when he tried to interrupt. "Despite being a woman, I'm a ship superintendent. People don't walk in off the street and get this position. I have an electrical engineering degree and six years of shipyard experience. My specific training has been in sonar and navigation systems, and I was one of three people from Electric Boat who were sent to SPAWAR to get trained in testing and installation procedures for the new ESGNs. The management above me and the crew and supervisors who report to me have absolute confidence in what I do, and in what I direct them to do."

"Ms. Russell…" He tried to interrupt again, but she shook her head and continued, her voice rising over the wind.

"I know the procedures, sir. I know the requirements.

I also know only an idiot would replace such an expensive and major system without first looking at the inspection and rejection reports. Yes, they were detailed—as much as they could be—but they didn't answer some specific questions that I have. I've done everything that can be done at my end." She shrugged. "Now, as far as how quickly you'd like to have your boat out of here, it's up to you."

McCann was impressed. He knew he could be arrogant, brusque and even intimidating. He knew he'd been all that over the past few minutes. In fact, he probably had been ever since he'd woken up to Parker's phone call this morning. Still, she'd stood up to him, her voice never wavering while she'd listed her qualifications and her beefs.

"All right. I'll ask again," he said in what he felt was a more civilized tone. "What do you need from me?"

"Permission to come aboard, sir, and test the system ahead of the production crew's arrival."

"You have papers?" He extended a hand.

She quickly pulled the clipboard from under her arm but didn't open the hinged metal cover that protected the paperwork. "Let's duck into the Pipe Shop. I don't want my papers dissolving in the rain before I even get started."

Leading him around a corner, Amy pulled open a door and motioned him inside. The shop appeared to be empty, but the lights were on. It was dry and warm and had the distinctive smell of pipe welding. As they crossed the concrete floor, McCann saw a figure appear behind the glass window of an office door. A piping foreman, blueprint in hand, nodded to them when he recognized the ship super, before going back to work.

"I can't believe it," Russell said, walking toward one of a half-dozen work benches on the shop floor.

"Can't believe what?"

She put her clipboard down on the work bench. Clean sheets of cardboard had been taped onto the bench, and the rain that dripped off her hard hat formed dark spots on the work area. Opening the clipboard, she pulled out work orders and copies of the inspection reports. She handed him a work order before answering him.

"You aren't as bad as I expected," she said as he glanced at the documents.

"You were expecting Shrek?" he asked.

He could see her face clearly for the first time. He was right. She was young. Her face was pretty. Her eyes glistened in the shop light.

"I'm not talking about your looks, Commander."

"What then?"

She shrugged. "The other sub service officers I deal with. None of them are too comfortable with women."

"I beg to differ," he said absently, turning his attention back to the paperwork.

There was a long pause. "I didn't mean that the way it came out."

He raised an eyebrow and shot her a curious look.

She shook her head. "I'm talking about *working* with women. Especially women in management. As good as you might be working with other men, it seems like most of you guys lack confidence when you're dealing with women."

He fought back a laugh. "You think I lack confidence, Ms. Russell?"

"No, but you definitely have preconceptions. When I introduced myself, you automatically assumed that I wasn't qualified to do the job."

He was about to argue, but she was starting to roll. "Don't try to deny it, Commander. I don't blame it on individuals. The system breeds it into you. The male-warrior culture you live in."

"You seem to know a lot about it," McCann put in. "Was psychology your minor in college?"

"As a matter of fact, I do know a lot about the life-style, but that's not only from books. And I do think a certain mind-set develops in men who are stuck with one another for so many months at a time."

"We're not *stuck* with one another," he said, hiding a smile as he handed the paperwork back to her.

"Whatever. You know what I mean. I think it'd be healthier if they allowed women to ride these boats."

"Women are often on submarines."

"Yeah…as passengers." She carefully put her papers back in her clipboard and closed it. "Researchers, scientists, observers. And only on special occasions. I'm talking about regular crew."

"You build them, Ms. Russell, so you should know why that isn't happening. Depending on the boat and the mission, you could have three to a bunk in the crew's quarters. Hot racking." He looked at his watch. "Mixed-gender crews sleeping in shifts for five or six months at a clip? That's just looking for problems."

"*Hot racking.* Wonderful term. I always thought that it sounded awfully painful." She pulled up the collar of her jacket. "Sorry. No more questions unrelated to electrostatic gyro navigator testing and installation. Can you take me on board now?"

"Do you need to bring any of your people with you?"

"No. I'm only doing some testing." She cocked her head. "And I can handle it on my own, Commander."

The way she drawled her words told McCann that he must have sounded doubtful again.

"Glad to hear it. You have what you need?"

"I need to pick up a testing device at one of the shops. But it's practically on our way."

He looked up at the sky as they left the shop. The rain wasn't stopping. She kept his pace with ease.

"What's your work schedule?" he asked her.

"I have a crew of ten, with supervisor, ready to come aboard at 6:00 a.m." She touched his arm, pointing to the door to a large building. "Let's take a shortcut out of the rain."

McCann followed her up a short flight of stairs past a door. The building was a maze of corridors and offices, but she led him through it without hesitation. He knew that the shipyard superintendent had offices a few floors above.

"What's your plan for physically bringing the new system on board?"

"Bringing that crew on at six will give us time to break down the unit, move the malfunctioning components and prep everything for the new installation. That takes a little bit of time. No one will be standing around twiddling his thumbs. When first shift gets rolling after seven, we'll bring the new unit on."

They walked out of the building onto a paved street. The light green corrugated steel walls of the Ways loomed ahead of them, gleaming from the rain and the floodlights that illuminated the company's name high above.

The huge, cavernous building actually housed two work facilities. The near side consisted of a wide floor with steel rails embedded in the concrete to move the cylindrical sections of the Trident subs under construction. The sloping Ways took up the far side of the building. A few years ago, McCann had attended the launching of one of the last 688-class subs, standing atop the ship as it slid backward into the river. Since that day, the far side of the building had pretty much sat empty. *Hartford* was tied to the pier on this side of the Ways.

"Right here." She motioned to an ancient shop nestled against the high green walls. "You can come inside if you like, or wait here. It'll take me thirty seconds."

He welcomed any reprieve to get out of this weather, no matter how short the duration. Inside, there were three men working on an electronic panel. All of them looked up and nodded. McCann acknowledged them.

He waited right inside the door as Russell went to the back of the shop to get what she needed. The place was crammed with more equipment than the inside of a sub. Boxes, wires, benches, panels, all kinds of components crowded every aisle.

The men turned their attention back to their work, and McCann looked out through the dirty glass of a small window. As he watched the rain fall, a door opened and a man dressed in a security raincoat came out of the Ways, looked briefly down the road, and then turned up an alley next to the shop. A couple of moments later, a second security guard came out.

McCann immediately spotted the drawn pistol the guard was holding inside his partially snapped raincoat. Before McCann could think of the possible reasons for it, the guard tucked the weapon into the holster under his raincoat and followed his partner into the alley.

Three

Lee Brody filled his coffee mug and sat back down at the mess table. Taking a sip, he put the mug down on the padded plastic table cover and gazed with satisfaction into the black steaming liquid. Submarine coffee was the best in the navy. No question.

He looked around the mess deck. Everything shone. Shipshape and ready for sea. As it should be. After all, if everything had gone according to schedule, *Hartford* would be a hundred miles off Long Island by now. Even so, Brody felt good. Two crew members were sitting and talking at the far table. He took another sip. He could feel the soft thrum of the engines; it was a sensation that always gave him that warm feeling of anticipation, of a journey—no, an adventure—about to start.

Growing up near the shipyards in Newport News,

Virginia, Brody had always been fascinated by subma-rines. He'd been aware of them for as long as he could remember. He'd seen them being built, their cylindri-cal hulls peeking out of the corrugated steel buildings that hung out over the water. He'd seen them tied to the docks, and he'd seen their sleek black forms gliding through the choppy green waters of the outer bay. He'd known men who'd worked on them, sailed them.

Sailing on subs was what he'd dreamed of as a kid as he sat on the pier watching them. He knew from an early age that he would have a life at sea.

Being a sailor matched his personality. The summer he graduated from high school, he'd enlisted. Now, at twenty-three years old, he had no family that he was in touch with anymore. He didn't care much about the news. He might read the NASCAR results occasionally, but he didn't really care if Dale Jr. won or if Jeff Gor-don won. He never argued politics because he had a no-tion that government had too much power over people, but not everyone understood that and he couldn't really explain it. Actually, he had little interest in what hap-pened on the outside. The navy was his world. His fam-ily.

It didn't bother him in the slightest that, every time the hatches slammed shut, he was cut off from the rest of the world for months at a time. Not like some of the other bubbleheads on his crew. He never got close to marrying, never even had a steady girlfriend. No kids that he knew of. No mortgage payments to make. His home was right here. It was the sub he was riding, and the one hundred and thirty guys he shared it with were his brothers.

Three years he'd been riding submarines. Electronics was his thing, so he'd trained in sonar tech, working his way up to petty officer second class. Brody knew he was damn good at what he did. His commanding officer, McCann, knew it, too. The C.O. told him at his last review that, after this patrol, he wanted to send Brody to school for a new system that was going to be installed on the upgraded 688s and the Seawolf-class boats. That way, McCann said, he'd also be right in line for petty officer first class after he'd put in the requisite time.

Brody didn't know how to feel about that. The promotion was nice, but it meant that he'd probably be transferred to some other boat to work with another crew. He hated change. He liked what he had. He liked this C.O. McCann was a decent guy. He was tough, but he had a solid relationship with this crew. Brody had served under three different skippers, and McCann was the best he'd seen. But everyone knew that the commander wouldn't be staying long. Two more patrols and McCann would be up for captain. He'd get that fourth gold bar, too. He was on his way up. But before that happened, Brody knew he'd have to think hard about where he wanted to be.

The sonar man took his dishes to the galley. There were only the three of them in the enlisted mess; nine in total remained aboard for the twenty-four-hour turnaround it would take to fix what was wrong.

They had left their berth upriver at the sub base yesterday, the tug casting off when they reached the mouth of the Thames River. Everyone on the crew thought they'd be away at least six months. They were being deployed to the Indian Ocean and Persian Gulf. But they hadn't got much past Groton Long Point when the gyro navigator had shit the bed. Instead of coming about and going back up to the sub base again, the boat waited until the orders had come through to pull into one of the empty berths at the Electric Boat shipyard. These people had built most of USS *Hartford.* And from what Brody understood, they had a replacement system on hand and everything would be done today.

It was surprising when the C.O. had granted leave to most of the crew for the duration. The men loved it. Most of them had moved their families to the area when they'd first been stationed here.

But Brody had been happy to volunteer to stay aboard. The food was better, and he'd already put himself onto his six-hour sleep schedule. He was also looking forward to starting work on a training manual for one of the new systems in his free time. Without the hustle-bustle of daily duties, he could get a good start.

He nodded to the other two on his way out of the mess. They were thumbing through some motorcycle magazines.

"When are the yardbirds supposed to get here?" the new galley man asked. Dunbar had been brought aboard to replace one of the old cooks who'd retired after thirty years. The other, Rivera, worked the torpedo room.

"They're supposed to be on the job at 0600," Brody answered.

"Who's gonna babysit them?" Rivera called after him.

"No one's been assigned. The yardbirds will stick to the control room, and the officer of the watch will keep an eye on them. Also, I was told last night the X.O. will come back this morning to go over it all with them." Brody headed for the door.

"Want to play some poker?" Dunbar called after him.

"Nah." Brody shook his head. "I've got some work to do."

"Shit, man," Rivera complained. "You've got plenty of time for work once we get under way again."

Brody waved them off and stepped into the narrow passageway outside the mess deck. He wanted to get into the sonar room and take some notes for the manual. Remembering his notebook, he started toward the NCO's quarters.

As he passed the gangway leading down to the torpedo room, a movement below caught his eye. Someone was down there. Brody paused, doing a quick recount of who was on board. Himself. The two in the mess. The deck officer and a radio man in the control room. The reactor technician. In the engine room, the machinist's mate and one motor monkey. A seaman topside, standing watch.

Even though there were auxiliary power-plant units aft of the torpedo room, the reactor man wouldn't have been checking them now. He wouldn't leave his station in Maneuvering where he was monitoring the reactor. Nobody should have been in the torpedo room.

He peered down through the opening and listened. Two pairs of legs moved into his line of vision. Black stretch pants. Black sneakers. Nothing any of the crew would wear.

"Who the hell's down there?" Brody shouted.

A sharp blow to the back of his head was the only answer he received.

Four

Electric Boat Shipyard
4:25 a.m.

"**W**ould you mind giving me a hand with one of these?"

McCann turned around and saw the ship super walking toward him. She was trying to juggle her clipboard and two hard-plastic carrying cases. Another large bag hung from her shoulder.

He fought back any comment about her claim of being able to handle it on her own. "You got saxophones in those cases, Ms. Russell?"

"How did you know? I thought we could jam a little in our downtime."

He took one of the cases from her. The thing was damned heavy. "Sax, nothing. You've got a dead body in here."

"Yeah, but the identity of the body, I'm afraid, falls under the category of 'need to know.'"

He tried to take the other briefcase, too, but she shook her head and led the way out of the shop.

Crossing the road, McCann glanced up the alley where the security guards had gone. There was no sign of them. Amy led him through the same door into the Ways. The place was dark, except for a few security lights along the walls of the vast building. They walked along the wall toward the pier that extended out into the river. The fifty-foot-high doors at the end of the building were closed, but there was an exit door to the left of them.

"So, other than a dead body, what else are you hiding in these suitcases?" he asked as the two of them walked out onto the rain-swept pier.

"Testing equipment that SPAWAR insists on us using before we do an ESGN replacement," Russell explained. "It runs the diagnostics that tests the lateral systems, too, including the GPS."

"We don't have one of those on board."

"Of course. It takes a highly qualified individual to run and handle the data analysis."

He shot her a sideways glance. "Come again?"

"I guess the navy must be too cheap to buy you one," she deadpanned. She looked over at him and smiled. "Actually, this unit's brand new. And I'm not complaining that you don't have it yet. As one of three who went out for the training, it's job security for me."

A squall of rain whipped across the pier, and McCann breathed in the salty smell of the tide.

"It's Amy, you said?"

"That's right."

"You said 'job security.' I thought women engineers are in high demand."

"I hear they are, too. But not in Groton, Connecticut. And not anywhere around here, either. At least, not for someone with my specific qualifications."

McCann knew all about Electric Boat's layoffs over the past two decades or so. Only a skeleton of the old workforce remained. He doubted any of the remaining personnel had any feelings of job security. "You could always relocate if there are more cuts."

"Easier said than done. I have more than myself to worry about."

It was none of his business to ask, but his curiosity won out. "Family?"

She nodded but didn't elaborate.

Amy stopped when they reached the gangway leading out onto *Hartford* and looked across at the submarine. The curved top of the hull and the sail shone in the rain. McCann looked at her and was surprised by the expression on her face. It matched the one he used to wear whenever he looked at the boat. Those were the days when he was smitten with his job, his life. He'd been much younger then. The wind and rain swept around them, but she didn't appear to mind.

"She's beautiful."

He couldn't argue with that. "That's a nice thing to hear, coming from someone who builds them."

"What do you mean?"

"Well, the cabinetmaker is the one who sees all the flaws invisible to everyone else."

"True, but a *successful* cabinetmaker never points them out."

"Point taken."

"But she's still a beautiful boat," she said in a low

voice, adjusting her shoulder bag before stepping onto the gangway.

The sailor standing the topside watch saluted McCann as they boarded the vessel.

"Nice night, eh, Barclay?" McCann said. The seaman was from Mississippi and right out of sub school. *Hartford* was his first submarine after serving on two surface crafts. "Must feel just like home."

"I only came on watch at 0300, Captain. I can still feel my toes."

"That's good. We don't want to amputate anything if we can help it."

Amy put everything down next to the open hatch.

"After you," she told him.

Maneuvering down the ladder was a little tight. McCann knew it was often a challenge for surface types, especially when they were carrying gear. He descended first, pausing on a rung of the ladder to help her find her footing. Instead, she stood waiting to hand the test equipment down to him. He took down the case he was carrying and came back up to find the next case being lowered to him. When the equipment was all down, he didn't have to go back up because she was right behind him, climbing down the ladder like a seasoned sub rider. She landed on two feet, unzipped her jacket and wiped the rain off her face.

"I'll start in the control room." She pointed in the right direction, picking up all the equipment except the case he'd been carrying.

McCann followed her lead, heading for the sub's command center. The passageways were empty. It was quiet on board. The normal human sounds that were part of submarine living were not there yet. Still, it was cool and dry, and it felt like coming home for McCann. The pathetic thing was that *Hartford* was more of a home to him than his small, empty house overlooking the river in Mystic. Amy stepped into the control room ahead of him.

"Stop right there. What are you doing on board?"

When McCann heard his officer of the watch bark at the ship super, he pushed past Russell.

Paul Cavallaro immediately came to his feet. "Sorry, Skipper, I didn't see you." A lieutenant assigned to Navigation, Cav had been left in command of the vessel during the night when McCann had given the X.O. permission to go home.

McCann looked around and into the adjoining radio room and found his officer was the only one on deck. There should have been a communications man on duty.

"Lieutenant Cavallaro, this is Amy Russell. She's the ship super who'll be running the equipment installation."

The two nodded, and the ship superintendent began setting up her testing equipment in front of the GPS system. She was standing on the port side of the control room and didn't go any farther forward than the unit panels. McCann left her to her work and went to the conn.

"I didn't think they'd get started until 0600," Cav said quietly.

"I don't complain when they're early." McCann replied absently, peeling off his raincoat. "Where's your radio man?"

"I sent Gibbs to the officer's mess to get me the ESGN spec sheet. I left it on the table when the X.O. called me to take the conn."

McCann nodded and watched her take off her navy-blue management coat. She was wearing a green flannel shirt under a vest and heavy khaki pants. He couldn't help but notice that, even in the bulky clothes, she obviously had a nice figure.

"Where's the rest of her crew?" Cav asked.

"She's the expert. They'll come aboard once she determines exactly what it is they need." McCann was about to leave her with Cav and go hang his raincoat.

"This babe's going to handle it herself?" Cav asked.

Change of plan. Maybe these two wouldn't be best left alone.

"The 'babe' is an electrical engineer, and she's just finished a training course with SPAWAR," he said coolly, recalling what she'd said to him earlier about submarine officers and women. McCann wondered if he'd sounded as bad.

Cav glanced down at his watch.

"We're ahead of schedule," the commander reminded his junior officer.

"That's not it," Cav said. "Gibbs has been gone five minutes. If you don't mind, I'm gonna go find out what happened to him."

"I have the conn, mister," he said officially, mounting the step to the platform at the center of the control room. The twin periscopes were aft of him. As Cav went aft, McCann checked the status of the systems on the LED displays. When he was satisfied that all was correct, he stood on the port side and watched Amy work.

It was immediately evident that she was competent. She worked quickly and efficiently. The two cases lay open on the floor, displaying an assortment of tools, gadgets and testing apparatuses. The shoulder bag had been unzipped, and a laptop had been connected to the defective unit and to a couple of testing devices in the briefcase. She was on her knees on the deck, her head bent over the equipment. She was in full concentration, monitoring the changing screens on the laptop.

"Anything?" McCann asked, sitting down on the nearby chief of the boat's swivel chair. The COB had nearly torn the navigator a new butt hole when the ESGN had begun to malfunction.

"You're the impatient sort, aren't you?" she asked without looking up.

"No. I'm the hands-on sort."

She glanced up at him.

"I mean, it's tough for me to watch someone else have all the fun. Or doing all the work."

"Well, this is no fun. And so far, it's no work, either," she said, darting another quick look at him.

He leaned forward, planting his elbows on his knees. "What do you have so far?"

"Nothing," she said. "The preliminary scan tells me that everything is running fine. I don't see any malfunction in the software. It's checking the unit hardware now."

"Do you have the rejection report handy?" he asked, crouching down next to her.

Amy handed him the clipboard. McCann leafed through the documents until he found the initial report.

"Did you test these parameters?" He held the paper before her.

She looked up briefly. "I sure have. Those were the preset values I started with."

McCann turned to see if Cav was coming back. He was the one who'd originally signed off on the report. It would be good if he were in on this. But there was no sign of him. In fact, there was no sign of anyone. It was too damn quiet. He glanced at his watch.

"I'm only in a primary phase," she told him. "A lot more could show up once I run a more detailed diagnosis."

"Is that usually the way it works?" he asked.

She started to say something, then bit her lip and concentrated on the screen.

"Spit it out, Russell."

"You say that as if I'm a Russell terrier, choking on a bone," she said, looking at him sharply. "Everyone calls me Amy."

McCann smiled. She had a quirky sense of humor.

"Spit it out, Amy," he said.

"It'd be premature to say anything," she replied, typing in a couple of commands on the laptop. "You'll hold it against me if I'm wrong."

"There'll be no court-martial," he said lightly. "I'm just looking for your expert opinion."

He noticed her eyes were dark blue when she looked up at him.

"No," she said, turning her attention back to the screen.

"No, meaning you're refusing an order?"

"No, as in, the answer to your first question is no."

She was too clever. McCann had to think back to the exact wording of his question. "No, meaning…"

"No, that's not the way it usually works. The system failures should show up with bells and whistles in the primary test phase. We run the more detailed diagnostics after that to pinpoint the specific location, and to make sure every *i* is dotted and every *t* is crossed. We want to make sure we're replacing the right components."

McCann looked at the GPS screen. Once the COB had finished lighting into the operator, the navigation man and Cav were the only ones involved with the unit yesterday. The backup unit had worked fine.

McCann should have gotten involved. This was a new system, but he was fairly familiar with it. Not as familiar as he should have been, though. He knew every valve, pipe, panel, cable and piece of electronics inside this fast-attack submarine. But he should have been in Cav's back pocket.

He'd always been that way. On the wall above the engineering officer's desk was a large print of the piping and instrumentation systems of the nuclear plant, mapping everything from the core's main coolant piping to the last condensate pump pressure control valve. As part of one of his EO exams, McCann had to be able to reproduce it from memory, and he still could, he thought, if need be. As C.O., he knew *everything* about his sub—except some of the minute details of this new system. When they got out to sea, he'd learn the ins and outs of this, too.

"My men didn't imagine the system malfunction," he said, hearing his defenses kicking in.

"I'm not saying that your men *imagined* a problem yesterday," she said calmly. "What I'm saying is that, whatever the problem was, they might not have had the means of diagnosing it correctly."

McCann felt a little better about that. It would have been a major problem if he'd curtailed the start of a patrol over a couple of officers and operators misreading navigation screens. "What else could be wrong?"

"I can't tell yet. Give me a little time to work on it first."

She reconnected a couple of probes to the module and started running another program. Her face registered everything going through her head. He could tell the moment she had something.

"What have you got?" he repeated.

"Must be a pain in the *ass* to work for," she murmured under her breath.

"What did you say?"

"I said your crew must be *fast* workers, Commander."

"Right," he retorted. "Just tell me what you see."

"The first possibility is that you might have a local area network failure," she told him. "Everything looked good before, but as soon as I test for results through the next system, I pick up some malfunctioning."

"What could cause that? Wiring?"

She shrugged. "Any number of things. Could be faulty wiring. The good news is that, at this point, I don't think you'll have to replace the ESGN unit. The bad news is that unless we can retrace what specific functions were being performed when the problem started, we'll be searching in the dark for the faulty connections…if that's what it is."

He thought about that for a moment. "We'd barely

gotten out of the harbor. We didn't do anything complicated."

"In that case, we're searching in the dark," she
concluded.

"You're going to have to do better than that. I've got
a thousand miles of wiring on *Hartford*. I want a plan
on how you're going to resolve this."

"We'll start with a check of the connections that
feed out of the ESGN," she suggested. "I'll get a handful of guys in here and go to work. I'd say that if all goes
well, we should be able to pinpoint the problem in a
couple of hours. If we get really lucky, we might nail
it in just a few min—"

She stopped as her pager went off. She sat back on
her heels and dug the unit out of the pocket of her blue
coat. He saw her frown as she looked at the display.

"The boss. Have you already been complaining
about me, Commander?"

"Not me. It must have been some other pain in the ass."

She smiled at him. She was quite pretty when she
smiled, he thought.

"Just so long as it wasn't you. Do you mind if I use
your phone?"

"Not at all." He pointed to the quartermaster's telephone.

She pushed up to her feet, heading that way. McCann
watched the program that she was running on the computer, then followed the connection hookups she'd
made. Common sense stuff. Four months ago, *Hartford*
had been sitting in dry dock for a massive changeover
to fiber optics. He wondered if that's where the problem had originated. But they hadn't faced any trouble

on the subsequent sea trials or the trip south to load *Hartford*'s weapons.

Where the hell was Cav?

"Christ, it *can't* be," she snapped at the person on the line. "I was there ten minutes ago. How did it happen?"

He looked up at her. She was staring straight ahead and was clearly upset.

"Did they get everyone out?" she asked.

McCann guessed there had to have been an accident. The shipyard was a dangerous place to work. Inside the sub, though, you couldn't hear any of the sirens, if there were any.

Amy looked down at her watch. "No, we probably won't need it, but we still have to get the crew lined up for six o'clock." She nodded at something that was being said on the other end. "I'm coming over. No, that's okay. I'll take care of it."

McCann stood and watched her as she hung up. "An accident?"

"A fire." She moved briskly to the laptop and test equipment. "The same shop we were in few minutes ago is burning right now. I work out of that shop a lot."

"What about the three guys who were working inside?"

"They got out, thank God." She started disconnecting the wires, shut down the computer and quickly rolled the cables. She was all concentration, in spite of obviously being upset. "I have what I need for now. I'll be back at six with the crew. We'll comb through these units and find the culprit."

She closed one briefcase after the other with a snap, zipping up the shoulder case with the laptop in it.

"You can leave everything here until you get back," he suggested.

She looked around the control room. "I don't want them to be in your way."

McCann took the two heavy briefcases and stowed them away by the navigation panels. "We're not going anywhere. They'll be safe here."

"I have to take the laptop," she told him, looping the shoulder strap over her arm. "I can send some of this data to SPAWAR and leave a copy with our own engineering department so they can take a look while we're here going over the wiring."

She zipped up her jacket.

"How bad is the fire?"

"I'll find out when I get there. The main reason they called was to take a head count to make sure everyone was out."

"That's a shame," he said.

Amy gave a brief nod, still looking extremely tense. "Can I get out on my own or do I need an escort?"

"I can't leave the conn, and we can't let you roam around the boat alone, either." He was reaching for the phone to call Cavallaro back to the control room when he saw him coming down the passageway.

"Done already?" Cav asked Amy.

"With the preliminary testing, yes. I'll be back with my crew later."

This wasn't the right time to tell Cav that their findings yesterday had been off. "Did you find Gibbs?" McCann asked instead.

Cav nodded. "He's on his way up, Skipper."

"I'll walk Ms. Russell out. Then we need to talk,"

he told the officer before following Amy down the passageway.

"You said you worked out of that shop? How is that going to affect you?"

She shrugged. "I don't know how bad the fire is, or what caused it. Depending on how the investigation goes, I might have bigger problems to worry about than losing my desk and a couple of framed pictures."

She stopped by the ladder that led up to the hatch.

"If the need arises," he said, "I can testify that you didn't set a match to the place before we left."

She almost smiled. "Thanks, Commander. I'll let you know if I need you." She placed one hand on the metal ladder, then hesitated before climbing.

McCann waited, but Amy continued to examine the bank of cables just outboard of the passageway. She climbed one rung, paused again, and then came back down.

"What is it?" he asked, curious now.

"I'm trying to remember. Right under the control room, under the GPS receiver and ESGN unit, is that the enlisted mess?"

"There are a number of spaces under there," he explained. "The mess, the trash room, the officer's wardroom, the ship's office. They're all below us here. It depends on where you mean exactly."

"I'm thinking about the wiring under the unit."

He thought for a moment. "That wiring runs along the underside of the decking. If it's connections you're looking for, they could be anywhere."

She adjusted the shoulder strap of the laptop case. "On the last ESGN installation we did on the Seawolf, there was a panel in the overhead of the space below that we could remove. With that out, we could get a clear shot at a panel of wiring connections leading to the navigation systems. Do you mind if I check it out before I go, just to see if we can do the same thing here? It shouldn't take more than five minutes."

He stepped back, motioning the way. "Be my guest."

The stairs that led below were by the escape trunk. Shaking her head, she signaled for him to go ahead of her.

"After seeing your navigation officer's reaction, I think I'd rather have you lead the way. I don't want to startle anyone else."

McCann decided that a sailor might have a slightly different reaction to the sight of such a good-looking woman in their living quarters. The fact that she was wearing a white hard hat and shipyard management gear wouldn't really make a difference.

There was no one in the passageway. He led the way down to the enlisted mess. McCann poked his head in first. Surprisingly, no one was there, either.

This was the largest open area on the sub, capable of seating half of *Hartford*'s crew. The mess was a combination cafeteria, movie theater, game room, and training area. A place where the seamen could gather, it was rarely empty when they were on patrol.

Amy moved forward between the tables. Keeping her eyes fixed on the overhead, she turned into the adjoining galley.

"You're sure stocked with food," she commented, looking around.

"Before the problem with the navigation equipment yesterday, we had stores laid in for a normal patrol."

"I'll be really careful not to ruin anything." She pulled a small flashlight out of her pocket and directed the light above. "Never mind the nuclear reactor. I know how precious food is to these guys."

McCann leaned against the entry. The only galley crewman who'd stayed on board was Dunbar. He wondered why he wasn't here getting breakfast ready. Amy zipped open her jacket, and as she looked up, her hard hat tipped off her head and clattered to the deck. Light brown, shoulder-length curls were barely held together in a ponytail at the nape of her neck. Their heads were close together as they both bent to retrieve the hard hat, and he smelled the fresh scent of shampoo mixed with the smell of rain and shipyard on Amy's hair.

"This place is smaller than my kitchen," she said as she put her hat back on. He noticed she seemed a little flushed.

"I'd wager that you don't cook four meals a day for a hundred and thirty men in a space this size."

"No," she told him, eyeing the arrangement. "I only cook for three. My kitchen is a little larger, but I don't think it's laid out as well."

McCann wondered if the three were herself, a husband and a child. He hadn't paid attention to whether she was wearing a ring. That was no indication, anyway, as most shipyard workers didn't wear rings at work. One touch of a welding rod to a wedding ring would send enough electrical current through it to melt the ring right off your finger. Not a pleasant experience.

Amy was searching the overhead and above the appliances. She stopped suddenly and turned around.

"I just remembered where that connector panel is on

the 688-class subs. We're too far aft," she said. "We need to be about eight frames farther forward and about twelve feet starboard of centerline."

McCann understood her. The shipyard production crews identified the work areas in the submarines by the frames, or curved I-beams, that formed the "ribs" of the ship's hull. Those frames were numbered consecutively from bow to stern. The centerline was an imaginary line that ran right up the middle of the ship, dividing the sub into starboard and port sides.

"That would put you in the ship's office," he said, "below the sonar equipment room."

"That's right," she said, heading out of the galley. "You're my witness, Commander. I didn't touch any of the food."

As they went back out through the mess, McCann glanced at the steaming pot of coffee beckoning to him. His clothes were still wet, and he was ready for a hot cup of java. He considered asking Amy if she wanted a cup. He didn't get a chance to ask.

"I have to hurry," she said, looking at her watch. "I need to see what kind of damage that fire has done to the shop."

He nodded and followed her out of the mess. Amy moved forward along the passageway, past the trash room and his stateroom. She was looking into the overhead and following a bank of cables that threaded between piping systems and ventilation ducts.

She stopped to let McCann move ahead of her in the passageway. As he passed the officer's wardroom and enlisted quarters, he glanced in. It was strange not to see any of his crew at all. For a moment, he considered reaching for the nearest phone and having Cav get every crew on the watch to check in.

"I'm sorry this is taking more than five minutes," she called after him.

"That's perfectly okay," he said over his shoulder. "You mentioned that you've been at work since ten o'clock last night. Are we going to lose you when the first-shift people get here?"

"I don't punch a clock," she told him. "I'll stay with the crew until I make sure you're back in business."

He went by the NCO's quarters and stopped in the doorway of the ship's office. "Sounds like you work some crazy hours. It must take its toll on your family."

"It would…if it was a regular thing." She avoided meeting his gaze and brushed past him to get inside the narrow office space.

The ship's office was also a data center. It contained all the records and personnel files that were part of the submarine's everyday life. Packed with file cabinets, shelves, a computer, a printer and copier, the two-foot-wide aisle in the middle was filled with a single chair and several boxes of paper that must have been brought aboard at the last minute, before *Hartford* left the sub base. McCann frowned at the supplies that had not yet been stowed where they belonged.

Amy climbed over the boxes and pushed in the chair before turning to him.

"You don't waste an inch, do you?" she asked, peeling the laptop off her shoulder and placing it on the desk.

"We pack enough supplies to last us six months. There's a place to stow these, though."

"I'm glad I didn't open either of those refrigerator doors in the galley. I'd hate to see what you've got in there."

She looked away and took her hard hat off. Her hair looked soft, and it shone in the overhead lighting. She pointed upward and nodded toward a steel panel bolted to the decking overhead.

"Right there," she said. "We have to remove the light fixture to be able to access the panel, but this will be the perfect place to start. Above it is the first main connector out of the unit."

McCann climbed past the box to see if anything else needed to be removed to give her men access to the panel.

"Do you see it?"

He had to get very close to her in order to see past the light fixture. "It's a crowd with the two of us in this space. How many are you going to put to work in here?"

He saw her stare past him at the door.

"What's going on?" she asked someone behind him.

McCann whirled around in time to see the door to the ship's office slam shut on them. He reached across the boxes on the floor for the doorknob. Before he could turn it, the lock clicked on the outside.

Five

More than fifty feet above the blazing roof of the old shop, flames and sparks mingled with dense clouds of smoke. The roar of the fire was deafening now, and the heat was rolling off the building in waves. Most of the Groton firefighters and their trucks were already here. More from the neighboring towns were arriving by the minute. Three ambulances sat in a line by the main gate. So far, there had been no need for them. But smoke inhalation was always a serious concern.

Some of the firefighters battled the inferno while others hosed down the corrugated steel walls of the Ways next to the shop. No one wanted to let the high walls melt and buckle in the intense heat. If that happened, the structure of the building would be compromised, and the weight of the huge cranes situated just under the roof could bring the entire building down.

The old wooden shop would be a total loss; everyone could see that. A relic of the early 1940s, when the shipyard had expanded like a gold rush town to meet the wartime demand for fleet-type subs, the shop had gone up like a box of forty-year-old matches, in spite of the rain. The three men inside barely escaped the cluttered space, and the equipment left inside was history by now.

Everyone moved back from battling the blaze as the roof collapsed inward, sending another shower of sparks upward into the misting predawn sky.

The general manager of the shipyard had been called in, along with his top managers. Whoever hadn't arrived already was on their way.

Hale, the shipyard director of security, crossed the wet pavement to where the Groton fire chief stood looking for other potential problems that the fire might trigger.

"We've shut down the gas lines in the building," Hale shouted over the roar of the fire.

The chief nodded and gestured toward the huge bay doors leading through the Ways. A small door for foot traffic was swinging open in the breeze. The steel wall was showing signs of buckling.

"You need to have your guys make a more thorough sweep of that building," he said. "If that wall starts to come down—and it might—we want to make sure that there's nobody in there."

"I have a group going through there right now," Hale replied. "You'd figure that with all these sirens a person would have to be deaf or dead not to get his ass out of that building."

The security director's walkie-talkie crackled. He turned away from the fire, bringing it to his ear. "Hale here. Go ahead."

"Need…bod…" The words coming through kept breaking up.

"Repeat. Do you read me?"

"…bulances…"

The communication was from the men he had inside the Ways. Turning to a security guard and two firefighters standing by, he pointed to the building. "They need help in the Ways."

The three men rushed toward the door.

The walkie-talkie came alive again. "…need ambulances…"

Hale shouted to the fire chief over the din. "Ambulances. They need help in there."

As the fire chief called for ambulances, Hale rushed toward the door himself. The smell of melting paint burned his lungs. His men could have been overcome with smoke. As he reached the door, one of the security guards who'd been inside stumbled out, clutching the walkie-talkie in his hand. He doubled over, retching as Hale bent over him.

"What is it?"

"They're dead."

"Who?"

"Brian and Hodges. Dead." He looked wildly into Hale's eyes. "Somebody fucking stabbed them."

Hale straightened up, stunned by the words. It took a few moments for him to find his bearings. The names rushed through his mind. They weren't on the detail clearing the building. They must have been in there earlier. He thought of the young men, their families, their children. They were stabbed?

Hale yanked open the door. The handle burned his hand, and he jerked backward, startled. Before he could go through the door, an ambulance screeched to a stop behind him and the EMTs leaped out. He held the door open with his foot as they scrambled through, carrying tanks of air and stretchers.

Shouting cut through all the other noise, drawing Hale's attention. Everyone was looking toward the pier, and two security guards were running in that direction. Hale turned to look.

The footbridge to *Hartford* was dangling from the pier, one end of it in the river. With no tugboats in sight, with no one visible on the bridge at the top of the fairway, the submarine was backing away from the pier, operating under its own power.

Six

Amy would have crawled into one of the cabinet drawers to give him more room, but the narrow office had the maneuvering space of a coffin. There was no-where to go. She managed to wedge herself sideways into a corner between a floor-to-ceiling cabinet and the paneled outboard bulkhead.

McCann attacked the door like a raging bull, but there was no moving the steel barrier. He'd shouted from the top of his lungs, but no one answered from the other side. Calling the control room over the intercom had produced no response, either.

Neither of them considered for a moment that his crew was pulling a prank on them. Amy had seen a masked man with a pistol in his hand reach into the room and grab the door handle. Before pulling the door shut, she'd seen another masked man behind him. She'd immediately told the commander what she'd seen.

"I'll have every one of your sorry asses court-martialed," McCann bellowed into the intercom before turning to where Amy was pinned against the wall.

His sleeves were rolled up to his elbows. He was over six feet tall, very wide across the shoulders. He exuded an explosive power, and his physical presence seemed to fill the small office space. His anger heightened the feeling. He appeared angry enough to break the entire submarine in two. Turning back to the intercom, he punched a button and held it down as he barked into the unit.

"Captain here. Code red. Repeat…" He stopped, glancing at her and muttering, "The PA is down."

Amy nodded. A phone hung on the wall, and he picked it up, listened, and slammed it back in the cradle. Whoever was responsible for this had taken down the communications system.

Her mind raced a hundred miles an hour as she tried to consider every possibility of what could be happening to them. Suddenly, in the middle of the confusion, the faces of Kaitlyn and Zack—her seven-year-old twins—came into sharp focus. Her neighbor Barbara was with them. She came over and stayed with the twins five nights a week, while Amy was working third shift. Most days, Amy got home before the two second-graders had to leave for school. Not today, though.

She'd known that she might be running late this morning, and Barbara was going to get the children ready and walk them to the bus stop. Still, what would happen when she didn't show in the lunchroom? They knew Amy was scheduled for volunteer duty today. She'd never missed her turn before. The twins would know something was wrong. And what would happen when they took the bus home? No one would be there. Barbara had a doctor's appointment this afternoon. And Amy's parents were not flying back from California until Wednesday. Where would the kids go if no one was there to meet them?

She shook her head as panic clawed its way into her throat. She felt chilled and feverish at the same time. Amy looked around the tight quarters before her eyes settled on Commander McCann. He was doing something on the PC.

"What do you think is happening?" Her voice sounded strained even to herself. She tried to bind a tight rope around her emotions. The last thing the sub captain needed right now was a hysterical woman on his hands.

"Someone, a group of people, are trying to take over my sub," he said tensely, continuing to type on the keyboard.

Amy forced herself to move away from the paneled wall. Walking on rubbery knees, she moved behind him, looking past his shoulder. He was trying to get into different networks. Every one of them seemed to be down.

"Do you mean…like a hijacking?" she asked, shivering.

"That's what I'm trying to find out."

Amy didn't want to distract him. She knew there was no one more familiar with the systems and operations of this sub than the man sitting before her.

"The network is shut down. From what I can tell UHF, HF, VLF and ELF systems are locked down, too."

She knew he was talking about frequency channels in the communications system.

He continued to mutter. "That's against SUBSAFE rules and a dozen other regs."

He stood up. Amy backed away quickly as he started opening the cabinets and drawers. He was looking for something.

"Is there anything I can do to help?" she asked, feeling useless just watching.

"Do you have anything on you? Tools? A knife? Anything that we could use as a weapon?"

The joke around the shop had always been that if Amy ever fell in the water, she'd never surface. She tended to carry too many tools on her. In fact, the union had written formal complaints against her for carrying them. It didn't stop her.

She patted her jacket pockets and started emptying them on the desk. A crimping tool, a pair of pliers, a wire cutter, a screwdriver that doubled as a voltage detector. She stripped off her blue coat and threw it aside, taking out a tape measure from the pocket of the vest she was wearing under it. There were also some cable straps and banding crimps. McCann wasn't waiting for her to give him an inventory. He continued to search the drawers, pulling out anything that could be used as a sharp object or a tool and adding it to her pile.

"Do you think some of your crew is involved with this?" She realized this was the wrong question to ask the moment it left her lips.

His expression became even fiercer. The drawers opened with more vengeance. "I have no information on that right now."

No ship's captain would take the idea of mutiny lightly.

As she patted the back pockets of her jeans, her gaze fixed on the laptop that she'd hurriedly tucked under the desk.

She pointed to it excitedly. "Remote access to the network. I might be able to connect to the shipyard's system and send a message out. We could warn them what's happening here." The news she'd received not too long ago came back to her. "That fire…"

"What about it?"

"It was probably a decoy. They're trying to distract everyone."

He reached under the desk for the laptop and handed it to her. "Don't build your hopes up about getting connected. You're talking about a signal that has to penetrate two inches of HY-80 steel."

"We have to try." Amy unzipped the bag and booted up the computer. The wait felt like forever. Finally, the Windows start-up icons appeared. She searched for network access.

"It shows a remote signal," she said, turning the screen to face him.

"It could be from our in-house router in the control room," he said thoughtfully, "but we'll take whatever they give us."

He started typing, his fingers flying over the keyboard. Most of it was gibberish to her, codes, time, date. He pressed Send, and the computer started grinding. The cursor locked, nothing happening.

"Come on, damn it," he said under his breath.

The locked cursor stared back at them.

"We lost it. It's not there."

He was talking about the signal. The bars had disappeared. Amy forced down her disappointment.

He pushed the laptop toward her. "Don't give up. Keep searching for the signal."

She squeezed by and watched him go back to search the drawers and cabinets. A box cutter's sharp edge introduced a whole new realm of possibilities. Her attention returned to the screen. No signal.

"You were going to remove the paneling in this ceiling to get to the wiring of the navigation system in the sonar equipment room," he said. "Is there any chance of climbing through?"

She shook her head. "No. From the stage where they do the wiring installation in the modular sections at Quonset, there's no space. We've stuffed ten pounds of shit into a one-pound container…at your request. There's no way to get through up there."

He'd reached the last set of cabinets and methodically began to search them.

She now knew what he was planning to do. They had to work their way out of this room, since the door was locked from the outside. This was one of many restricted areas on the sub.

He pulled two pairs of scissors from a drawer before crouching down to inspect the bottom shelves.

Amy felt a faint shudder in the deck, and she knew something had gone wrong. McCann's gaze went to the door, then to the ceiling and bulkheads.

"What's going on?" she asked in a whisper.

He stared at her for a long moment before answering. "We're moving."

Seven

Admiral Norman Pottinger, commander of the U.S. Atlantic Fleet Submarine Force, was still asleep when the phone rang. He stared at the dark ceiling of the bedroom for a couple of seconds before rolling onto his side and patting the bedside table in search of his glasses. He glanced at the clock. His alarm would go off in twelve minutes. On a normal morning, he would have been awake in eleven. He turned off the alarm.

Patricia switched on the light on her side of the bed and checked the caller ID.

"Groton," she told him, reaching for the handset.

He knew his wife wouldn't bother to speak into the phone. No son of a bitch in Groton was stupid enough to call at this hour unless it was an emergency. She passed the phone to him.

Pottinger sat up and cleared his throat before speaking. Don Brown, the commander of the submarine base in Groton was on the line.

"We have a disaster on our hands, sir."

"Hold on."

Pottinger immediately put his bare feet on the carpeted floor and stood up. Padding across the floor to a desk by the window, he turned on a lamp and picked up the pen lying beside a yellow legal pad. Behind him, his wife turned off her light.

"All right. Give me the specifics."

"Seven minutes ago," Brown started, speaking formally, "USS *Hartford* left the pier of the Electric Boat shipyard without authorization and with unknown passengers aboard."

"What do you mean *left?*" Pottinger pulled out the chair and sat down. "They were deployed twenty-four hours ago."

"Well…yes, sir. They were directed to return to port because of a malfunction with their navigation equipment. Your office was notified, Admiral."

His office may have been, but *he* wasn't. Pottinger had taken a rare weekend off, spending time with his family on the Outer Banks and closing down their summerhouse for the season.

"Who's in command of the ship?"

"We don't know for sure who has the conn on *Hartford* at this moment, Admiral, but it's Commander McCann's sub."

"That's right." He jotted down the name. McCann was a good officer. "What the hell were they doing at Electric Boat?"

"The shipyard had a replacement system. A joint

decision was made by NAVSEA, the undersecretary of the navy's procurement liaison, the defense contractor, and Commander McCann, who was then directed to dock the sub in the shipyard. The system replacement was to be completed before 1200 hours today."

"But the replacement was not completed and McCann took his ship, anyway?"

"Not exactly, Admiral. The replacement was not completed, but we can't be certain of the circumstances of the undocking. In fact, we're operating under the assumption that *Hartford* has been hijacked."

"What are you talking about, Captain Brown?" Pottinger picked up the pad of paper and walked out of the bedroom. He could hear the volume of his voice rising sharply. "No one can hijack a fully-manned submarine."

"All but nine members of the crew were given leave, sir."

"Why the hell would McCann do that?" he barked. "That submarine was fully armed. That crew had already been deployed."

There was a pause on the other end. "Commander McCann ran that decision by me, sir. This crew's time ashore had been cut substantially short. McCann believed the sailors could use the extra day with their families before going out on patrol, and I agreed. There was no reason to believe the sub's security stood to be compromised in that short duration of time in a secure defense contractor's facility."

Pottinger considered the ramifications of this security breach. If that submarine so much as ran up on a sandbar, the potential for disaster was incomprehensible. If that sub had really been hijacked...

"Where the hell is McCann now?"

"He's aboard *Hartford,* Admiral."

"Say that again."

"One officer and eight enlistees were left on board. Per shipyard security, at 0400 today, Commander McCann arrived at the gate. He made a stop at the NAVSEA office and a few minutes later boarded the submarine in the company of a shipyard superintendent who was to be responsible for the navigation equipment replacement."

Pottinger ran his stubby fingers through his short, thinning hair. He walked into the kitchen. "So we have a civilian aboard, as well."

"Yes, sir. A woman."

"Jesus H. Christ." He sat down on one of the kitchen chairs. This was getting worse by the second. "What else do you have?"

"Around 0430, a fire broke out in one of the support shops in the shipyard. They're still battling the blaze right now. They suspect arson."

"No shit," Pottinger said, in no way trying to keep the sarcasm out of his tone.

Brown continued. "A few minutes ago, the bodies of two shipyard security guards were found in the North Yard Ways, the building adjacent to the fire. Both had been stabbed to death."

"Who killed them?"

"We believe it was the hijackers, Admiral. Oxygen tanks and other diving equipment were found abandoned in the vicinity of the killings," Brown said solemnly. "Shipyard security concurs. The director of security believes the hijackers swam in, murdered the guards, then boarded *Hartford.*"

Pottinger tried to absorb all of this. "And they sailed off with one of your subs."

Brown's voice was grim. "Yes, sir."

"What the hell happened to the floating booms?" Pottinger barked. "We spent $600 million to position those security measures *everywhere* that our submarines or our ships are docked in North America."

"The security boom was in place, sir. Shipyard security put the boom in place behind *Hartford* immediately after docking. The ship was penned in, but the divers must have known that they couldn't approach the boat directly from the water."

"And that boom did nothing to stop the sub from leaving?"

"No, sir. That was never the intention behind their design," Brown said. He was beginning to sound rattled. He had plenty to be rattled about. "They were just designed to keep intruders in small boats away. The security boom in place was an anti-motorboat, type-B device. Historically, smaller light-hull crafts belonging to protestors or curiosity seekers have been the only type of problem we've had in this area. The distinctive feature of this boom is the baulk—a heavy iron-strapped wood-and-metal tank fitted with eyebolts and links for connecting it to the boom jackstays. It stretches from pier to pier behind the vessel and..."

Pottinger let Brown talk for a moment. He knew the next steps in the notification chain, but he had to find out what measures were being taken.

"...two watertight iron tanks occupy the interior of each baulk and provide flotation. Each baulk is fitted with four steel spike cutters and connected by upper and lower jackstays. Along the upper jackstays, at intervals of four feet, four-pronged steel star cutters are—"

"But they didn't do jack shit to stop *Hartford,* did they?"

"No, sir. They wouldn't."

Pottinger stood up again, thinking. The consequences of what this all meant would be dire, no matter what the outcome. Rogue terrorists using a fully armed U.S. fast-attack submarine could hold the world hostage. If they had the know-how—and there was no reason to assume they didn't—they could use the sub's nuclear weapons to strike any number of targets in the northeast. The damage that one nuclear submarine could do to the East Coast, to this country, was almost beyond comprehension. MK48 torpedoes, Tomahawk cruise missiles with nuclear and conventional warheads…never mind a god-damn nuclear reactor. That one submarine carried more firepower than the United States ever released in any war.

Christ, he thought, they could hit Washington from where they were right now. Free in the Atlantic, they could start World War III.

Pottinger felt himself break into a sweat. Careers would be ruined for this, his included. Too late for that. What was important now was containing the potential damage.

"How many divers came in through the shipyard?"

"They found eight scuba tanks."

The navy put a hundred and thirty people on those subs, but Pottinger knew a crew of eight trained people was enough to sail it out of there.

"Shipyard security has to have more details," the

admiral demanded. "Surveillance cameras, eyewitnesses."

"It's too soon, sir, to have anything solid. *Hartford* is still backing into the channel."

"Is anybody taking responsibility for the hijacking? Any sign of foreign or homegrown terrorist group activity?"

"Not yet, Admiral."

Pottinger glanced at the clock on the kitchen wall. As much as Brown had to be berated, it was much too soon to get any information from anyone.

"What action are we taking?" he asked, starting to pace the floor.

"Two tugs and three smaller craft are en route from the sub base. They're approaching the I-95 bridge and should catch up to it in a few minutes. Coast Guard has deployed a cutter from New London to assist, as well." Brown went on to name another submarine, a sub tender and an aircraft carrier that were within four hundred miles of Groton. All had been put on alert and were moving in to head off *Hartford* if the sub tried to disappear into the Atlantic. The first real support to reach them, however, would be from the air—sub hunters flying in from South Weymouth, Massachusetts.

"Any communication with *Hartford?*"

"None, sir. All channels are down."

Pottinger ran his hand through his hair again. "What's happening now?"

"Hold on, Admiral." Brown was speaking with a subordinate. "The sub has completed its backing maneuver. *Hartford* is sitting in the channel, her bow pointing south toward the mouth of the harbor."

"How long before the sub makes open water beyond the lighthouse?"

"Depending on their speed, they could clear New London Ledge Light in ten to fifteen minutes."

Pottinger knew they couldn't do anything to them while the nuclear submarine was in such close proximity to the Groton-New London shoreline. Whatever group was responsible for this had to know that, too. They had to be preparing to make their demands.

"But they *are* moving, Captain?"

"Not yet, sir. Their bearing is south, but they are not… Correction, *Hartford* is beginning to move."

In an avalanche of shit, this would at least be a hint of air freshener. They could deal with this much better once the nuclear submarine was in the open waters of the Atlantic Ocean. With a full crew, *Hartford* might be able to evade detection and disappear, but not with a skeleton group. Once they were clear of the coast, the Atlantic Fleet would be able to do whatever needed to be done.

"Brown, I want you to get any information you have on the crew that you know is aboard, and the civilian, to my office in the next ten minutes."

"We're sending what we have right now, Admiral."

"Do you know anything about the civilian?"

"No, sir," Captain Brown answered. "We're bringing up the security clearance files now."

Pottinger sat down. The pacing wasn't going to prevent the inevitable.

"How much of this has leaked out?"

"Shipyard personnel were the first ones who realized *Hartford* was leaving. And with pursuit activity on the river, I believe it's only a matter of time before the press is all over this."

"Well, pick a spokesperson. But I don't want a word of any of this confirmed until you have clearance from Washington."

"Yes, sir."

Pottinger needed to call his boss, Bob Gerry, commander of the Atlantic Fleet. But that wouldn't be the end of the calls. The defense secretary was the next on the list. The Pentagon staff would take it from there. Considering the magnitude of the situation, the president would be briefed, as well.

Christ, all this the day before the election. That couldn't be any coincidence, he thought grimly.

"Brown. Listen hard. There will be no move to board or cut them off until I order it. That is a direct order."

"Aye, sir."

Pottinger hung up and stared at his notes for a few seconds. Punching the number of his next call, he thought that he should have retired the last time he'd had the chance.

Eight

USS Hartford
5:33 a.m.

They were a two-person wrecking crew.

Everything that was screwed, bolted or glued to the outboard bulkhead was being removed. McCann was determined to get the two of them out of this office. Their only possible escape lay on the other side of the wood-veneered, sheet-metal bulkhead that formed the outboard wall.

"Once we remove this bulkhead, you know we won't be able to go forward or aft," Amy told him as she moved the things he was ripping out to the far side of the office, near the door. "The frames running up and down cut off most of the space, and the piping and cable banks take up the rest. Going up or down is the only possibility, and I'm not sure we'll be able to do that."

"I know we can't go fore or aft," he replied. "Going

up won't work, either. Even if we *can* get up into the sonar equipment room, we'll be forward of the control room and cornered. The only way to go is down."

"To the torpedo room," she replied.

"Right."

McCann remembered that Rivera, one of the torpedo men, had stayed on board last night. He didn't want to believe that any of his nine men were involved in what was going on now. He imagined them in situations similar to this, maybe even worse. Still, someone was operating this sub.

Unlike the Florida flight school courses taken by the 9/11 hijackers, learning to operate a submarine wasn't available in any class open to the public. The people running the show here had to know their stuff. And this worried McCann even more. They also had to know the extent of the power of this single vessel—and how McCann's key-and-vault combination information made them an entirely different threat. That was the only explanation he could think of as to why they would keep him alive.

"Are we still on the surface or do you think we've submerged?" Amy asked quietly.

"We're still on the surface."

She took a clock and a file holder that he'd stripped off the wall and put it behind her. "The navy must know by now what's happening, don't you think?"

"A missing sub doesn't go unnoticed for too long," McCann answered, working on a final sheet-metal screw. "Yes, I guarantee you that the navy knows this sub has been hijacked."

Dropping the screw on the deck, he turned his attention to the other edge of the bulkhead panel. He had no access to the screws securing that side since they were buried behind the file cabinet. Using the screwdriver, he dug at the edges of the panel, trying to wedge it back enough to get a good grip on the thing.

"Then shouldn't they be stopping us?" she asked, adding as an afterthought, "They can, can't they?"

"They can blow us out of the water. But considering the nuclear reactor that powers us, I'd say they won't. At least not while we're in New London harbor." There was no reason for Amy to know that this submarine was also armed with two nuclear warheads. That was top-secret information. It was bad enough that he suspected the hijackers had this knowledge.

"Great." She sat down on one of the paper boxes, watching him. "I feel like a death-row inmate who's been given a second final meal while they tune up the electrical generator."

McCann jabbed himself on the hand with the screwdriver, but the surface wound was well worth it because the paneling was clearly starting to give in. She was right there, moving everything else away so he had elbow room. Driving the screwdriver back in at another point along the edge, he pried the panel back an inch. As he did, Amy leaned over him and jammed a stapler into the opening, effectively wedging the panel open.

He sat back on his heels, and she saw the blood on his hands.

"Use these," she said, retrieving a pair of work gloves from the pocket of the jacket she'd taken off. "You'll get a better grip."

The gloves provided the grip he needed. Bracing

himself against the cabinet, he yanked the panel back, exposing a small bank of cables, a pair of small copper pipes and insulation. The space was not the rat's nest he'd expected.

"A little space, but you'll never get through," she told him, looking over his shoulder. "On the other hand, I might."

"I'll get through," he said, determined. "We just need to cut those cables free and I think I can work my way down between the frames."

"We'll end up behind the starboard torpedo racks," she said thoughtfully. "We'll be able to climb out from there."

"I'll go. This is the safest place for you to be."

"I don't think so," she argued. "Right now, I feel like a sheep in a slaughterhouse. They locked us in here because they want to know where we are. If you get spotted out there, they'll come right back here looking for me."

"I don't know what I'll be facing, or who might be waiting down in the torpedo room to greet me."

"I think I'll take my chances," she told him, grabbing a pair of wire cutters off the counter. "We have to do some path clearing before we climb anywhere in there."

"Those are high voltage." He pointed to specific cables.

"I know that," she said. "I'm only going to cut the metal bands holding them together. I'm not going to cut the cables. May I?"

"I'll do it."

She motioned for him to let her by. "This is one area where I do have some expertise, Commander McCann."

It went against his principles to let her get involved, and not because she was a woman. She was an innocent civilian.

"Tell me what to cut and I'll do it," he told her.

"You really don't know how to let people work, do you?"

He snorted, taking the wire cutters out of her hand. Turning his back, he started yanking some of the loose insulation out of the opening.

She picked up another wire cutter off the counter and forced her way next to him as she crouched down.

"I'm helping," she said stubbornly. "This is a union shipyard."

"You're salary personnel. Besides, I guarantee you that we're not in the shipyard anymore."

"Look," she said seriously. "My life is on the line, too. There's too much at stake for me to be a passive observer."

He looked at her for a moment, then handed her the work gloves. "Put these on."

"Aye-aye, sir."

McCann noticed Amy glance at her watch before pulling the gloves on. The pained look in her expression was impossible to miss.

"This is the normal end of the shift for you, isn't it?"

"Another hour or so."

"Worried about your family?"

She nodded and looked away. Her eyes were glistening with emotion and she swiped impatiently at something on her cheek. She was doing her best to be tough.

"It's too soon for them to know what's going on here."

"I hope so," she whispered, focusing more closely on the puzzle before them. She started pushing at the cables.

McCann admired her strength. She was holding herself together better than he'd have thought. There were a half-dozen cable hangers holding the bank in place.

"You cut the bands on as many as you can see above us," she said. "I'll cut the bands on the ones below us."

He followed her directions, cutting and moving cables as she directed. In a few minutes, they'd cut enough of the hangers to allow McCann to shove the cable bank aside. Above the opening, several cables separated themselves from the bank.

"Let me have the gloves," he ordered. "I'm cutting a few of these lines."

"You do that and they'll notice some minor power outages here and there on the sub," she responded, peering up at him and handing him the gloves. "Nothing too major."

"That's too bad. I want major." He glanced up at the ceiling. "You mentioned something before about the main power cables to the ESGN being up there. I'm trying to think of what kinds of havoc we could do to the control room instrumentation if we were to disconnect it from here."

"I wish I had the schematics," she said, thinking. "My guess would be some malfunctioning of the sonar equipment, but that's it."

Time was of the essence, McCann realized. The space between the frames was now large enough for him to get through. Getting free of this office wasn't enough. Once *Hartford* reached the mouth of New London harbor and dived, the stakes rose substantially. Somehow he had to stop the ship.

For a brief second, the thought ran through his mind that maybe the hijackers' object wasn't just to try to disappear into the Atlantic. Perhaps, much like the terrorists who'd flown those planes into the buildings in New York and Washington, these people intended to cause major damage here on the East Coast.

But that was too grim a possibility. What they intended was outside of his field of action. McCann decided to focus only on what he could do.

As much as he loved *Hartford,* he'd tear his ship apart, piece by piece, if that's what it took to stop them.

Nine

The crew knew him only as Mako. He often went by other names, but this one, he felt, suited him.

Short and solidly built, he had a head of bristly blond hair that was heavily streaked with gray. Mako was in his late fifties, ancient by normal standards in his line of business—if there was anything called normal in the mercenary business. But clients never asked his age, and he didn't offer. He prided himself on a reputation for being intense, brutal, accurate, and he was the only absolute expert for hire in *this* field, as far as he knew. He spoke eight languages fluently, and he believed in no country or God. His loyalties were to himself and to the one who was transferring a fat amount of cash into his bank account at the moment. And of course, next week or next month or next year, when he was ready for a bit more excitement, the allegiance would shift to someone else.

Mako stood on the periscope platform a step above the conn. The crosshairs in the periscope view locked on the waterline of the Coast Guard cutter. The ship was on a course that would put them directly in the path of the bow of the submarine. It was a larger cutter, and Mako could see helmeted Coasties manning machine guns fore and aft.

Mako made a 360-degree sweep with the periscope. Two small navy launches were running alongside *Hartford*. There was another smaller Coast Guard cutter following in the sub's stern wake. He was keeping his speed at only three knots. They were staying close, obviously waiting for orders.

"Increase speed to five knots."

"Very good, sir." Paul Cavallaro was sitting in the X.O. chair, and he passed on the order. "Speed, five knots."

Mako looked away from the periscope optic module and glanced around the control room at his four-man crew. The geographic plot of their course and destination was already visible on the navigation screen.

"We have to shake them a little, boys. Show them we mean business. Have two MK48s loaded into the trays."

"We need to turn on the PA, sir," Cav reminded him.

"Do it," Mako ordered, looking back through the periscope. "I have a target. Now mark."

"Target mark set, sir. We have a firing solution."

"Offset zero degrees," Mako directed. "Low active snake. Give me a read back."

"Attention!" another one of his men barked. "Firing point procedures, tubes one and two, zero degree offset, thirty-second firing interval."

Mako watched the firing panel until the torpedoes were programmed. He looked through the periscope again. "Last call, shithead. You might want to move your carcass."

"Ship ready."

"Weapons ready." The calls sounded from the crew.

"Stay right there and I'll shove these torpedoes up your ass," Mako warned, looking into the periscope again.

"If we shoot now and hit that cutter, sir, we risk damaging our sonar."

He looked at Cavallaro for a moment and saw the doubt in the young man's eyes. It was more than sonar that he cared about. "We'll risk it. I want to show these morons we mean business."

Mako looked through the periscope again. They were near the mouth of New London harbor. Beyond the Coast Guard cutter, the rising sun was reflecting brilliantly off the New London Ledge lighthouse. This had to be done.

"Solution ready."

Mako looked one last time. The cutter wasn't giving up. You asked for it, asshole. "Tube one, shoot."

"Set," fire control responded.

"Fire."

Ten

Just a few seconds after a shudder went through the submarine, a loud boom nearly knocked Amy off her feet, and her ears felt a sudden change of pressure.

She stretched out her hands and arms toward Mc-Cann. She'd been standing on one of the boxes, working on removing the overhead panel. He reached for her, steadying her just as a second boom rocked the sub, tumbling her into his arms.

"What was that?"

"A pair of torpedoes hitting something."

She held on to him, every nerve in her body jumping. This was it. The end of her life. And she hadn't said goodbye to her children. She'd made no plans about who would raise them. Her mind raced in a hundred different directions.

Ryan would take the kids, since he was their father.

But his heart wouldn't be in it. His job and lifestyle wouldn't allow it. Kaitlyn and Zack would be better off with her parents, but the kids really had too much energy for them. They would be a burden. Her sister would be the most likely person. But she was on the West Coast. And did she tell anyone about the last life insurance policy she'd bought? Would they disqualify any claim because this hijacking would be construed as an act of terrorism?

She pressed her hands to her ears. They hurt.

"Yawn, Amy. The concussion causes a change in pressure."

He had to repeat it a couple of times before she shook herself out of the self-misery that was drowning her. Scared and confused, she looked up at him. Every line in McCann's face was tight. His dark eyes looked almost black, and they were blazing. He cupped her hands over her ears.

"Open your mouth wide. Yawn."

She did as she was told and felt her ears pop. She had to do it a few more times. "Who fired the torpedoes?"

"We did, I think."

She started shaking. She lived in Stonington, half a block from the water. How far out from the mouth of New London harbor would they have to be to get a direct shot at Stonington? Her two angels were still in bed. Her eyes welled with tears, but she didn't care.

He motioned over his shoulder at the outboard wall. "I'm almost there. I'll have to work my way through any other obstructions after I climb in. It looks like I'll have a clear drop to the torpedo room, though."

She nodded.

"I want you to stay here for now. Do what we decided on the wiring above the panel. Wreck that navigation instrumentation, if you can."

Amy was afraid, but she wasn't going to admit it. She wouldn't slow him down. It looked like he was the only one who could stop them. She gathered all of her strength, wiped away the tears on her face and nodded again.

"Go," she said as calmly as she could muster. "I'll cut the bastards' juice from here."

Eleven

Newport, Rhode Island
6:15 a.m.

Senator John Penn was, if nothing else, a creature of habit.

It didn't matter if he was in Rhode Island or in D.C. or on the campaign trail in some small town somewhere in the middle of the country. Good weather or bad, five days a week, he was up at 5:45 a.m. and out of the house or hotel or anywhere else he was staying by 6:15 a.m. for his morning run. Half a mile of walking and stretching, two miles of running, another mile of cool-down walking as he began to conduct business with one of his aides.

The exercise was a wuss workout compared to the standards of a lot of his colleagues, but at fifty-four years old, John Penn loved the routine. It kept his weight down, his stomach reasonably flat, and his cholesterol numbers within a healthy range without medication. And that was good enough.

Over the past year and a half of political campaigning, there'd been an additional advantage to the morning exercise routine. Acting on a suggestion from his campaign manager, Penn always invited one or sometimes two members of the media to join him on his exercise route. His aides called it a "casual chat" with the senator, as opposed to a formal interview. But the end result was the same, good publicity from a cadre of increasingly friendly reporters.

Before running for president, John Penn had always been extremely protective of his family's privacy. Even as a U.S. senator, he'd taken the position that his service to the nation did not make his family members celebrities. All of that had changed, however, the moment he'd put in his bid for the highest political office in the country. He and his family had agreed to make the sacrifice.

Oddly enough, he found he enjoyed the relationships that he was developing with members of the media. In creating a casual rapport, Penn found that the way the reporters dealt with his family was very positive. Many of the questions that came up during these jogs had to do with the melting pot that best described his family. Whether it was his nineteen-year-old son, Owen, who'd become a paraplegic after a car accident three years ago, or his gay, twenty-four-year-old daughter, Aileen, who was pursuing a career in the movie business, or his free-spirited and outspoken red-haired Irish-American wife, Anna, who didn't believe in or practice any specific religion, or the fact that Penn was African-American, the media had—for the most part—portrayed them with respect.

To the surprise of many political gurus, his family's diverseness had actually helped him in the opinion polls. They were unique, and the American public seemed to accept that. He and his family seemed to provide a refreshing change to the lack of humanity that characterized the sitting president's administration.

The best part of it all, John Penn found, was that in making himself accessible to the public through the media, he'd finally become truly comfortable with who he was and what he stood for. Smart, black, born and raised in a project in the Bronx, he brought to the table his vision of a government that he believed matched the qualities of the people of America—a government that was better, fairer, more compassionate and less belligerent than that of President Will Hawkins.

Greg Moore, one of his aides, was waiting in the kitchen of John Penn's small mansion in Newport. The young man's T-shirt and shorts were a contrast to his own long-sleeved, foul-weather jogging suit. But the senator figured their age difference was enough to explain Greg's tolerance for the weather. If Walter Cronkite was standing at the end of the drive in a T-shirt, though, John was going to be annoyed.

Greg told him about the weather and ran down the day's schedule that had been faxed to the house an hour earlier. The young aide never mentioned the next day's election. John had reached the saturation point after a dinner speech in California the previous night. He'd made a decision. No eleventh-hour campaigning, he'd told his team. They were to cancel everything on his schedule. There would be no two-dozen stops on the way home. He was going to spend today quietly in Newport, and that was that.

"Who do we have jogging with us today?"

"Two reporters. We decided to go with local connections for this final…uh, today." He told him the names of the reporters from the *Boston Globe* and the *Providence Journal*.

The senator knotted the laces on his sneakers as Greg rattled off the reporters' names and their recent work. Both papers had vigorously endorsed him. Penn's campaign manager had made sure they'd invited younger reporters, since their surveys showed that—as strong as he was in every demographic—nearly eighty percent of the under-fifty age group were Penn supporters.

"And where are they meeting us?"

"Considering the bad weather, we recommended that they join us along Ocean Drive by the start of the Cliff Walk. This way, you're done with most of your run, and they won't be too wet or pooped to want to talk."

Senator Penn trusted his staff's judgment for these types of decisions. He drank the glass of orange juice already poured for him by the housekeeper, did his routine stretches and glanced quickly at the headlines of the three newspapers sitting on the counter. His name and face were on the top half of each of the front pages.

Everything looked good. Too good, Penn thought apprehensively.

One more day. He took a deep breath, stretched again and nodded to Greg. By the door, two members of the secret service, also dressed in running clothes, joined them.

"Let's get this show on the road."

At the end of the winding driveway, by the gates of the mansion, the real show was already waiting for him. News vans blocked the street as a dozen or more reporters with microphones and cameramen in tow surged toward the gates past the line of additional secret service agents and state police. Some of his neighbors were even out on the sidewalks, raincoats on over their pajamas.

"What the hell is going on?" Penn asked his aide.

"I don't know, sir."

The reporters started screaming all at once as soon as John Penn walked within earshot.

"Has something come up that you guys forgot to tell me?" he asked quietly.

Greg put a hand on the senator's arm, motioning for him to stop as he reached for his cell phone. Senator Penn, putting on his best campaign smile, decided to continue on. Whatever it was, he wasn't about to turn tail now. After the craziness of this past six months, there was no question that he couldn't answer. There was no topic that stumped him. He was confident and ready for anything.

John motioned to one of the state police officers to open the wrought-iron pedestrian gate. John Penn waved back the secret service and stepped into what looked to be a feeding frenzy.

"Senator Penn," a reporter shouted. "Do you have any comment about what's happened at Electric Boat?"

"Who do you believe is behind it?" another one called out.

"Shouldn't there be an emergency broadcast?" a woman shouted from the back.

"Do you advise people to stay indoors?"

John Penn looked over his shoulder, searching for Greg. He wasn't going to admit to this throng that he had no clue what was going on.

"Senator…senator!" A female reporter shoved a microphone into his face. "What do the events of this morning do to your promise of bringing our troops home from the Middle East?"

"If you're elected president, are you just going to let the terrorists do whatever they want?" another one asked. John heard the note of accusation in his tone.

"If you're elected tomorrow, will you declare war on whoever is behind this?"

The crowd seemed to be growing in size. There was the same kind of borderline hysteria in the air that he remembered seeing in September 2001, right after the planes had crashed into the Twin Towers and into the Pentagon. But John had no clue what had happened this morning. Electric Boat made nuclear submarines. Had there been an attack on the shipyard?

For the first time in his career, the senator from Rhode Island found himself speechless.

"How about your platform of peace?" someone else shouted.

"Are there any nuclear warheads on that submarine?"

Penn saw Greg fighting his way through the reporters to get to him, motioning to him to retreat.

John Penn heard himself saying the one thing that he despised whenever he heard other politicians say it.

"I can't comment at this time," he said, backing toward the gate. "But I'll be communicating with the media as soon as I have something constructive to convey."

As he and his small entourage hurried back down the drive, the shouts of the reporters filling the morning gloom, he felt the cold, uncomfortable sensation that he was being set up somehow. What he had to do now, however, was find out what the hell was happening.

Twelve

Clearing the security checkpoint, Lieutenant Sarah Connelly hoped that she wouldn't be the last one arriving at the conference room on the fourth deck of the E-Ring. She'd received the call only thirty minutes ago from her superior, Admiral Meisner, the head of Naval Intelligence. Ready in ten, she'd had to put her fate in getting here on time in the hands of the driver they'd sent to get her. The car had barely touched the ground on the way to the Pentagon.

As an attorney and a senior naval intelligence officer, Sarah was regularly directed to sit in on hearings or emergency briefings beyond the full caseload of assignments that she and her staff were assigned. Nothing out of the ordinary there.

But today was entirely different. The admiral's news of a submarine hijacking had her scurrying to get ready.

When he mentioned Darius McCann's name, she'd come running.

In the car she considered how odd it was to hear the admiral refer to Darius. As she thought about it, Sarah had felt a sense of relief almost that her superiors didn't see a conflict in calling on her with this specific situation. She and Darius had known each other for thirteen years. For two of those years, they'd been lovers. For ten of those years, they'd been good friends. During the past year, however, their only communication had been a birthday card that she'd put in the mail for him. That was just last week. He hadn't bothered to remember hers.

To everyone who knew them, the relationship had run its course for both of them. They each had adjusted well to the breakup and had gone their separate ways. But Sarah couldn't ignore how she felt this morning when she'd heard he was in the middle of a naval investigation—in the middle of a potential nightmare. It was just another reminder of those invisible wires that still connected them.

She ran the last few steps to the elevator, just as the doors were closing. Someone near the door put a hand out, holding it open for her.

"Thanks," she said, stepping into the crowded elevator.

Wanting to keep her mind focused, she did not look at any of the faces around her. Instead, she stared at the panel displaying the floors. The elevator nearly emptied on the third floor. Stepping out on the fourth floor, she nodded thanks to a navy commander who motioned for her to go ahead of him. He was the same person who'd held the elevator door open for her.

After signing in at the security desk, Sarah started toward the large conference room where she'd been told the meeting would take place. Her companion from the elevator was right behind her, and they both stopped at a reception desk just outside of the conference room.

The young man behind the partition looked up from his computer screen, reading their badges. "Lieutenant Connelly. Commander Dunn. They're waiting for you inside."

"I guess that's as good as any introduction," the commander told her, extending a hand as they headed toward the conference room door. "Bruce Dunn."

"Sarah Connelly." Surprised at his lack of formality, she moved her briefcase from one hand to the other and shook his hand. Clear green eyes, strong chin, Dunn was definitely easy on the eyes. A nose that looked like it had been broken once or twice only added character to his face.

"How much time did they give you to get here?"

"Half an hour," she said. "How about you?"

"About the same."

"I live twenty minutes away," she added. Sarah noticed the tiny bit of tissue still attached to a cut right under his chin. She pointed to it. "Your stitches are showing."

He wiped a hand down his throat, brushing the tissue away. "Better?"

"Much."

He reached to open the door to the conference room. "They better have some cinnamon doughnuts in there."

She liked his sense of humor, but her thoughts about him were cut short the moment they walked in. Seeing the gathered brass, Sarah felt her stress level go to about a thousand RPMs. This was not a standard briefing. The tension inside the room was crisp, and the subdued conversations stopped as the admiral entered with the head of the joint chiefs. About two dozen uniformed and plainclothed personnel crowded around a huge conference table. She immediately recognized some of them, but her attention was immediately drawn to a large TV screen at the far end of the room. The volume was turned up as a reporter described the live footage of New London Harbor. The man's voice bordered on frantic. A large electronic map on the wall next to the TV screen highlighted the location of *Hartford*.

"...can see where the unmanned New London Ledge lighthouse has sustained damage. The landmark, a brick building that sat by itself in the water at the mouth of the harbor, appears to be totally destroyed. Smoke is rising from the ruin. From here, we can see smoke from the...get a shot of the Coast Guard cutter," the reporter said to his cameraman, "there, you can see it now. Smoke is engulfing the Coast Guard cutter that the submarine clearly fired on. It's hard to believe that this is taking place right here on the Thames River."

The network anchor cut in as the camera zoomed closer. It appeared that they were filming from the top of a building in downtown New London, overlooking the harbor. Groton was visible across the river. Just then, the screen split into two images and an aerial shot of the scene appeared. Sarah could see the submarine gliding through the dark water.

"The submarine looks to be heading for Fisher's Island or what locals call the 'Race,' the opening that leads to the Atlantic from New London harbor. But, of course, we can't tell for certain," the reporter said to the network anchorman.

The anchor cut in. "We're getting unofficial word that the submarine we're looking at from our New London affiliate's helicopter is the USS *Hartford,* one of the navy's improved Los Angeles-class submarines.

"What the hell is that news helicopter doing up there?" one of the generals barked.

A member of the admiral's staff picked up a telephone and spoke into it briefly.

"We've just been told that there will be a press conference at the navy submarine base in Groton any minute, now," the anchorman added. The image shifted to an empty podium in a briefing room. A number of officers were standing behind it, and others were coming in and out of the picture. "For those viewers who're just joining us…"

Sarah felt a touch on her arm. Commander Dunn pointed to two empty seats against the wall, away from the TV screen. Admiral Meisner had seated himself at the table in front of the chairs, and he nodded to the two of them as they made their way to be seated.

The admiral rolled his chair away from the table and leaned back as Sarah sat down.

"Are you up to this?" he whispered.

"Absolutely," she said confidently.

"We'll take care of the tactical side of things and any negotiations when they come up," Meisner explained. "You and Commander Dunn will handle the investigative side of it."

Sarah realized Bruce Dunn was listening to the conversation.

"By the way, have you two met?"

They both nodded.

"Your primary objective is to identify who is running the show inside. We want to know the man on top and everyone else on his crew," Meisner continued. "Most of us in this room believe that only a present or a former U.S. sub driver could pull this type of maneuver. Also, you should know right up front that we're not ruling out that some or maybe all of the ten crew members left on board *Hartford* are willing participants in the hijacking."

The sudden rush of temper set Sarah's ears on fire. She knew McCann, and so did they. She held back her comment, though. She knew she needed to come across as cool and objective or she would immediately be removed.

"Are you okay with this?" the admiral asked her directly.

Sarah's past relationship with Darius was no secret to anyone that she worked with. "Of course, Admiral."

Meisner turned his chair slightly. "And you, Commander Dunn?"

"We'll see what evidence presents itself, sir," he answered coolly.

The admiral nodded, satisfied. "We've set up a command center for the two of you three doors down. You'll have a staff of six investigators, but you have clearance to use anything and anyone you want...CIA, FBI, Homeland Security, and any local or national law enforcement databases or personnel. We're putting together your list of contact liaisons right now. We'll make sure that you're made aware of any or all communications that we might establish with *Hartford*."

Sarah nodded.

"When do we start?" Dunn asked.

"Commander McCann's records are to be reviewed before us in a couple of minutes. You'll want to be present for that," the admiral advised. "You're dismissed right after that."

"Why only McCann's records?" Sarah asked.

Meisner frowned. "McCann is the most knowledgeable and powerful person aboard that submarine. We know that and we're certain whoever is behind this operation knows that. He has the keys and the combinations that could result in a nuclear holocaust. You understand, don't you, Lieutenant Connelly?"

"Of course, sir. We'll assess the records of the others aboard *Hartford*."

Nothing more needed to be said by him, and Sarah didn't miss the warning look sent by her superior. She was to stay objective.

The television was turned off. Sarah had no doubt that the press conference would not actually take place for quite some time, if at all.

Admiral Meisner called the meeting to order and made a quick introduction of the major players attending. He finished with Sarah and Commander Dunn. Looking up at the electronic map on the other side of the conference room, she realized that the submarine was now southwest of Fisher's Island, but it had not yet made a change in its course to the east and the Atlantic. If it turned to the west, the sub would be bottled up in Long Island Sound. Not a good thing. It would be like having a tiger shark in a wading pool. A tiger shark with serious teeth.

A handout was passed around. Sarah received her copy and stared down at Darius's military résumé. Years of hard work jammed into a couple of paragraphs. The stamp at the bottom read "Under Investigation." She stared at the two-by-three photo of him in his dress whites at the top of the page. Professional and serious, but definitely good-looking. His piercing dark eyes and chiseled features made him the classic poster boy. Tough, but not unapproachable. Confident, but not arrogant. She knew for a fact that the navy had used this same picture of Darius in recruiting efforts over the past few years.

To calm her agitation, she reminded herself that this was only a briefing. As an attorney, she knew she could gather enough facts and figures to show that Darius could walk on water if it came down to it.

A navy lieutenant named Seth McDermott, who sat on the far side of the table from her, began reading McCann's fact sheet aloud.

"Commander Darius McCann is forty years old… today." He paused for a second. "Commander McCann graduated magna cum laude from Notre Dame with a bachelor of science degree in aerospace engineering. Upon graduating, he attended Officer Candidate School in Newport, Rhode Island. Received commission September 1989. Following commissioning, completed nuclear propulsion training in Orlando, Florida, and Idaho Falls, Idaho."

An older admiral that Sarah remembered being introduced as Smith cut in. "Married? Children?"

"No, sir." The lieutenant looked down at the sheet in his hand before answering. "Never married."

"Steady girlfriend?" the admiral persisted.

Sarah focused on the sheet on her lap, feeling the gazes of several in the room fix on her.

"No, sir."

"Let's stick to the résumé, Seth," responded Admiral Gerry, the commander of the Atlantic Fleet.

The older officer frowned at his sheet. "Go ahead," he growled, "but it's clear as day that this work is incomplete. I'm going to have some questions."

"I'm sure you won't be alone, Admiral," Gerry replied. He nodded to the lieutenant, who continued.

"After completing Submarine Officer Basic Course, he completed three North Atlantic deployments before reporting to the naval postgraduate school in Monterey, California."

A light tap on her arm drew Sarah's attention to Dunn, who tilted a pad of paper toward her. She read his scribbling. *Old goat…retired Rear Admiral Joseph Smith, assigned to the panel by President Hawkins this morning.* She nodded. That explained why she didn't know him.

Dunn scribbled something else on the paper. Sarah looked over.

Smith doesn't like me much.

She gave a small nod and turned her attention back to the room.

"Graduated with distinction, earning a master's of science in physics with a military professional subspecialty in nuclear and directed energy weapons. He was presented the Naval Sea Systems Command Award and the Superintendent's Most Outstanding Thesis Award for his work on nuclear propulsion."

"That's impressive," someone murmured. There were a number of other comments.

"After completing Submarine Officer Advanced Course, subject reported as engineering officer on USS *Rhode Island,* completing two deployments, including numerous surfacing in the packed ice and open water polynyas of the Arctic."

Sarah remembered those blocks of time very well. That was when they'd first become romantically involved.

"Immediately following second deployment, served as assistant force nuclear power officer reporting to the Commander Submarine Force, U.S. Atlantic Fleet."

There was another tap on her arm. She looked over at Commander Dunn again. He had another note for her. *Seth McDermott. Good guy. He'll be working on our team.*

"During this assignment, instrumental in developing advanced submarine firefighting tactics, damage control equipment and active ventilation procedures. Additionally, subject earned his professional engineering license in the Commonwealth of Virginia."

This time, there was no tap, but the legal pad slowly slid in front of her. Sarah looked down.

Let me take the first swing.

Surprised, she read it again before turning to Commander Dunn. He was all attention, focused completely on the speaker. She didn't know what he meant or how to take his comment.

"In his next deployment, he served as executive officer on a five-month deployment around South America on USS *Omaha,* during which time he conducted top-secret weaponry testing. Following that tour, he was assigned his first command, USS *Hartford.*"

Seth McDermott finished reading and looked up. To Sarah's relief, for a couple of moments, absolute silence ruled the room. Now she understood that it was actually advantageous for McCann to have his impressive record read by these people.

"All the makings of a fine *early* career," Rear Admiral Smith said curtly, flipping through his pages. "Now, let's get back to basics. Commander McCann. What was his first name?"

"Darius, sir."

"Darius. What is Commander McCann's ancestry?"

Sarah had to fist her hand in her lap and bite her tongue so she wouldn't stand and object to the question. She couldn't believe what Smith was implying. The innuendo was hardly subtle. McCann's flawless record spoke for itself.

Lieutenant McDermott looked across the room at Admiral Meisner. Sarah saw her superior hunch over the table, his elbows planted on the dark mahogany. She knew that was a sure sign that Meisner wasn't any too pleased with the question, either.

"What is it that you want to know, Admiral?" Meisner asked.

"I'm interested in his ancestry."

"How many generations would you like to go back, Admiral?"

"One will do."

Sarah knew her superior was well aware of this information, so she was pleased when Meisner took his time and thumbed through a manila folder on the conference table first before answering.

"Father, fourth-generation Irish. Cork City, I believe. Commander McCann's mother was born in Iran."

Smith looked positively smug as he turned to Admiral Gerry, the commander of the Atlantic Fleet. "Has Commander McCann ever expressed anything that might demonstrate disagreement with our Middle East policy?"

"Of course not," Gerry said.

"Does he have any family members that still reside in Iran?"

"Admiral Meisner?" Gerry said, fending off the question.

"He does, sir."

Sarah saw the head of the joint chiefs scribble a note that he handed off to an aide. The man left the room immediately.

"Is this his first patrol in the Persian Gulf region?" Smith asked the Atlantic Fleet commander.

"Yes, sir," Gerry answered, obviously showing deference to the president's adviser.

"Did he have any objection to this assignment?"

"No, sir."

"My apologies for interrupting, Admiral Smith," Dunn said before Smith could fire the next question. "But we're wasting valuable time discussing information of very little relevance."

"Very little relevance, Commander Dunn?" Smith asked critically.

"Yes, sir. My understanding was that this briefing

was being held for the purpose of understanding the credentials of the ranking officer so that strategies can be developed to counter the potential actions of the unidentified hijackers. It serves no purpose to assume that Commander McCann has betrayed his trust."

"Do you think it is irrelevant that McCann has family connections with a rogue nation that is a sworn enemy of the United States?"

"Yes, sir. It is entirely irrelevant to the purpose of this briefing," Dunn responded sharply. "Unless, of course, we had all been told beforehand that you wanted to conduct a genealogy club meeting, then I could have brought pictures of my Russian great-grandmother who, as you know, was a diehard communist. Perhaps you have something to share about your own great-grandfather, whom I believe stole horses for the South during the Civil—"

"That's enough, Commander," the head of the joint chiefs snapped. "But I have to agree that we are digressing from our purpose, Admiral."

Sarah didn't miss the daggers that Dunn and Smith sent each other. He wasn't kidding when he said they didn't like each other.

Admiral Pottinger, commander of the Atlantic Fleet Sub Force, spoke for the first time. "We need to discuss a plan for taking back control of this vessel. We cannot afford to leave that submarine in the hands of hostile forces for even a minute longer than we have to."

"Whatever is decided upon must be quick and decisive," someone else replied from across the table. "We cannot allow any half-assed cowboy stunts like the one the Coast Guard pulled this morning."

Others began to weigh in with their opinions, but Sarah knew she'd have no involvement in any of those decisions. Admiral Meisner was on the same wavelength, for she saw him stack up the files in front of him and turn around and hand them to her.

"McDermott will stay and bring you anything pertinent from this meeting," Meisner said. "You've got a lot of work to do."

Sarah nodded and grabbed her stuff. Commander Dunn was on his feet, and the two of them left the room.

Outside, she turned to him. "You're lucky you're not being escorted to the brig, talking like that to Admiral Smith."

"He's retired," Dunn said coolly. "He just doesn't know yet that he doesn't run every show."

Sarah looked at him as they walked down the corridor. "So what's the real bone of contention between the two of you?"

"If you really have to know," he replied, smiling as he pulled open a door for her, "I'm his former son-in-law."

Thirteen

USS Hartford
8:01 a.m.

Amy glanced over at the hole in the wall where McCann had disappeared before reaching up to make the first cut into the wires overhead. Without the schematics, she was no better than a bull in a china shop. But it really didn't matter. Any kind of damage was a positive step.

She felt partially responsible for this whole mess. She'd ignored the immediate warning flag that had gone up in her head the moment she'd started testing the navigation system in the control room. The rejection report completely disagreed with the actual sequence. From the first readouts, it was clear there was nothing wrong with the system. The local network malfunction could have only been caused by someone intentionally disconnecting a wire or loosening a connection. She had a good idea that it must have been something right there in the control room, too.

From the moment she'd been given the job, she'd operated on the defensive, looking for screwups that occurred during production. She'd searched for catastrophic system failures and had totally disregarded the possibility of operator sabotage.

She knew now why it happened, too. Someone had wanted to bring *Hartford* back in for this, the hijacking, and Amy had missed the opportunity to send up a flare. She'd never even voiced her concern to the sub's commander.

Idiot.

She snipped away with her cutters, determined to do some real damage to the navigation system that she guessed was probably working perfectly now.

Fourteen

Mina Azizi was born and raised in Iran.

Iran was a different place then. It was a different time, long before the Islamic revolution that shattered the bond between East and West, before the revolution that set women back decades in their freedoms and in their perceived value in a society that was suddenly so foreign to Mina. So medieval. It was a place where families were not torn apart at the whim of a local mullah, a place where politicians and governments had no divine power to deny sisters and brothers, parents and children, the simple act of visiting one another.

Mina came from a large family where having an opinion was as vital as bread and water; it was the sustenance of their very existence. Voicing that opinion was as natural as the water that ran over the stones in a river at the base of the garden. When she was growing up, every Friday, without fail, her parents' house was filled with people. Young and old, cousins, aunts, uncles and friends who happened to be passing by descended on their house, since her father was the eldest in his generation. No matter how many came, there always seemed to be enough food. The conversations were lively, the arguments loud.

She remembered sleeping on pallets on a second-story porch with her cousins on warm summer nights. The smell of the flowers from the gardens still came back to her sometimes on warm evenings. She recalled the arguments she and her cousins had until her grandmother would come out and tell them to go to sleep. They were good days.

Mina came to the United States in 1961 at the age of eighteen to attend George Washington University. That same year, she met and fell in love with a hazel-eyed, sweet-talking senior who proposed marriage to her at the end of their first date.

Mina and Harry McCann married a year later, and Mina's life took a different path than she'd ever imagined just a few years before, lying on her pallet on that summer porch, the scent of her family's flowers in the air.

Now, nearly fifty years later, she was happy to think that path had been a good one.

There had been many sacrifices. From the very beginning, she'd missed her parents, her brother and sister. Early in their marriage, she and Harry made a point of visiting Iran every summer. But as their four children came along, each two or three years apart, the trips had become more difficult to make, less practical, and therefore less frequent.

And then the revolution changed everything. Travel between Iran and the U.S. stopped completely. When her mother died, Mina couldn't return for her funeral. She couldn't visit her father after his stroke. She'd missed his funeral, as well.

She still had a brother and sister who lived in Iran. She talked to them occasionally on the phone. But that was the extent of her connection with people who had been everything to her in the early years of her life. She sometimes felt it was as if she'd lived two separate lives.

Harry filled many gaps in Mina's life, and she loved him for it. He wore many shoes. As the years passed, they had created their own kind of Persian-American family. Mina had no immediate kin nearby to stop by and fill her house on weekends, so they had created a new extended family that included their three sons and their daughter and an endless array of friends who had each carved their own permanent place in her heart and at their table. And now her family included five grand-children that she and Harry were extremely proud of.

Mina hadn't been too keen on moving to Key West after Harry's retirement. But with the way their children's lives and jobs had developed, there hadn't been that one place where they could live and be close to all of them. She finally gave in to Harry, and two years later, she had to admit that he'd been right. Her family loved to come to the Keys for visits. The grandchildren were more attached than ever to Mina and Harry. And the times when there were no impending visits, the two of them were flying to California, Wisconsin, Massa-chusetts or Connecticut to see them.

In fact, this morning Mina was already planning to start packing for their Thanksgiving trip to Massachusetts to visit their daughter and her family, even though they weren't leaving for another two weeks.

Following her everyday routine, Mina slipped out of bed around seven-thirty, started a pot of coffee for her husband and made herself a cup of tea. She stepped out the kitchen door onto the brick path already warm with the sun. The hibiscus in the back was blooming beautifully, and she marveled at their colors before walking around the side of their little house.

On both borders of the walk, she and Harry had planted a rose garden, and the scents of the roses filled the morning air. Some of the prettiest had no scent, and Mina could never really understand why a botanist could breed a hybrid for beauty at the expense of smell. Still, she mixed the different varieties and was happy with the end result.

It was Mina's habit to take her time on this walk. It was her "moment of Zen," as Harry joked. As she ambled along, she liked to search out every new bud and tend to every fading bloom. Along the brick walk, two or three feet apart, she'd placed clay pots of fragrant flowering jasmine. As she passed them, she collected pocketfuls of star-shaped flowers, knowing how much Harry enjoyed the fragrance at the breakfast table. Reaching the gate by the driveway, she opened it, picked up the morning paper and paused before starting back along the brick path.

Most mornings, she also stopped to talk to their neighbor Nora Smith. A retired schoolteacher, the ninety-two-year-old was an early riser, but Mina knew

that the older woman timed her own walk to get the
newspaper to have a chance to visit with Mina. They
exchanged news of everything from their children and
grandchildren to politics to flowers to tourists to gas
prices to whatever Nora had seen on CNN that morning. Unlike Harry and Mina, who never turned on the
TV unless they were watching a movie or a ball game,
Nora's never went off.

This morning, Mina saw that Nora's paper was still
lying on her driveway. Looking up at her neighbor's
house, she saw the shades still closed. There was no
sign of her elderly friend on the wraparound porch, either.

Concerned, she started across the small border garden to knock on her door, just to make sure everything
was okay. Nora never slept in.

"Mina…"

She turned around, surprised to see her husband.
Hastily dressed in jeans and a T-shirt, Harry was coming out their front door. They were both creatures of
habit. But it wasn't the fact that he hadn't showered and
shaved before stepping out that worried her—it was the
look in his eyes. He didn't have to say a word for her
to know something horrible had happened.

"What's wrong?" she asked. "Who called? Who's
sick? Was there an accident?" She stumbled as she
came back through the strip of garden, and the handful
of jasmine flowers she was carrying spilled onto the
driveway. She recovered her footing and ran toward
him.

He didn't say anything but only gathered her in
his arms.

"Please tell me. How bad is it? Who called you?" She couldn't stop the questions any more than she could prevent the tears welling in her eyes.

"Nora called. She said we should turn on the TV."

Perplexed, Mina looked up into his face and saw pain there. Something made her think of the September 11 attack. It had happened first thing in the morning. She thought of the afternoon of the Challenger explosion. She still remembered where she was and what she'd been doing.

"What's on TV, Harry? Who's destroying our world this time?"

"I don't know the details yet." He took a deep breath. "There's something going on with Darius's submarine."

The world tilted. Her vision blurred. Darius was the only one in their family who'd wanted to join the military. She'd been furious with him when he told them. She'd used so many arguments against it. Her parentage. The possible questioning of his loyalty. The rejection of the belief she and Harry had tried to instill in all of their children about the peaceful resolution of problems. They'd tried to raise peace-loving, responsible adults. Not soldiers.

All her tears had been for nothing, and Darius had done what he felt he was meant to do. In the end he'd managed to succeed in his career, and he had made his parents proud of him. They were proud of him and everything he'd accomplished.

Now she could only think the worst. *Hartford* had sunk. There had been a nuclear accident. Where was her son? It was his birthday today. Forty years old. It felt like only yesterday that he was just an infant. A little boy…

"What are they saying?" she asked, feeling her body go numb joint by joint. But not her grieving heart.

He shook his head. "They suspect hijacking. But nothing is for certain. We've had no calls from the navy. We don't even know if he was on board. They were docked at Electric Boat for some reason. This could all be nothing. I *want* to think it's all nothing."

"Did you try to call him?"

"I called his house. No answer."

"Then we have to call someone else," she said passionately. "His superior. That admiral…what was his name…the one we met at that dinner in D.C. last year. I'll call the secretary of the navy. I'll call the president directly. I'll demand to know what he's done to my son."

Mina's emotions swung from one end of the spectrum to the other. Grief turned to anger. Numbness was replaced by uproar.

"We're his parents," she cried. "We have the right to know what's happening to him."

"We'll do all that, my love," Harry told her, placing a kiss on her forehead. "But for now, let's not think the worst. We just have to assume that Darius is fine. We have to."

Harry took her by the hand and led her back onto the porch. But before they could go in, they heard the sound of the cars. Two state police cars, escorting a black SUV with tinted glass, pulled in front of the house.

Mina leaned against her husband. Suddenly, her legs weren't strong enough to carry her weight.

Two state troopers got out of the vehicles. Two navy officers stepped out of the SUV, looking at the McCanns intently as they crossed the lawn.

The men were all strangers. It couldn't have come to this, she told herself. These strangers couldn't be bringing news of their son's death. She bit her lip as a knot formed in her chest, stopping her from breathing. Her head was pounding. She brought her hands to her mouth. Everything around her started to blur, as if the lens on a camera had become loose.

"Mr. and Mrs. McCann?" one of the navy officers asked, stepping onto the porch.

As Mina's world went dark, she was vaguely aware of the fragrance of jasmine on her fingers.

Fifteen

Mako glanced at his watch. Everything was moving according to schedule. Perfect. He mounted the conn and looked at the displays, the status board and the plotting of the course. He reached up and pressed a button.

"Radar? Conn." His voice rang on the communication system. "Anything happening with the sub hunters overhead?"

A couple of planes equipped with air-drop torpedoes had joined them a few minutes earlier. Now that they were almost out in open water, Mako wouldn't put it past the brass at Atlantic Fleet to return his earlier gesture by launching a couple of torpedoes at them.

"Nothing, sir. The three choppers are holding their position and the two planes continue to circle."

Mako stepped up onto the periscope platform and

swung around, looking to their stern. Far off in the distance, smoke continued to belch into the air above what was left of the lighthouse. The New London Ledge lighthouse had been a square, stone-and-brick edifice rising right out of the water, but now it was smoke and rubble. Beyond the lighthouse, the Coast Guard cutter they'd clipped with the torpedo was listing to one side and a tug was alongside, assisting her. He swung the periscope around and noted that the two navy launches were now keeping a respectful distance.

Above them, he could see the three helicopters. One was from a news station; two belonged to the navy. Mako guessed that they were not firing any torpedoes because they were about to drop a dozen navy SEALs out of those helicopters in an attempt to try to land them on the bridge at the top of the sail. A few minutes later, they'd blast open the hatch. That meant he had another ten minutes, tops.

He wouldn't need that much time.

They were vulnerable as long as they stayed on the surface, but he knew these waters like the back of his hand. He knew when and where he should dive. And they were almost there. In another thirty seconds they'd be in water more than eighty feet deep. Twenty seconds. Ten.

"Down periscope." Ten seconds. "Take her down to sixty feet. Ten degrees down angle. No alarm prior to diving."

"Aye, sir." The orders were repeated.

Seconds later, the deck angled downward as the helmsman followed the orders. The hull groaned slightly and the sub leveled out moments later. Mako ordered some quick checks for water integrity. Everything moved smoothly. The boat settled. The first leg of the mission was complete.

There was no point to go any deeper now. He didn't want to hide. The threat had to lurk right at the edge. He just had to stop them from trying to land on him.

From the periscope stand, Mako studied his crew. Every one of the men in the control room was an absolute expert in taking and executing his commands. But something in the navigation area caught his attention. A screen blinked a couple of times and went dark.

"What the hell is going on there?" He crossed to the panels.

Paul Cavallaro, noticing the same thing, was there before Mako and sat in the chair in front of the dead screen.

"They must be cutting the juice to it." He started running some tests. "Shouldn't we let them know?"

"Hardly," Mako replied. "You know what your orders are."

The screen at the next panel started acting up, going blank a couple of seconds later.

"If they keep this up, we'll lose sonar," Cav said over his shoulder.

Mako motioned his man Kilo to the conn. He spoke in a low voice to him.

"Send two men down there now." Kilo and his men had been signed to handle situations such as this. He'd done a good job taking care of the security guards. "Make sure they keep McCann alive. We might need him yet. Just stop him from doing any more damage. But that yardbird is a nuisance. We should have finished her hours ago. Have them do it now."

Sixteen

McCann didn't know if they were still in Long Island Sound or in the Atlantic, but from the pitch and length of the dive, he knew they had taken *Hartford* to periscope depth, which meant they were now capable of using the vertical launch system.

His time was running short.

Working his way down to the torpedo room, McCann had found the last few feet the tightest of all. Hung up at one point when his clothing caught on a pipe hanger, he'd finally been able to work his way through, emerging outboard of the torpedo racks. A torn shirt and a few scratches were all he had to show for his trouble.

The area was the arsenal of the attack submarine. Three sets of double-decker racks held twenty-two smooth white torpedoes. Four more fish sat ready in the tubes. Two of those were already fired, though, Mc-

Cann recalled. On less critical missions, a couple of racks were usually left empty for the purpose of maintenance and movement. But that wasn't the case on this patrol. Their destination in the Persian Gulf mandated that *Hartford* should be fitted with every ounce of firepower that she could carry.

He worked his way to the aft end of the rack and around the tail end of the fish to the aisle that separated the side and center racks. With the exception of the soft hum of the ventilation system, it was very quiet. But he knew someone, most likely two people, had to be working the tubes. He had to find out if they were still down here. He had to assume they would be.

They. The word stuck in his craw. He still didn't want to believe that any member of his crew could have anything to do with this. McCann had been caught unawares. The same thing could have happened to the rest of them.

He touched the keys hanging on a chain around his neck under his shirt to make sure they were still there. His first stop had to be the weapon's locker. This meant that he had to get out unnoticed.

Crouching low, he moved around the loading and ramming gear across the narrow aisle. That's when he saw them. He was right. Two men were loading a torpedo into a tube that had fired before. They worked in absolute silence.

The one closest to him had narrow shoulders and long arms and was wearing coveralls. McCann saw immediately that he wasn't a member of his crew. The hijacker wore a shoulder holster. When he turned slightly, McCann could see the butt of his firearm.

The man stepped aside and the submarine commander had a clear look at the second man. Square upper body with the sleeves of the coveralls rolled up to his elbows. Tattoos down both arms and on the back of his neck into the hairline. This one didn't have to turn around for McCann to know who he was. Juan Rivera.

He would have liked nothing better than to wrap his fingers around the man's thick neck right at this moment. The enlisted crew of *Hartford*, the officers, the X.O., everyone including McCann, had looked after him and tried to be there for him when Rivera's mother struggled with cancer a year ago. She'd died, but McCann really thought that the torpedo man had walked away from that loss with a gain of a new family, at least new friends. But he'd guessed wrong. From his hiding place McCann could tell Rivera was armed, as well.

Suddenly, he wasn't too sure of anyone's innocence. Rivera was here, obviously cooperating. And after hearing what Amy had said about the navigation system, McCann figured Cavallaro must have known there was nothing wrong. That spoke of his involvement. Barclay, who'd been topside on watch, could be part of this. There had been only one hatch left open, and anyone wanting to get inside the sub would have had to pass by the young sailor. Of course, Barclay could be dead, but McCann didn't even trust his own shadow right now.

He slowly backed up. He had to get to the weapon's locker and go from there.

By the stairs, McCann stopped and looked back over the racks just as the hijacker started up the aisle between the racks. Quickly, McCann ducked back into the auxiliary machinery room, which was just aft of the torpedo room. The huge auxiliary diesel engine was located here, as well as quarters for some of the crew. Pressing himself against a bulkhead, he could see the hijacker through the doorway, standing near the tail of the fish. He had his back to McCann, but if he turned around, the intruder would see him.

McCann edged away until he was out of the hijacker's possible line of vision. Suddenly, his foot caught on something on the deck and he nearly pitched backward, barely catching himself before he fell. Looking down, he saw Lee Brody's body partially stuffed under one of the massive engine mounts. His mouth was covered with duct tape. His hands and feet were bound. The man was totally out.

McCann crouched over Brody and looked closer at the source of blood that stained the young man's collar. There was a nasty contusion on the back of his head and a bruise on the side of his face where he must have hit the deck.

McCann checked for vital signs. Brody was alive. He didn't know if the sonar man would be any use to him anytime soon, but he used the box cutter to cut through the duct tape on his hands and ankles. He gently pulled the tape from Brody's mouth. He couldn't do anything more for him now.

McCann edged his way to the door and looked in. Rivera and the hijacker were forward, by the tubes. The fish was no longer on the rack. The two men appeared to be just finishing up loading it.

He had to get to the weapons locker. Darting around

the corner, he moved quickly to the stairs but stopped dead at the sound of footsteps directly above him.

Someone was going down the passageway toward the ship's office...where he'd left Amy.

Seventeen

Pentagon
8:25 a.m.

If Bruce Dunn had any reservations about working with Sarah Connelly on this investigation, they were gone in the course of the first hour. On the professional side—an area in which he considered himself a good judge—she was smart, efficient, persistent and obviously a mover and shaker. She knew how to get people to do what she wanted. On the unprofessional side—an area in which he considered himself even more of an expert—she was five-ten, had blue eyes, sexy short dark hair and an athletic build that could have been on the cover of a glossy magazine, not in the strict confines of the navy uniform.

And this wasn't the first time he'd admired this specific facet of her *personality*. He'd attended at least three different navy functions where he could remember Lieutenant Connelly being there. He'd never been able to get within an arm's length of her because of her other eager admirers. But he'd made sure to ask a few questions about who she was. It never hurt to learn a thing or two about a beautiful woman.

Bottom line, she had it all. But if the telephone call Bruce had gotten this morning had been any indication, the navy brass wasn't giving Sarah her due. He'd been told that she'd been chosen for the job because of her personal relationship with McCann. Moreover, to learn more about the sub commander, Dunn was to use her however he needed.

"Eleven of them. They're all here." Sarah dropped a stack of folders in the middle of the conference table and took the seat across from him. "A personnel file for everyone that we know is on the boat, including Amy Russell."

"Where did you get her file?"

"EB faxed what they had, and I got the rest from files the FBI keeps on defense contractor employees who have top-secret clearance," she told him. "Anything on the surveillance cameras?"

"They have clear pictures of McCann in the parking lot, by the security booth, and going in and out of NAVSEA barge," Bruce explained. "The cameras in the North Yard Ways were supposedly destroyed by the fire. I have one of my NCIS guys ready to go over the tape from the cameras that were trained on *Hartford*."

"Are there problems with those, too?"

"We don't know yet. The bad weather, time of night, they're all factors. They told me on the phone from Groton that they can see some shadows. There's a lot more digital enhancement we can do, though."

"Have they sent them over?"

"They're here, being analyzed."

She had shed her jacket, and the sleeves of her white shirt were rolled up to the elbows. His gaze lingered briefly on her forearm. The muscle beneath the smooth skin was firm and toned.

Sarah reached for the folders she'd dropped on the conference table. Bruce noticed that she chose Amy Russell's first. He couldn't help but wonder if the navy lieutenant still carried a torch for her ex-boyfriend.

Bruce turned his attention back to the laptop screen and the list he was putting together. Submarine skippers and experts, both retired and still in the navy. He didn't personally believe that an American sub driver had to be the only one capable of engineering this kind of hijacking. His list already included British and Russian commanders.

Unfortunately, what he had before him was a long and impressive collection of names. The difficult part would be to narrow it down to those who might have a bone of contention.

"This is interesting," Sarah said under her breath.

Bruce realized she was still paging through Amy Russell's files. "What did you find?"

"This woman. Amy Russell." Sarah looked up. "She could easily be connected."

Eighteen

Sitting in Amy's kitchen, Barbara Quayle let out a frustrated breath and hung up the phone. All the circuits were still tied up. She couldn't call out. Nobody could call in. The last person who'd called them was a parent from the twins' elementary school phone chain. That had been around seven o'clock. They closed the school right after the attack in New London harbor.

Right now, Barbara didn't know if she should be taking the kids somewhere. If she should, she didn't know where. The twins' grandparents were still away, but she didn't really know what help they'd be, anyway.

She'd been occasionally sneaking into Amy's bedroom, keeping an eye on the news on her television. She didn't want to let Zack and Kaitlyn see what was going on where their mother worked. Not that *anyone* really seemed to know what was going on. The only things that the news reporters appeared to be certain of, so far, was that a fire had broken out in the shipyard and something unexplainable had happened in the harbor. They kept showing the Coast Guard ship that had been damaged, and the New London Ledge lighthouse that had been demolished. Although witnesses in Groton and New London claimed to have heard and seen explosions, the news people were being very careful with their speculations. Whether the submarine leaving the harbor had done the damage or not, no one would say officially.

Barbara reached inside her pocket and opened the cap to her blood pressure pills. She wasn't due to take one until tonight, but she didn't care. Her heart was pounding, and she felt lightheaded. Her blood pressure had to be up. She took one.

There was something terrible going on. She knew it, and she could see it on every station that she turned the channel to. And she was scared—not for herself, but for the twins and for Amy.

Where was *she?*

She'd hoped Zack and Kaitlyn would sleep late today, but both of them were up and looking for their mother as soon as the call had come from the phone-chain parent. Barbara hadn't said anything about what she'd seen on the news. She even let them watch one of their Disney movies while they ate their breakfast, sitting on the sofa in the living room. That was a huge treat. She knew for a fact that Amy never allowed TV and meals to go together. But even that kind of indulgence hadn't fooled them.

Kaitlyn barely touched the waffles Barbara had

popped in the toaster. She had no interest in the movie, either. She was cuddled on the window seat, her face pressed against the glass pane, watching the rain outside and the quiet street. She was waiting for her mom to come home.

Zack wasn't much better. He pretended that he was watching the movie, but Barbara knew the young boy was aware of every move she made in the apartment. His gaze followed Barbara whenever she disappeared into Amy's bedroom. He watched her pick up the phone a dozen times as she tried to get through to the shipyard, or to Amy's pager, or to her cell phone. She wasn't able to get through on anything.

Barbara grabbed her cup of tea. It was already cold, but she didn't care. She joined Zack on the sofa. He was just a few bites ahead of his sister when it came to breakfast.

"Not hungry today?" she asked him.

He shook his head. "Did Mommy call?"

"No, sweetheart. There's something wrong with the phone lines this morning. They'll be fixing them soon."

Sirens from the borough and the neighboring towns had been blaring intermittently for the past hour. The twins hardly seemed to notice them. Barbara figured she was mostly responsible for the children's nervousness; they were too smart not to see and sense her restlessness.

"So, how's the movie?" Barb asked.

Zack shrugged and his gaze moved to his sister again. Kaitlyn was still in her pajamas, and her short, curly hair framed her innocent face like a halo. She wasn't paying attention to anything but that road.

"How about a game of Sorry!" Barbara said, trying to put some enthusiasm into her voice. As painful as that game was for her to play, it was always good for at least an hour's distraction.

Kaitlyn didn't answer.

"No, thanks," Zack murmured.

He drew his knees to his chest and laid his head on Barbara's lap, his eyes on his sister and the window. The older woman ran her fingers through the young boy's silky hair. She had to put the minds of these two at ease, somehow. The problem was that she wasn't really in any better shape than they were.

She was worried sick about Amy. The young mother always called home from the shipyard at six-thirty on the dot. That was their morning routine, Barbara's wake-up call. They always had a few minutes of quiet conversation about how they'd each lasted through the night.

There'd been no call this morning. That was a first. The phones were working at six-thirty, too. She wondered if it was worth it to try the phone again. Maybe the lines were operating now.

Barbara had experienced a very difficult time emotionally after her husband's death five years ago. She hadn't known where she wanted to go, what she wanted to do. Her four kids were scattered around the country, living their own lives. She even had three grown grandchildren out on the West Coast. There was nowhere else she wanted to move to permanently. Three or four times a year, she traveled a week or two at a time to see her kids and grandchildren. But Connecticut was home, in spite of the frigid winters.

Having Amy and her twins move into the renovated school building in Stonington Borough had been an absolute blessing. Although they were strangers, she and Amy had become friends in no time. The young mother's tireless energy and her dedication to her children were remarkable. But that wasn't all of it. Being a single mother and holding a full-time job didn't force Amy to spend the rest of her time in a shell. She made a point of getting to know Barbara, involving the older woman in her family's activities. Amy had forced her out of the cocoon she'd begun to construct around herself.

Before Barbara knew it, the four of them were a family. The fact that Amy actually paid her for staying with the kids was ridiculous. Barbara felt she should pay *them* for the joy they gave her. But Amy was as stubborn as she was proud. She wouldn't have it any other way.

Barbara wasn't a churchgoer—hadn't been for years—but sitting in Amy's apartment now, she found herself praying for these precious children and for their mother's safe return home.

"Someone's driving up the street," Kaitlyn announced excitedly. She raised herself on her knees. Her hands and face pressed against the window. Drops of rain formed rivulets down the outside of the glass.

Barbara didn't have the heart to remind the child that there were a dozen apartments in this building and the car could belong to any of their other neighbors.

"Two cars," Kaitlyn reported happily.

Before Barb could get herself off the sofa, Zack was on the window seat next to his sister.

"Neither of them are Mommy's car," he said.

"Oh," Kaitlyn said, disappointment in her voice.

Barbara reached the window and looked out. A sedan, followed by an SUV and a third car, had turned on the street. A state police car brought up the rear. A little caravan.

Her heart pounded so loud that she could hear it in her head. A cold feeling of doom edged into her blood-stream. All the other excuses she'd been preparing for the children withered on her lips when the four cars pulled up in front of the building. As they looked down on the cars, people started to get out. Official-looking people in raincoats.

"Who are they?" Zack asked.

Barbara's knees were weak. She lowered herself onto the window seat next to the twins. They were walking toward the main entrance of the building.

"Strangers," Kaitlyn answered her brother. "They have nothing to do with us."

As the intercom buzzed from the front door, Barbara stared at the twins, wishing the little girl had been right.

Nineteen

USS Hartford
8:30 a.m.

At the sound of a key sliding into the lock, Amy jumped off the box.

She scrambled to pick up a wire cutter and her needle-nose pliers—anything sharp—and slipped them in her pocket. Quickly, she pushed the boxes of paper hard against the rest of the stuff she and McCann had piled against the door. She knew that none of this would stop anyone who really wanted to come in, but she wouldn't go down without a fight. Now she jumped back up on the box and threw her shoulder against the door, too.

Her stomach jumped with fear when she heard a click on the other side. Someone tried to push open the door. It opened a fraction of an inch, but Amy slammed it shut again.

She doubted she could hold them off for long. She

glanced at the hole in the outboard wall where Mc-
Cann had disappeared. She considered making a dash
for it and trying to slither through the opening.

But Amy didn't think she could make it. She also
didn't know if McCann had worked his way down to
the torpedo room yet. She had to buy him time, try to
hold them off as long as she could.

The next shove against the door was strong enough to
bounce her away from it. The door opened a couple of
inches this time, but Amy hung on and threw all her
weight back against it, shutting it one more time. She
heard someone curse in the passageway outside. The only
chair in the office was within her reach, and Amy grabbed
for it, looking for some way to use it to wedge the door.

"Commander McCann," a muffled voice called
through the door.

She didn't know friend from enemy. She set her
body hard against the door.

"It's Dunbar, Skipper." The voice became lower in
volume, more confidential. "There are only eight of
them aboard, sir. Brody and Rivera and I were able to
break free. They had us tied up in the torpedo room."

Amy stood her ground, not trusting anything that
was being said. She told herself the only way she'd
move away from this door would be when she heard
McCann's own voice.

"Skipper, are you in there?" the man asked. "Time
is running out. We need your help if we're gonna do
anything to take back the sub."

Amy put a hand in her pocket and took out the pliers. Pressing her heels into the deck, she pushed her
back against the door.

Her eyes fell on the cables dangling from the ceiling. Did they think she was stupid? It was no coincidence that right after she started doing some real damage to the wiring, they'd showed up at the door.

Her gaze swept across the rest of the room, searching for anything that she could use to fend them off. A printer at her feet, the paneling they'd peeled off the far wall to her right. None of it would be any help.

The next blow on the door was harder than any of the earlier attempts. Amy wasn't prepared for it. She cried out as she was thrown forward and into the file cabinet to her right. Before she could regain her balance, the door was shoved open, pushing into her legs all the trash she and McCann had gathered up. Someone kicked the chair at her and it struck her in the shoulder as she ducked away. When Amy whirled to face her attacker, the first thing she saw was the barrel of the gun pointing at her.

"What the fuck is that?" the one holding the gun blurted.

There were two men, both dressed in seaman's coveralls. The first one was in the room. The second hovered in the doorway. At least the distraction caused by the hole in the wall had extended her life for a few more seconds.

"Let Mako know McCann is loose," the first man ordered. The second one immediately backed down the passageway out of her line of sight.

The gun lifted to her head, the barrel actually touching her forehead. Amy didn't know where she found the strength or the courage, but it was kill or be killed. She shoved the gun to the side and threw herself against the man holding it, stabbing at his stomach with her needle-nose pliers.

The attacker grunted, not in pain, but in annoyance. The damage she caused must have been minuscule. His layers of clothing, the coveralls, acted like a shield. She'd only managed to throw him off balance for a moment, and he stumbled backward over the trash.

Cursing, he pointed the gun at her head again before regaining his feet. She kicked at his groin this time, with less effect than her previous effort, and she threw the pliers at his face.

Before the attacker had a chance to recover, a wrench swung down through the doorway, connecting with a sickening thud on the man's skull.

The intruder sank down into the debris before turning facedown onto the floor with a loud thump. Amy looked up in relief to see McCann standing in the doorway with an oversize wrench in one hand.

"There are two of them," she whispered quickly.

He nodded, reaching down and collecting the weapon before slipping back out of the room. He came back a moment later, dragging the body of the other man. He piled one on top of the other and reached for some plastic cable ties.

Amy crouched down, trying to help him tie their hands and ankles. But he was too fast, efficient. Or maybe she was too slow because she was in shock. She remembered that sometimes that happened to people. She dismissed the thought, though, because shock meant numbness, and she was hardly numb. A range of emotions raced through her. Relief fought with waves of anger and fear.

"One of these two said his name was Dunbar," she said accusingly. "I think your crew *was* involved with this."

"Not all of them," he responded in a sharp tone, standing up. He gestured with his head for her to follow him.

"Don't I need a gun?" she said at his back. He'd collected both of the pistols.

"Do you know how to use one?" He looked up and down the empty passageway.

"No, but there's always a first time."

His snort told her that now wasn't going to be that time. As she started after McCann, her boot caught on one of the men's legs. The leg of his coveralls had ridden up, and she saw a knife in a sheath he had strapped to his ankle. It was a vicious-looking thing. Amy reached down and grabbed it, slipping it into her belt. She gave a final look back at both of them. They didn't look to be dead. In fact, the one who'd been holding the gun to her head was starting to stir.

She couldn't just leave him. He could start to yell for help at any minute. She'd never hurt anyone before. She hadn't even done a good job of fighting him when he'd been ready to shoot her in cold blood. She thought, growing angrier, that her efforts had been little more than a joke. Totally ineffective.

Frowning, she picked up the printer off the floor, held it above his head, mumbled an apology and dropped it with a crash.

Her attacker stopped stirring. She bent over to see that he was still breathing. He was.

McCann's head appeared in the doorway. He looked

at the two motionless men, at the printer, then back at her.

"Follow me," he ordered.

She must have been too slow, for McCann reached inside the room, wrapped his hand around her wrist and physically dragged her out.

"I'm coming," she whispered, following him.

He signaled to her to be quiet as they hurried down the passageway.

Amy was relieved when he gave her wrist back, and she kept up with him. She didn't know what his plans were or where he was headed, but she figured she wasn't going to be left alone again.

McCann had different ideas. In a moment they turned into one of the ship's crew's quarters. She lingered by the door. He took a quick look around and did a search of the bunks.

"You stay here until I come for you."

"No," she said, blocking his exit.

"Amy."

"I refuse, Commander. You can court-martial me when we get back or get me fired or whatever, but I'm not going to be a sitting duck again. I refuse to hide in a closet and not have a chance to fight for my life. I'm coming with you."

"That's impossible. The only thing I want to think about right now is how to get this sub back. Having you with me is a distraction."

"I can be a help," she argued. "Honest. You won't even notice I'm with you." She turned to walk out ahead of him, but he grabbed her arm, pulling her back through the door.

She heard men's voices coming up the ladder from the lower level. They turned in the passageway, headed in their direction.

McCann shoved her into the closest bunk, drew his weapon and aimed it at the door.

Twenty

"We can't just write this off as unrelated," Sarah argued. "Of all the people who work in management for that shipyard, how many of them have a submarine officer as an ex-husband?"

"I'm not big on coincidences, either," Bruce Dunn replied, shaking his head. "But it's too far-fetched. Ryan Murray was only a communications officer before he transferred to the surface fleet two years ago." He thumbed through the file she'd been looking at before. "Amy Russell looks squeaky clean. Look at this—mother of twins, active in school PTA, volunteer at a local shelter. That's in addition to having an excellent work record. She has no excessive debt, no criminal file, not even a speeding ticket."

Looking at Amy's file, Sarah was reminded of what was missing in her own relationship with Darius. Even when their romance had been in bloom, she knew that he was looking forward to leaving the navy someday, moving into some three-bedroom suburb, having half a dozen kids and just spending time with them. He was looking for the kind of life he had growing up. Family mattered to him. A lot. The relationship he had with his siblings and his parents was unlike anything she ever had with her own.

He'd never popped the question with her. She didn't think he'd ever even come close to proposing.

Sarah hadn't been ready for that back then, anyway. Her career was on the move. She enjoyed the challenge of the job, the lifestyle. She wasn't sure she would be ready for marriage now, either.

Across the table, she looked at the picture of the young woman.

"I'm not accusing her of masterminding this operation," Sarah said reasonably. "What I do believe is that there had to be some serious coordination involved to have the right players at the right places for this hijacking. She could have served a function at the EB end of things, and that was why she happened to be on board at the precise time *Hartford* left the dock."

"What do you mean, 'the right players in the right places'?"

"The most obvious is the X.O., Lieutenant Commander Parker," she told him. "I find it extremely coincidental that a parked U-Haul truck should roll down the street and smash into his front door at three o'clock in the morning, resulting in McCann being called, in order for Parker to leave the ship."

She saw Dunn scribble Parker's name at the bottom of a long list he was keeping on a legal pad.

"Whoever is behind this wanted McCann there for the reasons that Admiral Meisner already listed. They also wanted a navigation officer and someone in maneuvering, and—"

"You're implicating the entire crew. Basically, what you're saying is that the hijackers wanted specific members of *Hartford*'s crew there, and these men are cooperating."

She sat back, feeling frustrated. "No, what I'm trying to say is that there had to be someone knowledgeable enough to run the reactor and the engine room and fire a torpedo with accuracy. That means the hijackers have successfully gotten the right people on board. Now, as far as whether they're cooperating or not, your guess is as good as mine."

Dunn tapped his pen on the pad a couple of times. "I agree with your hypothesis regarding McCann. He is their key to arming any nuclear warheads, not that they can't do plenty of damage with the conventional weapons they're carrying." Dunn thought about that for a second. "And I agree with your idea about the accident in front of Parker's house. It looks as phony as a televised town meeting."

Sarah was pleased that he was listening.

"I'll even go so far as to question why Paul Cavallaro was left on board that sub." He reached for the navigation officer's file and opened it up in front of Sarah. He pulled out a copy of the rejection report that was left at the NAVSEA office in the shipyard. "It was his call that brought *Hartford* back to EB."

She looked at the document. Darius's signature was also on that piece of paper, but she didn't want to go there. In her mind, McCann was one hundred percent innocent. But she was going to be smart enough to keep that opinion to herself.

"At this point, it's too big a stretch for me to believe every other person on that boat was put there for a purpose. Amy Russell, specifically, was only given the assignment the night before. She had specific qualifications that made her right for the job, but could have been one of several ship supers. In addition, Russell was only scheduled to go aboard at 0600 with a crew and not before. No, I think she surprised them. I think she was in the wrong place at the wrong time."

"And Darius McCann would never have escorted her aboard *Hartford* if he thought something was about to happen," Sarah asserted.

Dunn scratched his chin and nodded gravely. "Unfortunately, if our assumptions are correct, then she's of no use to them."

"Which means…" she paused.

"Which means," he continued grimly, "there would be no reason for the hijackers to keep her alive."

He closed Amy Russell's file folder and slid it across the table. As the file came to a stop, a sheet of paper protruded from the file.

Sarah glanced at the heading as she pushed the paper back into the folder. She'd read the information on that sheet. It pertained to the woman's personal life and referred to her children. An unexpected sharp pang ran through her.

"Do you know if anything has been done about seeing after her twins?" she asked.

"We had the locals and the Family Services people pick them up." He looked at her intently. "We wanted to bring them in before the sharks got to them."

"What do you mean?"

"I mean the media."

She hadn't considered that. The media was already all over this. Her thoughts shifted to Darius's parents. They'd be in the Keys this time of the year.

"How about Commander McCann's family? Has anyone been in touch with them?"

He nodded curtly and looked away. He was avoiding eye contact.

"What's wrong?" she asked.

He paused before looking back at her. "I don't know the details. But I received a text message about an ambulance being dispatched to the house."

"Harry?"

"No. Mrs. McCann, Darius's mother."

Twenty-One

The hour-long meeting in the Situation Room with the secretary of state, the secretary of defense, the secretary of homeland security and a number of chief advisers had given President Hawkins all the information he needed. Now he knew exactly what he had to say.

The earlier news conference held at the sub base in Groton had only whetted the media's—and the nation's—appetite. In a prepared statement, the navy spokesperson had told the country only that a submarine had left the Electric Boat Shipyard ahead of schedule. The damage to the Coast Guard cutter and the New London Ledge lighthouse were under investigation. In the statement, no fatalities had been reported and no mention was made of any threat. There was also no mention of a hijacking.

Minutes later, however, the terror alert was raised to

the highest level, and the public was repeatedly given the statement that the president would be speaking to them shortly. In the meantime, everyone should be observant but should go about their business as they normally would.

Now it was up to Will Hawkins to show them that calm heads were in control of the country. This was not going to be an ordinary briefing. The White House leaked word that the speechwriters were taking a back seat on this one. The president would address the nation and tell them the truth—to the extent that he could without creating mass hysteria.

An impossible task, the president thought as he half listened to his aides remind him of last-minute details. The director of the camera crew started his countdown. Fifteen seconds to air.

Hawkins downed half the cup of scalding coffee and handed it to an assistant to be taken away. He looked down at the notes he'd rewritten on a piece of paper. He glanced up at the door, behind the camera crew. His campaign manager, Bob Fortier, had just slipped into the room. He received a reassuring nod from him.

The director pointed at the president, gesturing to him that they were live in three seconds. Two. One.

"Good morning, my fellow Americans. For the second time in this decade, our way of life is today being threatened by terrorist actions. One of our most powerful weapons of war, the fast-attack submarine USS *Hartford,* has been hijacked from a pier on the Thames River in Groton, Connecticut. The nuclear-powered *Hartford* is equipped with Tomahawk cruise missiles, vertical launch system missiles and MK-48 torpedoes."

Hawkins paused to make sure the significance of this registered with the audience. He'd been advised to make no mention of nuclear warheads, since there was a possibility that the hijackers might not be aware of them. Even now, the president considered telling them. He told his cabinet that he believed the people of this country had the right to know the extent of the danger they were exposed to. He told them that he believed the hijackers knew a lot more than his intelligence advisers were giving them credit for. *Hartford* was handpicked for this disaster. He'd let the country know when it was necessary.

"Of the regular crew of 121 enlisted and thirteen officers, only two officers and eight enlisted remain aboard. In addition to those, a member of Electric Boat Shipyard management is on board the submarine. At this time we have no information about their safety. We are concerned about their well-being, as we are concerned for the safety of others."

He accepted a piece of paper that was handed to him by an aide. He glanced at it and put it down.

"As your president, I am not only concerned about those brave sailors and that innocent civilian. My fellow Americans, this hijacking of a powerful weapon in our arsenal of freedom represents a direct attack on our nation. I cannot express this clearly enough. The United States of America is under attack.

"At the present time, *Hartford* is traveling at a speed of approximately fifteen knots in a westerly direction beneath the surface of Long Island Sound. Yes, the submarine is headed toward New York City. But the people of that great city and its boroughs aren't the only ones in danger. Each of the VLS weapons on *Hartford* is capable of traveling thirteen hundred miles and hitting targets with an accuracy of a bull's-eye the size of a picture window.

"And what is within range? In short, every major metropolitan area and every nuclear power plant east of the Mississippi are within striking distance. Even as I sit here in the White House, my advisers tell me that Washington, D.C., is a prime target for the terrorists' missiles."

Hawkins briefly looked down at his notes and then looked steadily into the camera, talking to each individual viewer.

"I'd like to remember now a clear, bright September morning in 2001, when hijacked airliners were flown into the World Trade Center, the Pentagon, and would have undoubtedly struck another target were it not for the courage of a few Americans in the skies over Pennsylvania. I'd like to remember now the horrible images of fires burning, structures collapsing. I'd like us all to remember the thousands of lives that were lost.

"That said, I want all my fellow Americans to know that we're doing everything possible to stop another act of mass murder *before* it occurs."

He leaned forward in the seat, his voice rising.

"First of all, we will retake that submarine or destroy it before it can do harm to our cities, our towns, our people or our democratic way of life. To that purpose, I have ordered the entire Atlantic Fleet in pursuit of USS *Hartford*. I have also ordered the immediate implementation of our nation's emergency response plans. Our emergency teams are already in place in Boston, New

York City, Philadelphia and Washington, to help direct the orderly evacuation of those cities. Because of the dangers that exist in having a nuclear reactor in the hands of untrained personnel, state and local law enforcement agencies have also been mobilized to help our citizens vacate the areas on either side of the Long Island Sound.

"Our two-pronged goal right now is to stop any attack by these madmen and to take every precaution to protect Americans at home and around the world.

"Despite the dangers we are facing at this very moment, I have ordered—under the provisions of the Homeland Security Act—that the government continue to function without interruption. Federal agencies in Washington are all open and will remain open. Though I am ordering the New York stock exchanges to remain closed today, the nation's banks and businesses will remain open as usual. We will not allow these barbarians to succeed in disrupting our lives."

The president knew this was more rhetorical than true, but he needed to present a forcefully positive outlook on the situation.

"In the meantime, the search is under way for the identities of those men or nations who are responsible for this evil act. I am directing the full resources of our intelligence and law enforcement communities to find and bring to justice these faceless jackals. I promise you that these men will not remain faceless for long. I also promise you that we will make no distinction between the terrorists who are involved with this act and those who have funded or harbored them."

He sat up straighter, tried to brighten his expression.

"On behalf of the American people, I want to thank the many world leaders who have called to offer their assistance this morning. As always, America stands shoulder to shoulder with our friends and allies in the ongoing war against terrorism."

In a perfect world, he thought, Americans would be aware of any threat against them before the rest of the world even had a hint of a problem. But they weren't living in a perfect world.

"Standing before you this morning and informing you that we are facing such a threat is not a pleasant duty. Nonetheless, with the clear and decisive plan of action that I have just laid out, we will move forward to meet this threat head-on."

Hawkins spoke fiercely into the camera. "You who are right now listening aboard the USS *Hartford,* you who have chosen to bring your evil to our door, will soon feel the full weight of American might. Surrender now, or prepare to pay fully for your actions."

Hawkins took a breath and then spoke again in a civil voice.

"My fellow Americans, over the past four years I have worked tirelessly to make America strong and respected in the world. As your president, I come before you this morning prepared to fulfill my sworn duty now, as well. America has faced down its enemies before, and we will do it again this time. No one can stop us from moving forward in our defense of freedom and all that is good and just in our world."

He nodded, without smiling.

"Thank you. And God bless America."

The cameras stopped. The president sat back as one

of the production assistants rushed over to disconnect the microphone from his tie. An aide handed him another scalding cup of black coffee.

Hawkins's chief of staff stepped over to tell him that Rear Admiral Joseph Smith was on the line for him from the Pentagon.

The president answered the phone on his desk. "What do you have, Joe?"

"They're talking. We have an official demand from *Hartford.*"

Twenty-Two

USS Hartford
9:10 a.m.

There was no safe hiding place where he could leave her on the submarine. Right now, the key to their survival was to keep moving. After Rivera and the other man who'd been working with him in the torpedo room ran past the crew's quarters, McCann realized that Amy should indeed stay with him.

The two men were undoubtedly heading for the ship's office, and McCann momentarily considered trying to surprise the two from behind, but then decided against it. He couldn't risk a shoot-out with Amy on his heels. Not with the possibility of other hijackers coming to help. They'd be caught in a cross fire with nowhere to hide.

Now, however, they had to keep moving.

"They might be trying to fix the wiring I cut up there," Amy whispered when he motioned for her to climb out of the bunk.

She looked wild-eyed and a little frightened. But she was holding up surprisingly well.

"We can't worry about that now." He looked her over. She had taken off her vest back in the ship's office. The sleeves of her green flannel shirt were rolled up. He looked down at her steel-toed boots. "You've got to change those. They'll be too noisy."

"Change into what?"

"Check in the lockers, quietly. You might find a pair of sneakers that fit. If not, go barefoot."

As she went searching the lockers, McCann looked out again. All was quiet in the passageway. He considered the officer's wardroom. In it, one of the ship's Multi Function Display terminals was mounted on the outboard bulkhead. The unit, which was tied into BSY-1 combat system, showed current data on position, course, speed, heading and depth of *Hartford.* The device also had different modes, including a new closed-loop video hookup that showed views of strategically important spots throughout the ship. The purpose of the MFD system was for the officers to know the boat's status even when they were away from the control room. He had an identical MFD unit in his cabin.

He could use that now.

Though it was impossible, McCann would have liked to get up to his cabin. His safe contained classified documents that should be destroyed, but also additional weapons. Even taking up a position in the officer's wardroom was indefensible. He'd be in worse shape there than they were in the ship's office.

There were a total of eight MFDs around the ship. He needed to access one of them, but it had to be one that was in a less obvious place. At the same time, they had to be really careful not to be caught on one of the small surveillance cameras providing images into the system.

"A size too big, but I think they'll do."

She was holding a pair of soft-soled sneakers. He saw her sit down on the edge of a bunk and pull off her work boots.

Seconds later, two others came along the passageway, also going forward toward the ship's office. Hearing them come past, McCann waited behind the door, weapon drawn, ready to kill whoever poked their heads in.

As the hijackers continued along, he turned to Amy. "Hurry up."

Her face was pale with strain, but she quickly pulled on the second sneaker and laced it tight.

Whoever was running this show must be short-handed, McCann thought. There hadn't been any kind of thorough search on this level, which meant the men they had must be needed to operate the ship. That was definitely one point in the good guys' favor.

Amy stood up and he pulled her behind him as two sets of footsteps came back down the passageway. McCann was certain that the two men went down the steps to the torpedo room.

"Let's go."

"Where are we going from here?" she asked.

"We're heading aft."

"What are you trying to do?"

McCann wasn't accustomed to giving reasons for decisions and orders on his own ship, but he knew this was a special case. Having already seen her persistence in action, he figured it was easier and quicker to explain.

"We know there are at least two of them forward, probably in the ship's office. There are two below us in the torpedo room. I don't know how many of them are up in the control room, so it would not be too wise charging up there and trying to overpower them."

"Good thinking," she said encouragingly. "Especially when your own men are against you."

"Not all of them," he said for the second time. "I found my sonar man knocked out and trussed up in the torpedo room. There could be more of them on board in the same situation as him."

"Then, aft it is. But we have to pass the stairs to the torpedo room. They might spot us."

"We just have to be quick and careful." He was ready to go, but Amy grabbed his arm, holding him back.

"In case we're separated, where are we going exactly?"

"We'll be taking the tunnel through the reactor."

"To the engine room?"

He nodded.

"You're going to try to shut down the reactor, aren't you?"

She was reading his mind. And if he didn't get her moving, she'd be asking next for the sequence of what he planned to do. She'd even have him draw a schematic of it.

"We've got to go, Amy." He took her by the hand and pulled her out into the passageway.

Twenty-Three

USS *Hartford*
9:15 a.m.

Once the BSY-1 sonar consoles started coming—one by one—back to life, Paul Cavallaro began running tests on them. Mako waited until the navigation officer gave him a thumbs-up before he turned to his security officer.

"They went out the hole on the outboard side of the office," Kilo told him. "I had one of the men follow the passage they cut. They went down to the torpedo room."

"The two stationed down there to work the tubes didn't see them?"

Kilo shook his head.

This was a problem. Mako had wanted the commander where he could keep an eye on him. He considered the situation from McCann's perspective. He wanted to believe that Darius McCann wouldn't destroy his own submarine, but he wasn't so sure about that.

Navy officers—and submarine commanders, in particular—can be real cowboys at times, and they can do incredibly heroic and stupid things in situations like this.

He would have liked to keep him alive. But Mako didn't foresee any complications in their plans. They'd sent off the first communication. Everything was moving ahead right on schedule. McCann was just making his own survival less viable.

"How are the two they knocked out?"

"Still out," Kilo told him. "They'll be no good to us considering our schedule."

Mako would have liked to have more under his command, but it wasn't possible. He couldn't afford to lose many more at this point. "Have you been monitoring the multifunction display terminals?"

"We have, but nothing's shown up. McCann knows where the cameras are and he's been avoiding them."

Mako thought about that. McCann also knew where the other MFD units were located, which meant he'd be able to access views of the control room. He frowned, mulling over the possibility of the sub driver being able to identify him. That made McCann's survival even less tenable, but Mako didn't like it. McCann might have already seen who his enemy was.

He motioned toward the two cameras in the control room. One was trained on the conn itself.

"Have these disabled now," he told Kilo. After the command was passed along, he motioned Kilo to join him in the radio room, where he was out of earshot of the others in the control room.

"Take another man and start a search through the boat. Start in the captain's stateroom, just in case. Make a quick sweep of the living quarters. McCann is too charged up to hide in some bunk or under a table."

"The woman might."

"That would be good news for us," Mako said thoughtfully. "Find her and we'll be able to use her as a bargaining chip with the commander. He's the hero type. He might not want to let the girl die."

Kilo nodded curtly. Mako knew his man wouldn't have any problem killing a woman or anyone else. He would do what he was ordered to do. Case closed.

"Lock doors as you go. Searching the torpedo room thoroughly is critical. With all the munitions there, we don't want to tempt him with the opportunity of doing any serious damage. Also, make sure the engine room is sealed off."

"That will take some time. There are a lot of places to hide on a submarine."

"Then start now," Mako ordered. "Keep thinking what would be the biggest bang he can get for a buck. And buy us time. Even if you keep him on the run, we're moving closer every minute to our objective. That's the most important thing."

"What do you want done with him when we find him?"

"Either he surrenders or you kill him."

"And the woman?"

"She's of no real use to us, and you know the complication she'd be if she lives."

"Very good, sir."

Twenty-Four

Seth McDermott cruised into the conference room waving a copy of *Hartford*'s hijackers' demands before Bruce and Sarah even knew that communication had been established.

"They don't identify themselves," Seth told the gathered team. "But it sounds strictly al-Qaeda. They've identified two dozen prisoners at Guantánamo Bay. They're demanding their immediate release."

Bruce Dunn took the piece of paper and quickly scanned the names of the prisoners on the list. He didn't recognize any. He passed the list to Sarah and turned to one of their assistants.

"Don't bother with an A to Z yet. I need to know where they came from, how they got there, the charges against them, what kind of court proceedings they've had and where they stand now. I also need to know how long they've been there. Anything you need besides that?"

"No," she said, handing the list to the assistant.

"Then get going," Dunn snapped. "I want it done ten minutes ago."

The young officer took off with the list.

"Is that all of it?" Dunn asked Seth.

The young man shook his head. "They're demanding the transfer of five hundred million dollars to a bank account in Switzerland and safe transport out of the country."

"Or what?" Sarah asked.

"If their instructions aren't followed, they intend to detonate the submarine in New York Harbor at 0600 tomorrow morning," Seth relayed. "And if there is any attempt to stop them, they'll launch every Tomahawk cruise missile on the sub at targets up and down the Eastern Seaboard and then self-destruct right there in Long Island Sound."

"The end result is the same," Sarah said.

"Worse," Dunn replied grimly. "We'll have mass destruction in the cities from the missiles and radiation poisoning that will make much of the region, including New York City, uninhabitable. It'll make the meltdown at Chernobyl look like an afternoon in the park."

Long before the 2001 terrorist attacks on New York and Washington, Dunn had felt that the East Coast was much too vulnerable. The entire region was so densely populated, and in the event of an emergency, there was really no place for people to go. Not in a short time frame like the one they were facing now.

Seth wasn't finished. "You're right. They say they have the VLS weapons locked in on an unspecified number of nuclear power plants—starting with Waterford, Indian Point and Three Mile Island."

"The question is whether the president will order a strike," Sarah said, looking at Dunn.

"They're also claiming that their sonar is fully operational," Seth added. "They say they have the ability and the will to sink any ship and down any aircraft that directs hostile action against them."

"Jesus," one of the team murmured.

Dunn put a checkmark next to the name of Paul Cavallaro before looking around the room. Between those assigned to the job and others who were in and out with information, there were a dozen people in the conference room. But after Seth's news, you could hear a pin drop. The impact of this could be so far reaching, the fatalities unimaginable.

"What's the mood next door?" Sarah asked the question that had also been forming in Bruce's mind.

It was all fairly straightforward, Bruce thought. Does the U.S. lie down and submit, hoping that these hijackers would honor their promise? Or do we take the old approach of acting tough, of charging in and having the situation very literally blow up in our faces.

Seth said, "No one is committing to anything yet. They're trying to sort out the information before putting together a number of possible responses."

And most of the senior officers were probably already aboard choppers en route to the White House. Potential plans would be formulated next door, but the final decisions would be made by the man on top, President Hawkins. Well, Bruce thought, by Hawkins and the string-pullers behind the curtain.

"New reports are in from the FBI on the pictures from the shipyard's surveillance cameras," Sarah announced, looking at her computer screen and the message that had just popped up. "Let's get back to work, people, and see if we can figure out who these bastards are."

Twenty-Five

Newport, Rhode Island
10:00 a.m.

All modes of transportation on the East Coast had come to a screeching halt. The airlines were grounded. Private planes were not being given permission to fly, either. The skies had to be left clear for military aircraft. The rails for most of New York, Connecticut and Massachusetts ran along the shoreline, so Amtrak and all commuter lines shut down, too. The traffic jams on every highway leading from the coast—from Atlantic City to New York to Boston—had paralyzed the entire region.

In short, the East Coast was in a state of panic.

Anthony McCarthy could handle panic. For three decades, he'd been in the business of politics. He worked on his first presidential campaign stuffing envelopes while still in high school. Now a nationally connected political operative, he was a principal in one of Washington's most sought-after lobbying consulting firms. Many present and would-be political figures believed that, if you wanted to get elected, Anthony McCarthy was absolutely the best man out there to run your campaign.

He had skills, he thought matter-of-factly. And he had a few gifts.

One gift that McCarthy had recognized in himself early on was his ability to predict during the last three months of campaigning the outcome of any race. Not just most of the time. One hundred percent of the time. In presidential races, he'd been correct in every one of the past seven elections, and his own candidate wasn't always on the winning ticket. Even very close races like Bush-Gore of 2000 and Bush-Kerry of 2004 had presented no challenge for him. There was no need to recount anything. They just had to ask him.

The Hawkins-Penn presidential race had been in the bag for the past six months, if not longer. Hawkins had done everything he could to alienate the world, and the American public had grown tired of it. In fact, McCarthy was so relaxed about the outcome of the election that he'd gone along with his client's decision not to campaign the final day. When John Penn wanted to go home, he'd just passed the word, made the requisite cancellations and apologies, thanked everyone for their support, and let the affected organizers know that *President* Penn wouldn't forget them down the road.

But then the tide had turned.

This morning, in his house in Georgetown, McCarthy woke up sweating, staring up at the dark ceiling, knowing that the bottom had dropped out. A moment later, his phone had started to ring.

Transportation was a colossal problem for everyone on the East Coast. But for a man who'd helped generals and admirals and astronauts win Senate seats, it was a nonissue.

McCarthy had pulled out all the stops. He twisted arms and called in favors. Inside of an hour, he was on an air force jet that took him from Washington to Quonset Point, Rhode Island. And from there, a navy chopper delivered him to Newport, depositing him on the front lawn of Senator John Penn's mansion on the water.

Striding across the soft wet ground now, looking at the mist clinging dismally to the white edifice, McCarthy wasn't worried that a nuclear submarine was about to blow a few million people off the face of the earth. No, he had more important things to worry about. He wasn't ready to arrange for the burial of a campaign. They might be done. Defeated. Kaput. But they could at least go down with some dignity.

Inside, the mood of his client and his staff and aides was far worse than McCarthy had foreseen. Congressman Peter Gresham, Senator Penn's running mate, was stranded in Ohio where he'd been campaigning the day before.

McCarthy rolled his sleeves up and went to work.

"There's a line of reporters at least ten deep out by the gate," he announced to the roomful of gloomy faces. "We're calling a news conference, Senator."

"And say what?" the senator asked. "Repeat what they already know? I've made a dozen phone calls to the

Pentagon, the secretaries of defense and Homeland Security. I've even called the White House, but there's not one iota of material that they're not controlling carefully."

Despite McCarthy's connections, he hadn't been able to get anything out of Washington, either. "President Hawkins had a press conference at nine o'clock. The White House has already announced that he's planning to have another one at eleven. And knowing the crew that's pushing his campaign, he or the vice president will continue to have one every two hours after that."

"He's updating the people with what's going on. He has a legitimate reason to be on camera," Penn argued. "I don't. This isn't the time for politics."

"Excuse me, Senator, but why do you think he's on? He could put any number of his people in front of those cameras. He has a press secretary to do the job."

"This is different."

"Is it?" McCarthy argued. "In 2001, Bush only appeared on camera *once* on September 11."

"That wasn't an election year," Greg Moore chirped in.

"You got it." Anthony pointed to the young man. He looked around the room, waiting for his enthusiasm to start to ripple through the rest of them. Everyone seemed to be avoiding eye contact.

Two of the aides rushed to get a fax that was printing in the next room. Another aide rubbed on an imaginary spot on the coffee table. A young woman reached for the phone practically before it rang. They were all scared shitless. This was not the same firecracker bunch that had helped get them to this point.

"Anthony's right, honey," Penn's wife said from the doorway. "We have to find a reason to put your pretty face on TV."

McCarthy hadn't noticed the willowy redhead come in. She was wearing a white turtleneck shirt under faded jean overalls and holding her wet lapdog, a yappy and beloved shih tzu, under an arm. As always, Anna Penn looked so completely opposite to any potential First Lady ever. But Anthony didn't think her husband minded, nor did the segments of the population they'd polled over the past year. People simply liked her as she was—crazy and unpredictable to the bone. Somebody else would have to rein her in once they were in the White House. It was just his job to get them there.

"Actually, coming up with a reason for a press conference is easy," she continued, winking at McCarthy. "We'll just have Aileen take Owen out for some air in his wheelchair and push him down the forty steps and off the Cliff Walk."

The suggestion elicited a small gasp from one of the junior aides. McCarthy eyed the young woman. She obviously hadn't spent much time in the company of the senator's wife. If she had, she'd have known of the woman's sometimes bizarre sense of humor.

"It's raining outside," Penn responded to his wife with a smile. "Even if Owen is willing, I don't think Aileen will go for it. You know how she hates getting wet. No, honey. We'll save that one for another day."

"Just trying to help, dear."

As she went out, the senator turned his attention to McCarthy. "Look, Anthony. I already looked like a fool

once today. I'm not doing it again. I'm not going before TV cameras knowing less than they know."

"We can come up with a reason," McCarthy said,
looking around the room, hoping for some contribution.
"Perhaps not what Mrs. Penn is suggesting, but something legitimate and meaningful."

"You can volunteer to be on any team that will ne-
gotiate with the hijackers, Senator," Greg Moore suggested.

John Penn shook his head. "No. You can bet Jesse
Jackson is already putting together an expedition."

"Maybe he hasn't," McCarthy said with enthusiasm.
"We should try."

"I'm not about to risk making this situation worse
by jumping into the middle just to get a little attention,"
Penn said shortly.

"You brought up Jesse Jackson. If the hijackers
aboard that ship will respect a black American—"

"Stop right there," Penn said, standing up. "I want
everyone out…except Anthony and Greg."

The aides quickly cleared the room. Greg Moore
looked uncomfortable. When the door closed, Penn
turned to McCarthy.

"Look, Anthony. I'm in the position I'm in today
because, in the view of my party, I represent a phi-
losophy of governing that is better than the man in
the White House. They back me, perhaps in part because I'm black, but also because I have a record in
the Senate that says exactly what I stand for. I'm a
lawyer and I stand firmly within the mainstream of
U.S. political thought. Jesse Jackson has made a career out of being an outsider. Whether he really is an

outsider or not is beside the point. He has met with successes negotiating with some of America's enemies *because* of his status as an outsider, not because he's black."

There was no point in pursuing this argument. The senator was right. McCarthy decided on stating the obvious.

"Because Hawkins is in the White House, and making himself appear to be in total command of the situation, your run for the presidency is about to crash and burn," he asserted. Picking up a pile of faxes they were just receiving, he glanced at the pages and held them up. "These are the raw numbers from this morning's polls. We couldn't get any from New York or Philly, but look at the early numbers from Chicago and St. Louis. We're not slipping. It's a goddamn freefall. Look at these comments. The people of America suddenly think we're at war. Forget about any kind of change in presidents. All Hawkins's sins are forgiven."

John Penn walked to the hutch to pour himself another cup of coffee. "Sometimes we're faced with events that are out of our control."

"All I'm saying is that we need to be part of these events, sir." McCarthy looked at the glazed expression that had slid across John Penn's face. "You like to quote Shakespeare, Senator. How about, 'There's a tide in the affairs of men, which, taken at the flood, leads on to fortune.'"

"Interesting that you should pick that speech, Anthony. When Brutus says it, he's trying to convince Cassius to attack Marc Antony. It's a great speech, but Brutus turns out to be wrong. He wins the argument but loses the battle, and democracy loses out to monarchy in ancient Rome."

"I just mean that we need to be proactive now, show the American people that you're the leader they think you are."

"Hawkins might have been my opponent for the past year," Penn replied, waving his coffee mug at Mc-Carthy. "We've referred to each other in some pretty unflattering ways. Some of his negative smear ads were downright hateful. But on this day—even if it is the day before the election—Will Hawkins is my president, and I won't do anything that might jeopardize what he's trying to do to save the lives of people who are counting on him."

"Senator—"

"We're wasting our time here." Penn shook his head. "For the rest of the day, we're going to go to work to see if we can help prepare shelters, hospitals, law enforcement agencies…whatever…for what we could be facing at any moment. I'm going to work and help and it's going to be done without TV cameras. We're not going to do this for publicity. We're going to do it because it's the right thing to do."

Damn it, if Penn couldn't talk when he got pumped up, McCarthy thought. Glancing at Greg Moore, he saw the aide discreetly turn off his tape recorder.

Oh, yeah. This was better stuff than he could write himself.

They weren't done campaigning. Not by a long shot.

Twenty-Six

USS Hartford
10:15 a.m.

"What are we looking at?" Amy whispered.

"Those are the control consoles in Maneuvering, just above us," McCann told her, pointing at the red gas-plasma monitor display on the MFD. "If I can get in there without them knowing up in the control room, we'll be able to shut *Hartford* down."

"What exactly do they do?" she asked.

"Those three consoles monitor and control the submarine's entire nuclear power plant."

She leaned over his shoulder to get a closer look. Despite the sweat and dust and all the places he had to crawl through to get here, there was something raw and intoxicating about his scent. To keep her balance, she rested a hand on his shoulder and felt his muscles immediately contract beneath her fingers. She instantly withdrew her hand, tucking it between her knees, while still leaning forward.

"I've never seen the inside of Maneuvering. Once we build the structure, we're not allowed in there at all."

"I know." He pointed to the monitor. "The console to the left controls the electrical system, the center one is the nuclear reactor control panel, and the right one controls the steam turbines."

"The person manning the panel—" she pointed to the man seated at the consoles "—is he one of yours?"

McCann didn't answer immediately, but their faces were close enough that she could feel the heat rise from it.

"Yes, he is," McCann said finally. "He is a reactor technician, one of my petty officers."

"Was he the only one on your crew that was left back here?"

"No, three were stationed aft of the reactor—the reactor technician, the mechanist's mate and a machinist. I haven't seen the other two. That's why we were so careful coming through the reactor tunnel."

"You thought they might be guarding the entrance to the engine room?"

He nodded grimly.

She watched as he switched the image on the screen to another camera. It was the view they'd looked at a moment earlier. Two armed men were visible, obviously searching the outboard areas between the frames back at the extreme aft end of the engine room.

"These two are strangers," he told her.

As they entered the engine room through the watertight door at the end of the reactor tunnel, McCann had led Amy into the closetlike engineering office. He'd wanted to know what they were dealing with, and she watched him switch the screen to more than a dozen views of different locations on the boat. Several cameras appeared to be blacked out. He'd blacked some of them out himself as they'd worked their way to the engine room.

To get here, they'd sneaked past the crew's mess and down half a deck to the entrance of the shielded tunnel that led straight through the space that held the nuclear reactor. At the end of the tunnel, they'd entered the engine room, a noisy and crowded area that consisted of three decks containing the submarine-propulsion plant. McCann told her that when they were operating with a full crew, the reactor tunnels, the control areas that included this tiny office and Maneuvering, were manned stations.

He'd been cautious coming into the engine room, but there'd been no one at the entrance. A key that he wore on a chain around his neck had opened the door to the engineering office and locked it again from the inside.

He switched back to a view of Maneuvering, and Amy thought about all the different warning signs from the DNR, Director of Naval Reactors. The signs were clear about just who on the boat was allowed past certain points. It didn't matter that regular people, like Amy, who built these subs, looked at the top secret blueprints every day. Once the sealed reactor unit was delivered and installed in the submarine, the navy controlled it and no one trespassed.

McCann quietly opened the desk drawer and came up with pen and paper. He started taking notes on something he was seeing on the consoles.

Amy's gaze drifted to the hazard signs that were posted on the walls of the small office.

She worked in the shipyard. Day in and day out, she was exposed to all kinds of hazardous substances, high voltage and smoke and gases. She was thirty-two years old, but there were times that she thought she'd be lucky to make it to forty. As far as retirement age, forget it. There was no chance. Accidents happen.

And now this. She was caught inside a hijacked submarine heading God knows where. Never mind forty. Amy realized that she probably would never see the light of day again. She'd never see her babies again.

She forced back her tears and focused on the radiation warning signs.

On top of all the other fears and anxieties, it was a little unnerving to be sitting this close to a nuclear reactor. And it wasn't even being operated by the good guys.

"Do people who usually work back here have to wear dosimeters?" she asked, thinking about the clip-on radiation-detector monitors that looked like tiny flashlights.

"Nervous?"

"A little." She nodded, already feeling embarrassed at interrupting what he was doing.

"They do. But that's really precautionary. The reactor has extensive shielding. Not one American submariner has been treated for excessive radiation in four years. If we were aboard a Russian sub, I'd be worrying, too. Their sailors don't do so well."

That should have made her feel better. But the panic sensation wasn't going away. She stared at the screens he'd been taking notes on for the past few minutes. She realized he was making some kind of diagram and using code words. He also seemed to be marking the location of men on the boat, or at least those he could see as he switched between the views.

The same two armed men were still searching the engine room. They'd moved to the starboard side of the middle-level deck. And the petty officer before the consoles hadn't moved. She guessed they were stuck here for a while.

"How old is the reactor unit on *Hartford?*" Amy whispered.

He looked at her over his shoulder. His hand reached for hers, gently squeezing. "You really are nervous, aren't you?"

She shrugged, feeling her face going warm in embarrassment. His hand was warm, strong. Hers was sweating, and her fingers felt like ice cubes. He didn't recoil in disgust.

He looked at the screen first. No one seemed to be going too far. He turned back to her. "The entire reactor unit was replaced as part of the general refit four months ago."

That sounded like good news, and she thought it should have made her feel better. But her nerves hadn't stopped eating away at the lining of her stomach.

"I know you're not a nuclear physicist, but this is how the radioactivity works. The longer a fuel rod is in a reactor, the more radioactive it becomes."

"So when a submarine reactor is close to being replaced, it's extremely radioactive," she said.

"That's right."

"But in the case of *Hartford*, since the reactor is new, we're relatively safe. Right?"

"Theoretically." A half smile broke across his lips. "I can't really explain that soft glow around you, though."

"That's not very funny." Amy shook her head and withdrew her hand. There was something enormously charming about him when he smiled. "What else is there that I need to learn about the nuclear reactor?"

"I think I've already said too much. Some of what I told you is highly classified."

"Well, I won't tell anyone."

"That's what all the spies say."

She glowered at him. "You can shoot me if I try to sell it to our enemies."

"I'm afraid I'll have to."

She looked at the screen. One of the armed men was looking right at the camera. "You probably won't have to."

McCann glanced at the monitor and his face was grim when he looked back at her.

"Have faith," he told her. "You'll see your family again."

Amy nodded, wanting to believe it. The faces of Kaitlyn and Zack passed across her mind's eye. She tried not to think of them now, fearing she'd become weepy.

"Hopefully, we both will," she whispered back.

There was a long pause.

"Married?" he asked.

The question was unexpected and made a blush creep into her cheeks.

"I'm divorced."

"I'm sorry."

The way he mumbled the words made her think he really wasn't. She decided to let him in on all of it, all the info that generally started men running in the other direction. "I have twins. A boy and a girl. They live with me in Stonington."

"How old are they?"

"Seven."

"What're their names?"

She was somewhat disarmed by his interest. "Zack and Kaitlyn."

"Second graders?"

She nodded.

"That's so cool. I'll bet they're great kids."

Amy nodded again, feeling that tightening in her chest again.

"Do they look anything like you?"

"Kaitlyn does," she managed to get out. She planted her elbows on her knees, leaning forward, wiping at a nonexistent spot on the toe of her borrowed sneaker. A teardrop fell on her wrist.

He reached down and wiped the tear off.

She sat back and wiped her eyes with the back of her hand. "Sorry. I have myself back together again."

"Are either of them as smart as their mother?" he asked gently.

"Don't start with any compliments," Amy said, letting herself smile. "I'll really be a mess."

"It slipped out. It won't happen again."

Twenty-Seven

Commander Dunn and one of the aides had headed down to the labs to look at the image enhancements from the shipyard security camera. Seth had again been sent next door to keep track of developments. Everyone else working for them in the room had been assigned to find what they could, including the whereabouts of everyone that Bruce had included on his list.

Sarah used this opportunity to call Key West. No one was home at the McCanns'. She hadn't given up, though, and was able to find what hospital Mina McCann had been transferred to. But everything after that had been inconclusive. Harry wasn't talking to anyone while Mina was undergoing a battery of tests. No one knew anything yet. Her rank and government connections had at least been enough to get the news that Mina was now conscious.

This entire situation was so unfair to the McCanns.

Sarah had first met Darius's parents when she was in college. Over the years, she'd spent many days at their house. She'd eaten many meals at their table. She'd been treated just like a member of the family, even though there'd never been a serious commitment between her and Darius.

Harry and Mina were simply just about the nicest people she'd ever met in her life. She'd taken shelter more times at their home than she had at her own parents' house.

Sarah wondered if Darius's brothers and sister were on their way to Florida. She didn't imagine they could be, with all the airlines grounded and the East Coast highways being the mess that they were.

It was becoming increasingly difficult to concentrate on the work before her, but she forced herself to look at the list. She read over the names of the eleven people that they knew were on *Hartford*.

She'd checked off Darius and Amy Russell. Dunn had included Paul Cavallaro on his list, so their people were already doing some research on him. Lee Brody, the petty officer second class in charge of sonar, was the next name on her list, and he was turning out to be a real puzzle.

The young man had his own page on Sarah's legal pad. She had organized the different kinds of information she'd collected on him into two separate columns. It was very peculiar. The man's personal and professional lives were one massive contradiction.

"I think it's the way you like it. A touch of milk and half a teaspoon of sugar."

A cup of coffee slid in front of her. She looked over

her shoulder and smiled at Bruce Dunn. They'd known each other less than four hours, and he knew how she liked her coffee.

"Thanks." Her gaze moved to the cinnamon doughnut in his hand.

"I know all about the love-hate relationship women have with doughnuts and pastries. So would I dare get one for a woman?" he asked, looking into space philosophically.

"The answer is yes," he said, answering his own question. He put down the small tray he was carrying next to her. On it was a pastry bag that he promptly offered her.

Sarah opened the bag and peeked inside. "An apple turnover?" She looked at him, puzzled. "Good guess."

"You think so?" He put the files he held under his arm on the table and sat down next to her instead of across the table.

"This is my favorite pastry."

"I know," he said in a matter-of-fact manner.

Sarah stared at him. He was good-looking, charming, and from the quick search she'd done on his military background in the past half hour, Commander Dunn was destined to move quickly up the Pentagon ranks. He was also divorced, Sarah reminded herself, and he was definitely making some less-than-subtle moves on her. A very dangerous situation.

"Thanks for the pastry," she told him. "So what did you find out downstairs?"

"Their best resolution still isn't good enough to give us faces," he told her. "But forget about how many scuba tanks they found in the Ways. Not counting Mc-

Cann and Russell, twelve other people crossed the catwalk and went down the hatch."

"That means they had help from inside the shipyard, too."

He nodded, taking a sip of his coffee. "And they had help from the crew of *Hartford*," he said in a confident tone. "The same sailor who was on watch for the hijackers was also guarding the hatch when McCann and Russell boarded."

"Do you know who that was?"

"Kevin Barclay, twenty-one years old, originally from Winona, Mississippi. He's right out of sub school. *Hartford* was his first submarine after serving on two surface ships," Dunn explained. "I've already arranged for a crew to be sent to Mississippi to question the parents, neighbors, high school friends and anyone else willing to talk. We have some NCIS agents going through his apartment in Groton right now."

"How would a young kid like him turn on his own country?" she murmured.

"How did Timothy McVeigh, a decorated army veteran of the Persian Gulf War, get to the point of launching his own semiprivate war on the United States government?" he asked rhetorically.

"From what I remember, McVeigh was described as an extraordinary contradiction," Sarah said thoughtfully. "Which brings me to what I've been able to find so far on Lee Brody." She pushed her notes in front of him.

As she talked, he started perusing the lists she'd made. Brody had a lot of characteristics regarding his family and school and lack of social life and restlessness that were actually similar to McVeigh. There was even some mention of him being spotted with a friend at a couple of right-wing, fringe-group meetings over the past five or six years.

"There's a basic difference between Brody and McVeigh, though," Dunn said.

"Yes. The rage that builds up and makes him feel he needs to do one horribly violent act. I don't see it, either," Sarah explained. "But it could still be there and we're just not seeing it."

Bruce stared at a bookcase across the room. She could see he wasn't thinking about books.

"This entire situation is very fascinating. This could be a rerun."

She waited for him to say more, but Dunn sat back in his chair. He took a bite of his doughnut, drank his coffee. He occasionally opened one of the folders that she had on the table and glanced inside. He went through his own notes, too, and checked a couple of things on the laptop. He was concentrating fully, and she found herself watching him. She wondered what was going through his mind.

She also wondered what he was all about. As a person.

He had a wiry build, maybe five foot ten or eleven. Definitely a runner. He walked and moved with confidence. At the same time, he didn't overpower. He shared his knowledge but welcomed what others had to offer. Sarah had already seen that, not only in her own dealings with him, but in the way he worked with the rest of the people in their group.

He was not standard navy issue.

She stole a look at him. He had a thin face, broken nose and short, thinning hair that he was definitely not ashamed of. She'd seen a number of officers who were letting their hair grow a little longer on top in a comb-over attempt. He had a strong jaw and a well-defined chin. But his eyes were the best part of his face. They were amazing. Green or maybe hazel. No, she definitely thought they were green. They seemed to change every time she looked at them. And they were intense. As reasonably handsome as the individual parts of his face might have been, his eyes pulled all the elements together.

Those eyes turned on her, and there was a long moment of awareness. She shook herself out of it.

"What do you mean, this could be a rerun?" she asked, not too comfortable that he'd caught her looking at him.

"Do you know that demand for the release of the two dozen prisoners at Guantánamo Bay? It's all bullshit."

He'd just thrown her for a loop. "What do you mean by that?"

"I had them run a check on the names—looking for any possible connections—and as far as I can tell, none of those people mean anything. From what the preliminary reports show, they're Afghani nobodies who have just been cooling their heels there for the past few years. They were all scooped up during operations south of Kabul in 2004 and, based on what's on file, should have been released long before now."

"That makes no sense."

"My point exactly."

"And how is this related to your comment about this situation being a rerun?" Sarah asked again.

"I was thinking back to your comment about the Oklahoma City bombing."

She nodded. "What about it?"

"Early reports after Oklahoma City suggested that a Middle Eastern terrorist group may have been responsible for the bombing," he explained. "Even liberal Democrats in Congress were saying it."

"But within days, federal authorities linked the attack to McVeigh," she countered.

"Yeah. Days," he repeated. "We only have hours. Maybe minutes. And while the president is a guy who'd nuke the entire Middle East if *Hartford* makes one false move, we have enough to suggest that the hijacking might be the work of homegrown boys."

Sarah swiveled her chair to face him. "You thought that an outsider could be running that submarine."

"It was a possibility, but the hijackers must be mostly mercenaries hired to do the job. Now I believe that these are men acting on their own. And that means we could meet all of their demands, real or fake, and they'll still go out in a blaze of glory, blowing up the entire East Coast."

She knew he was just thinking out loud, but something about his analysis wasn't sitting right with her.

"If what you say is correct, then why are they waiting? Why make ultimatums? Why not do what McVeigh did and go after the greatest carnage? Hit us hard and do the most damage possible?"

"Maybe it's not political. Maybe they're just after the money and the rest is just a smoke screen." He shrugged. "The truth is, I don't know. But I think that's what we need to go after. Motivation. We have to figure out what the hell is going on in these people's minds. But the bottom line stays the same. The combination of guys on that boat just doesn't sound like a foreign terrorist group."

One of the aides called out that President Hawkins was going on air with another address to the nation.

Twenty-Eight

"That's a wrap," the director of the camera crew called out.

President Hawkins waited in his chair until the microphone was removed before getting up. He walked past the cameras and lighting equipment to his staff, who were waiting at the other end of the Oval Office.

"How did I come across?" he asked.

Three of the aides blurted out compliments in rapid succession.

"Excellent."

"Tough and in charge, sir."

"The country is lucky to have *you* in that seat, Mr. President."

Hawkins was pleased with the response, but he knew he'd only hear the truth from his campaign manager, Bob Fortier. The old pit bull never minced words. He didn't care about hurting the president's feelings or chewing him into little pieces and spitting him out. He was a no-nonsense, straight-from-the-hip guy who, when it suited him, could be a wheeler and dealer who knew exactly how to get a job done. Right now, Fortier was standing behind the military advisers near the window. His stony expression revealed nothing.

They needed to wait for the camera crew to leave the room. Someone handed the president a cup of coffee. He gulped half of it down, not minding the hot liquid burning his tongue and throat. He was in overdrive now, and he needed to stay that way until this thing was behind them.

When the television crew finally went out ahead of most of the staff, Joe Smith jumped to get his two cents in before anyone else could talk.

"Mr. President, your stance of not giving in to these thugs' demands is rock solid," the rear admiral said passionately. "I think it's brilliant to lay out a detailed counterattack strategy of your own before the American public. Put these barbarians on the defensive and keep them there."

"Thank you, Admiral. I appreciate your support."

"What I must disagree with," Smith continued, "is your insistence that you remain at the White House and announcing this to the country on live TV and radio. Everyone, Mr. President, including these hijackers, is listening, and you know damn well that we're within the range of a Tomahawk cruise missile from *Hartford*. At this very minute, a missile could be headed for us, and there's no guarantee we'll be able to knock it down before it strikes."

"Do you think I should be afraid, Admiral?" Hawkins asked with a smile, glancing out the window at the sunny skies of Washington, D.C.

"Not afraid, sir, but cautious."

"I'm taking precautions. The vice president has been taken to a safe location. If the worst should happen and these thugs, as you call them, are not the cowards they appear, then I am sure that this great country of ours will continue to function even if the White House comes down around my ears."

"Mr. President," Smith started again.

"I have great faith in our military superiority," Hawkins continued.

"Naturally, sir. But that doesn't mean you should be exposed. Take yourself out of the line of fire." The rear admiral wasn't about to give up. "We don't want to give these people a target."

Hawkins passed on his cup to be filled again. "Life is about choices, Joe, about roads that we decide to take or not to take. Each step paves the way for the next. Each road leads us to a new adventure," he said. "The events of this morning stand in history as the greatest threat ever raised against the American people. The magnitude of evacuation that is going on all along the East Coast is the largest ever engineered anywhere. People are scared, Admiral Smith. There is chaos across the country. I've ordered every facet of our government to do what we can to assist our people."

"All completely admirable, Mr. President—"

"Now, by staying at the White House, Admiral, I'm doing exactly what I'm ordering my troops to do. A captain remains at the helm of his ship until the very end.

People need to see that I'm calm, in charge and not afraid. The American people need to see that, and the hijackers need to see that. This is the road that I'm determined to take. Whatever road my actions lead me to, then I shall welcome that venture, as well. But in the end I believe the men aboard that submarine will back down. If they don't, they'll rue the day they were born, Admiral."

With a nod, Rear Admiral Smith acquiesced. Hawkins looked over at Bob Fortier. The old man was watching someone beside him. It was a reporter from the *Post,* and the man was writing notes ferociously on a pad.

The president turned back to Fortier, who gave him an approving look.

Twenty-Nine

USS Hartford
11:30 a.m.

When the two men paused outside the locked engineering office, McCann stood with Amy behind him, his pistol leveled at the door. He didn't think either of them were breathing as they waited. They knew when the hijacker put his hand on the door latch, but the door didn't open.

A moment later, they saw the men on the monitor. They'd moved to the next level up and were working their way past Maneuvering.

That was half an hour ago.

McCann looked at the monitor of the Multi Function Display. The two men had finished their search of the engine room and had moved into the forward compartment of the sub. He could see them now in the torpedo room.

Rivera and his coworker were keeping their attention

on their own jobs as the other two checked outboard of the racks. There was no view of where he'd left Brody, so McCann had no way of knowing if the sonar man was still unconscious, or whether it had been discovered that the duct tape that bound him had been removed.

McCann switched views and stopped at a blank screen. He frowned.

"What was this supposed to be?" Amy asked.

"The control room," he told her. "They've disabled the cameras, figuring we might get access to an MFD. Whoever's running the show up there doesn't want us looking over his shoulder." *Whoever is in charge*, McCann thought to himself, *knows details even as minute as this.*

McCann guessed he had Cav to thank for that.

"And maybe they're afraid you'd recognize them."

McCann's thoughts had been more along tactical lines, like how many men were in the control room, what stations were left unmanned, and if there was any way he could force his way in. Fear of recognition on the part of the leader of the hijackers had never crossed his mind.

"I have a question for you," Amy whispered. "Do you think they might have sealed off the engine room at the reactor tunnel?"

He thought about that a moment. "They might have, but I doubt it."

"Why?"

He'd already accepted the fact that Amy Russell was no doormat, no matter how dangerous a situation became. He was also resigned to the fact that she expected answers.

"Because once they've locked down that door coming through the reactor tunnel, they'd need a combination code to reopen it. That code is locked in the safe in my cabin." He shook his head. "They can't risk not having access to Maneuvering or the engines at this point."

"So how are we going to shut down the reactor?"

"I'll show you when we get there. But first we need to get our bearings on where this sub is headed and what they want to do. I also need to figure how much time we have."

McCann jotted down a few notes on his pad.

"Those two torpedoes were the only ones that were fired," Amy said quietly. "They've got Tomahawks in the vertical launch tubes, don't they?"

He heard the quaver in her voice and turned to look at her. Her chin was high, her blue eyes clear and direct. She was doing her best to stay strong, and he admired her for that.

"Yes, they do. And it's possible they won't use any of the weapons remaining on board," he suggested. "We've been cruising at periscope depth. That tells me they're in communication with the surface. Most likely they're making their demands."

"How do you know we're still at periscope depth?"

"I just know." He thought about it for a second. "The pitch of the deck hasn't changed since we submerged…and from this." He grinned and pointed to the MFD.

"What else do you know?"

"That these guys are not in any hurry to get wherever they're going."

"How do you know that?"

"We haven't gone over eighteen knots since leaving New London harbor."

Amy's expression brightened a little. "What do you think their demands are?"

He shook his head and then stopped. "There might be a way to find out."

McCann could have kicked himself for not thinking about this before. He looked around the small room and pointed to a seven-inch screen two panels away.

"Use the headset and check it out. Normally, it's not live TV. The set runs off the communications system, which was shut down before. But our friends in the control room might be as curious as we are about how this hijacking is being played on the networks. They could be bringing in the news live, or taping the broadcasts from satellite. Either way, check out the channels and see what you find."

Amy moved to the chair before the unit, put on the headset and went to work. "Maybe I can pick up *Regis and Kelly Live*," she said, smiling.

McCann realized this was exactly what she needed. To get involved.

He switched the MFD from the surveillance displays to the ship's stats. He brought up navigation. The GPS system screens came up with no problem, and McCann cursed under his breath at the thought of Cav sabotaging the unit with that phony failure. He looked at the three-dimensional navigational fix, getting the latitude and longitude. He then turned to SINS, the ship's inertial navigation system used to keep constant track of the sub's position by way of an advanced three-dimensional gyroscope system that followed the movements of the ship from a known starting point. As skipper, he always used both systems to keep *Hartford* on course. He could see the same thing was being done now.

When he'd come into the submarine service, the plotting on the submarine was done manually, by a junior officer, on tracing paper over a standard navigational chart. Now, in spite of the electronics, he still insisted on using that method as well.

A thought occurred to him and he pushed to his feet and opened an upright steel box secured to the bulkhead. Aside from diagrams of the propulsion system and the associated electrical components, he knew there were a number of duplicate charts kept here. He searched until he found the specific chart of New London Harbor and Long Island Sound. He spread the chart over a table and started plotting the numbers the navigation screens had given him before.

"Where are they taking us?" Amy asked a couple of minutes later.

McCann looked up to find that she wasn't checking the TV screen. She was watching him intently.

"New York City," he told her.

"Jeez! What do they have against New York City? Why is it that all these terrorists have to focus on that one city? Why not Chicago or Miami or Houston or L.A., for God's sake? Haven't those poor people suffered enough?"

McCann worked quickly to finish graphing the charts. "I don't know why you're being so negative. Maybe this is not intended to be an attack," he suggested. "Could be it's just a sightseeing tour. A little Christmas shopping."

"Commander, I didn't know you had a sense of humor."

He gave her a quick glance. "I don't. I'm serious."

She smiled and turned her chair back to the small TV screen and ran through the channels.

Hartford was traveling at exactly fifteen knots now. Based on the graph, they were on a line directly between Hammonasset Point in Connecticut and Orient Point on Long Island. With the kind of firepower they were carrying, there was no point in moving any closer, as dozens of cities, including New York City, were within striking distance. Their slow but steady approach toward Manhattan probably had more to do with strengthening their negotiating position than anything else.

If they weren't after something, they could have let the missiles fly the moment they went to periscope depth outside of New London harbor.

"I think I have something here," Amy said from her chair, readjusting the earphones on her head and leaning closer to the screen.

McCann switched to the surveillance displays first, making sure everything and everyone was where they were the last time he'd checked. The two men searching the torpedo room must have moved on to the next section, for they were no longer in view of the cameras. He thought about Brody. There was nothing he could do for him now, but he hoped he was all right.

He considered the two men. He couldn't imagine they'd be backtracking to the engine room. But even if they did, the locked door and the two guns he'd taken from Dunbar and his friend gave them more protection than they'd had in the ship's office. Besides, it was a big submarine and there were a million places to hide.

Amy let out a gasp. "That's unbelievable. Look at this."

He moved behind her to see what she'd discovered. The broadcast was live. Just as he'd expected, the only way for the hijackers to know how their destructive plans were playing out was by getting the news via satellite.

The broadcast was from Fox and the aerial shots were of different boroughs of Manhattan. An ocean of people and cars and trucks and buses had flooded the streets. The pedestrians were the only ones who were moving. Total pandemonium reigned.

"What is he saying?" he asked as a reporter came on. He placed his hands on her shoulders, leaning close to her face. The news bands at the bottom of the screen were too small to read.

"He's recapping a speech the president must have just made." Amy took the earphones off, holding one side of it to her own ear and the other next to his.

McCann pressed it to his ear.

"...not meeting their demands. America will not give in to terrorists. As you know, those were President Hawkins's exact words."

The screen split, showing an anchorman along with a shot of people leaving the city.

"What does that mean to the people of New York, exactly?" the anchor asked. "Should we be evacuating the city?"

As the reporter started to answer, McCann thought he saw a flicker on the MFD displays. Moving back to them, he switched through the functioning camera views. There was still no sign of the two goons who'd been searching for them. The tunnel to the nuclear reactor was clear, too, and back in the maneuvering room, his petty officer was still at his station.

"He's saying he has great faith in our military's ability to defend the country," Amy recapped for him. "The president refuses to leave the White House, in spite of *Hartford*'s ability to reach Washington with a missile."

She paused for a moment. McCann focused on the MFD screen.

"Is that true?" she asked. "Can the hijackers hit the White House with these weapons?"

"Yes, they can," he replied, not taking his eyes off the screen.

Things were happening in the torpedo room. Rivera and his helper were shuffling the fish.

He didn't like the look of this at all.

"There seems to be a demand for lots of money and freeing of some Middle Eastern prisoners," Amy said, repeating what she was hearing. "An unnamed Islamic terrorist group appears to be behind it."

McCann doubted the truth of that statement. They were easy scapegoats. If Fox News used the word *Islamic* in a sentence, nine times out of ten they'd finish the phrase with *terrorist*.

"You're of Iranian descent?"

"Yes, I am." He looked at her and then turned back to the screen. "Are they saying that?"

"Yeah." She paused. "McCann doesn't sound like an Iranian name. I hate it when the media does that."

"What?"

"They focus on what they want to see and not the whole person. And what does parentage have to do with this, anyway? They're so full of shit."

He glanced at her. She continued to curse under her breath as she watched the screen.

McCann figured he was the most Middle Eastern of anyone he'd seen on the ship so far. Money had to be the motivator, especially for someone like Cav, or Rivera, and whoever else on his crew was involved. None of them were Muslims. None had any ties to the Middle East at all. He was familiar with the backgrounds of his entire crew. He knew their personnel files inside and out. They wouldn't follow the orders of an Islamic terrorist even if they had guns held to their heads. He looked at the petty officer in Maneuvering. No one was holding a gun to his head. What they were saying on the news made no sense at all. It had to be something else.

"They think the nuclear power plants are more likely targets than the cities," Amy relayed. "But they're not ruling anything out."

McCann looked down at his chart. They were already past the Millstone Nuclear Power Plant in Waterford, Connecticut. But the structure was still an easy target for the Tomahawks.

He'd waited long enough. He had what he needed. His plan was clear. Shutting down the reactor wasn't enough. He had to go on a search-and-destroy mission before attempting to shut down the reactor. That wouldn't force the sub to surface. With enough of the hijackers still armed, they could use the auxiliary power, remain at periscope depth and fire some of the weapons. But once on the surface, they wouldn't be able to use the vertical launch system.

Amy was white-knuckled and pale when McCann turned her chair around to face him. He pulled away her headset and crouched down until they were eye to eye.

He pulled out one of the two guns and held it in front of her.

"This is very easy to use," he told her, showing her the gun and the little there was to know about it. "Keep the safety on until you want to use it. I don't want you shooting yourself or me by accident. If the situation warrants it, though, I want you to shoot. Don't hesitate, because I'm telling you, the bad guy won't hesitate. Someone tries to come through that door, you aim at the middle of his chest and shoot them dead."

"Where are you going?"

Her eyes were huge, and he could see the mist of tears forming. "I'm going forward to the torpedo room."

"What about shutting down the reactor?"

"I'll come back for that."

"Can I come with you?"

He shook his head. "This is the safest place on the sub for you right now."

"What are you going to do there?"

"They're getting ready to do some damage. I have to try to stop them." McCann gave her the weapon. Her fingers were like ice cubes, but they wrapped around the handle. She looked down at the weapon in her hand.

"Will you please reconsider and take me along?"

He pushed back the hair that had fallen across her brow. He lifted her chin until she was looking into his eyes again.

"I need to know you're here," McCann said softly. He pushed to his feet. "Lock the door from the inside. I'll come back for you."

She nodded reluctantly. "You promise?"

A chuckle rose in his chest. He imagined one of her twins asking that question in just the same way. "I will. I promise to come back for you."

McCann was on the loose, so Mako was not about to use the PA system for communication. What he wanted done needed to be conveyed from the conn to the torpedo room only, and the headsets were the way to go. Kilo distributed the equipment to the rest of their men. It was time that they kept Commander McCann guessing.

Standing on the conn, he strapped on his headset, adjusted the boom mike and single earpiece, switched on the wireless transmitter. He left one ear open for the room.

"Man battle stations." Mako stepped up onto the periscope platform and made a preliminary sweep of the surface as everyone moved into position.

"Battle stations manned, sir."

"Attention, fire control team. Attention, sonar," Mako ordered.

He glanced at his watch. They were right on schedule. He looked around at his men. All eyes were on him. The room was quiet.

"This is the plan, gentlemen. Four torpedoes. We'll hit them where it hurts most—in their pocket. We'll target that brand-new exploratory oil rig that has been going up this year off Orient Point. I want a firing solution. Prepare to engage."

As the men in the control room turned to their tasks, Mako watched Cavallaro mark the coordinates on the charts.

"Prepare for the firing sequence."

Thirty

The floor shook as another torpedo fired.

With his weapon drawn, McCann rushed forward along the passageway. No one appeared to be around. It all came down to a matter of priorities. He had to do what he could to lessen the damage they could inflict upon innocent people on the outside. Keeping *Hartford* intact was no longer the primary objective of his plan. As bad as a reactor leak would be if the submarine were to sink in Long Island Sound, the resulting problems would be secondary to the damage the hijackers could wreak on the population of the East Coast if they started firing the missiles.

Two of those Tomahawks in the VLS were tipped with nuclear warheads, and McCann was beginning to wonder if they didn't need him to arm the weapons.

He now had to operate under that assumption, and his first priority was to stop them from firing anything.

At the top of the stairs to the torpedo room, McCann got down on his hands and knees, peering as far as he could into the lower level. He could see no one, but the sound of operating torpedo racks reached his ears.

Before moving, he assessed his position. At the bottom of the stairs, three sets of torpedo racks stretched forward, filling the room. On either side of the center rack, a narrow passageway led to the torpedo tubes.

As McCann slid down the stairs, he saw Rivera operating the small crane while the hijacker helping him muscled the nose of the torpedo into tube number 3. He quickly dropped behind the starboard rack and then cautiously peered up over it. Both men were wearing headsets.

McCann, keeping his head below the level of the center torpedo rack, moved silently down the aisle toward Rivera's back. The time to let anyone surrender was past. The numbers had to be diminished. What he knew about each member of his crew was sealed and put away in the recesses of his mind. They were now the enemy.

He reached Rivera just as the hijacker shut the breech door. McCann was close enough that he heard the order from the conn through Rivera's headset.

"Match bearings and shoot."

The firing of the torpedo coincided with McCann shooting point blank into the back of Rivera's head. The muscular seaman went down like a rock in the passageway. McCann stepped past him and fired again as the other man turned, his hand still on the tube's flood-drain mechanism. The second shot echoed loudly throughout the torpedo room, but the shot was true. The bullet struck the man in the chest and he went down, dead before he hit the deck.

McCann took another look at Rivera, who was lying in a spreading pool of blood. He had been a trusted crewman. A shipmate.

"Stay focused," McCann muttered to himself.

He glanced at the VLS control panels, located in the center of the ship, between the torpedo tubes. It would take him only a moment to remove the back of the panel and rip out the internals of the firing connections.

Before moving to that task, McCann turned and fired two shots at the camera above the racks.

Thirty-One

Bruce Dunn considered the avalanche of information on the computer, in the phone calls, in the hundreds of pages of files that were stacked up on the conference table. These contained what he needed to know about everyone possibly connected with the hijacking.

But Bruce was more confused now than when he'd started.

He felt as if he knew less about some of these people *after* reading their files. Nothing made sense. Ends didn't meet, and from the phone conversations he was having with Admiral Meisner, it seemed that no one realized that something was wrong.

He shut the file on Paul Cavallaro and leaned back in the chair, his hands threaded together behind his head. He stared into space, but a muted TV screen at one end of the conference room caught his attention.

The TV cameras were inside the White House. President Hawkins and a group of high-ranking military advisers were going into a conference room. The president waved at the camera and shook hands with reporters before going in. He acted like it was a normal day. La-di-dah. Nothing much happening. If the sun stayed out, he'd probably get in a round of golf later. Just another day like any other in his presidency.

There wasn't even a sense that it was the day before the elections.

As the door of the conference room closed on the president and his advisers, the shot changed to views outside the White House. Pennsylvania Avenue was deserted, and cameras zoomed in on the military snipers on the roof while F1 fighters flew by overhead.

Dunn swiveled his chair away from the screen and realized that, across the table, Sarah had done the same thing. She'd been watching the same segment. He wondered if he looked as perplexed as she did.

"Do you want to step out for some fresh air?" he asked.

"Yes, that sounds great." She pushed to her feet and grabbed her jacket from the back of the chair, pulling it on.

Dunn didn't bother to tighten his tie or put on his coat. He just said a couple of words to one of their group and hurried to catch up with Sarah as she left the room. It had been his suggestion to step out, but she appeared more eager to get out of here than he was.

"Where do you want to go?" he asked, once they were out of the conference room.

"Outside," she said, never slowing down as they headed toward the elevators.

"I have my car keys."

"Good. I don't care where we go, but I need to get away from this place. Even just for a few minutes."

His mind immediately moved into the gutter, for the first thing that ran through his head was taking her back to his apartment. Actually he'd thought that every time he'd seen her at one function or the other. Not that she'd even noticed him. He pushed away the ridiculous thought. He'd certainly never had the opportunity of getting her attention.

They shared the elevator with four other people, so neither said a word until they were out of the building and walking to the parking lot.

"I've never seen anything like this before," she blurted when they were out of earshot of every one else. "Nothing makes sense."

"Thank you," he said, taking her by the elbow to hold her back as a car sped past in the parking lot.

"Thank you for what?"

"For speaking my sentiments. You must be reading my mind."

They reached his car, and he opened the door for her. But she just stood there, staring at him. "Are you pulling my leg, Commander Dunn?"

"Hold on. Let's not start with formality now. It's Bruce. And no, I'm dead serious. There's definitely something out of whack with this case."

She got in. Bruce hurried around the car and got behind the wheel. He turned on the engine and stared ahead, trying to decide where to go.

"I don't know where to start—"

"Wait," he interrupted.

He couldn't explain it, but after a career of military service, he was suddenly feeling a little paranoid. The sense that someone might be listening in on their conversation. It would be easy for someone to plant a bug in his car. He'd learned long ago to trust his instincts.

"Wait until we can compare notes."

He pulled out of the parking spot and headed for the exit. Sarah didn't require any explanations. Bruce sensed that she understood. Outside of the parking lot, he took a couple of quick turns.

"Where are we going?"

"Arlington Cemetery." He saw her smile. "What?"

"I would have picked the same place."

Bruce checked the rearview mirror before giving Sarah another side glance. He saw her look in the side mirror, too. They had more in common than both of them had realized. And he figured this was what happened when you planted the seed of suspicion. Nothing was safe. No one was to be trusted.

"I know why I was picked to work on this case," she said to him. "Why were you?"

"I don't know," he replied.

"There has to be something," she insisted.

"Although it was a long time ago, I did one tour of duty on a 688-class sub. Actually, it was about a zillion years ago. Right after that, I transferred into Intelligence. And I've headed a few NCIS cases." Dunn would have liked to think that his stellar career put him head and shoulders above everyone else who might have been given this assignment, but he wasn't that naive. "I can think of at least half a dozen people out there who are better qualified for this specific case."

"More submarine experience?"

Bruce looked up at the sky as an air force fighter jet made a maneuver overhead. "Yes, every one of them."

"Do you know or have you ever met Darius McCann?" she asked.

"Know him, like a friend? No. Know of him? Yes. Have I ever met him? Yes. In fact, the one time that I met him was at a function where you were in his company."

"*I* was?" She sounded surprised.

He flashed his ID at two armed soldiers standing at the entrance to the Arlington National Cemetery and drove up through the rolling lawns and gray-and-white stone monuments. The grounds were covered with yellow leaves, although there was still quite a bit of brightly colored foliage in the trees. He pulled over at a spot overlooking the Potomac River.

"You were attending a reception at Annapolis," he told her. "We weren't introduced, though. While McCann and I spoke, you were talking to some admiral."

"I ignored you?"

"No, the old geezer pulled rank."

She turned around fully to face him. "How many years ago was that?"

"Two, maybe two and a half." He wasn't going to say any more, or she'd be scared shitless. Exactly two years and two months ago was the first time he'd seen her. The event had been a cocktail party that was held after a speech at the naval academy. Bruce could provide more details about the longer length of her hair and how she wore flat shoes, and that her hand had barely dropped from McCann's arm that night. But he decided not to share any of that.

He also decided not to tell her what he'd thought that night—and still thought—Darius McCann was one lucky son of a bitch.

Suddenly, his sports car seemed a little small. He needed some air to clear his head and get that tempting scent of her out of his head.

"Let's walk."

She nodded, not waiting for him to come around to open the door. They met in front of the car. The air was brisk and the earthy smell of autumn was strong.

"Will you be warm enough like that?" she asked him.

"Hey. I'm a tough guy."

She smiled and he had to force himself to keep his hands at his sides. She wasn't wearing a hat, and the wind had her hair dancing in every direction. He guessed the strands were silky soft.

They walked for a few paces in silence before she spoke. "Would you like to go first, or would you like me to?"

"You start," he said.

She looked around them. There were no schoolchildren, no tourists, no families. The guards at the Tomb of the Unknown Soldier stood at their posts some two hundred yards away. The sky and the trees and the graves of countless American heroes were their only witnesses.

"Do you know Kevin Barclay was engaged this past summer?" she asked.

Bruce nodded. He'd seen it in the young man's file this morning.

"He and his fiancée were picking out china patterns

two weekends ago," she continued. "He was helping her make the guest list for the wedding they have scheduled for next summer. I don't mean to sound sentimental, but the hijacking of *Hartford* this morning had to be in the works for a while. So why bother? Why go through the paces of wedding planning?"

"You're absolutely right," Bruce told her. "He doesn't fit the profile for a member of a conspiracy that, at best, will require that he disappear out of the country. And he's not the only one."

She put her back to the wind. The breeze blew her hair into her face. "Who else?"

"I don't know how a young man like Paul Cavallaro could be part of the conspiracy. The guy comes from three generations of navy officers," Bruce told her. "He has two uncles and five cousins who are all in service *today*. His grandfather was a Purple Heart and Bronze Star recipient and his father received the Navy Cross from President Nixon. Their entire family has 'Property of Navy' tattooed to the soles of their feet."

"And yet, you sound like you're certain he's in league with the perpetrators," Sarah said.

"He's got to be, but I don't know how he could." Bruce stopped near a grave of a twenty-two-year-old who'd died in Vietnam. He looked up at Sarah. "Three days ago, Paul Cavallaro told his wife that some special duty was coming down. He told her it didn't matter what they told her—everything was fine, and she shouldn't worry."

"When did you find this out?"

"About half an hour ago. One of our agents was able to talk to her. The young woman is seven months pregnant, and she's a total mess worrying over her husband."

"They were being deployed. What kind of special duty?"

"She thought he was talking about some kind of promotion."

Sarah rubbed her arms and rocked back on her heels. "It doesn't make sense. These are clean, straight, all-American kids. Why, all of a sudden, would they be tempted to flip?"

"Exactly my point," Bruce said. "With the exception of two crew members, I can give you a similar story about the devotion of every one of the men who were left on *Hartford*. These aren't the kind of sailors who threaten to bomb their own people and tear their country apart."

The breeze was picking up. Bruce saw Sarah rub her arms again. She started walking. He fell into step.

"Which two?" she asked.

"Juan Rivera, a torpedo man, and Michael Dunbar, who works in the galley."

"And Darius McCann?"

He shook his head. "It's impossible. Other than the ridiculous ancestry issue that Smith brought up, and the media is feeding on, there's nothing in McCann's records that indicates he would go over."

Bruce didn't think Sarah realized it, but her sigh was audible. He gave her a quick side glance. She was watching her step as they walked along the path between fields of white grave markers.

"He's a lucky man."

Her blue eyes rounded as she turned to him. "What do you mean?"

"McCann," he said simply. "You really care about him."

"I care about his honor," she said tensely. "I know what he's stood for all his years in the navy, serving our country. It hurts to think that there'd be the slightest doubt about his allegiance."

He didn't say anything.

"If you were in his position and they asked your ex-wife to investigate your involvement in a situation like this, don't you think she'd defend you if she believed in your innocence?" she asked.

He didn't know what Claire would do, other than go to her father. Dunn looked down at the tips of his polished shoes. He was being unfair. He and Claire had their differences, but she was as much navy as any military brat. The navy's code of honor was as ingrained in her as it was in her father or her brother, who'd chosen that way of life.

"Yes, she would defend me," he admitted.

He could see that some of the tension had drained from her face.

"Thank you."

He grinned.

The wind had picked up. The temperature was dropping. Sarah pushed her hair out of her face and glanced back toward the car.

"By the way," she said, "I agree with your suspicions about Dunbar. There's nothing out there on him that's meaningful. Nothing personal that gives a glimpse of the kind of person he might be. As many pages as I looked through, he's just as innocuous as a brick in a wall. There's nothing in his file that distinguishes him. Nothing that draws your eye positively or negatively."

"Right. Nothing about Dunbar says he's connected to any community." He moved to Sarah's left to block the wind for her as they walked. "In the case of Rivera, it's the other way around. Too much baggage. He's gone through some real tough times this past couple of years."

"It appears he was seriously affected by the death of his mother."

"His girlfriend filed assault and battery charges against him but later dropped them. He was into roughing her up. He got busted for a DWI and a number of lesser charges. He's been on a self-destruct path for a while now, but everyone around him has been trying to be understanding because of his mother."

Sarah looked around again. Their arms touched as they walked. "We didn't come out here because of Dunbar and Rivera, did we?"

"No," Bruce said honestly.

The intensity of her blue eyes struck him when they turned on him. "Do you feel it, too?"

He didn't want to tell her exactly what he was feeling.

"You mean that feeling of being snowed under with information?"

"Like they're using us as puppets to push lots of paper around and pop the right questions every now and then," she clarified.

"Well put," Bruce agreed.

"We have a qualified group of investigators and law enforcement agencies and the CIA and everyone else helping us. But where are the top submarine experts?" she asked. "The ones who know that systems A and B were installed in which submarine and that only Captains X, Y and Z were trained to operate them?"

"That's a good point. And I don't bring that level of expertise to the investigation."

She put a hand on his arm. "I'm not denigrating what you do bring to the investigation, Commander."

"I didn't take offense to what you said, at all. And it's Bruce." He regretted when Sarah pulled back her hand. "But I'll tell you the truth. I'm still at a loss for a motive."

Sarah nodded. She looked back in the direction of the car. "There's one thing that keeps nagging at me."

"What's that?"

"We've talked about it before," she said. "It's no secret that there are a lot of countries and political groups in the world that hate us right now. But if they've hijacked that submarine to do serious damage, then why haven't they done it already? Why all this song and dance? Why are they playing hide-and-seek? Why not make the ultimatum for two hours, rather than twenty-four? They're not dealing with some poor schmuck who has to pry money out of a rich uncle. We're talking about the United States government, with cash by the ton at the ready."

"I don't have any answers to that," Bruce told her, taking her by the arm and starting toward the car. He could tell she was cold by the way she leaned against him. "But it's good to get these things out in the open."

"I think so, too. In fact, I'm feeling better."

"Not me. Not yet," he replied. "I feel like we're either working on this case too late, or too soon. We're not in a position of stopping anything, nor are we really in a position to start building a case to prosecute. There's only one thing that needs to be done right now, and that's making a preemptive strike on that submarine."

She listened, but clearly had doubts about his suggestion. "That would result in a lot of fatalities."

"True. But if we don't stop them, the number of fatalities will be much higher," Bruce said. "And I'll tell you what's nagging me. President Hawkins has established himself as a warrior. To wait eight hours and still not issue the order to have them blown out of the water doesn't ring true to me."

She shook her head and chuckled. "Now, that's some good venting. You must be feeling better."

"Not yet." He really didn't. There was still something more that he couldn't put his finger on. Something else that he couldn't quite see. "But I'm working on it."

"Tell you what," she said. "When we get back to the Pentagon, I'll buy the coffee and cinnamon doughnuts at the Center Court. Would that make you feel any better?"

Bruce wanted to touch the smile that was tugging on her full lips. He'd skip the doughnuts for a taste of that. "That wouldn't hurt my mood any."

"Good," Sarah said cheerfully. She casually looped her arm through his. "But can we walk faster? I'm freezing."

He had no jacket on to offer. And he didn't get a chance to make a joke about it, either, because his cell phone rang. He unclipped it from his belt and looked at the display.

"It's the Pentagon," Bruce told her before answering. "They found us."

Seth was on the line. He relayed the bad news. Admiral Meisner wanted them back at the office.

"What is it?" Sarah asked as soon as he ended the call.

"*Hartford* has fired more torpedoes."

"Where?" she asked, lengthening her steps to match his as they headed for the car. "Who did they fire on?"

"You know the exploratory rigs the oil companies—with the president's backing—put in Long Island over the environmentalists' squawking?"

"They fired torpedoes at that? The rig isn't even operational yet."

Bruce shrugged. "Forget about everything we said before. The president burned a lot of political capital on that project. Those bastards just made the biggest mistake of their life. Hawkins will definitely blow them out of the water now."

Thirty-Two

"Rivera, what's the goddamn status?" Mako snapped into the headset.

Silence greeted him. But the noises he'd heard before still rattled in his head. He thought he'd heard a gunshot that coincided with the firing of the torpedo. Seconds later, more shots. But nothing after.

"Outer doors three and four open, self-checks complete, no fish loaded," the man at the firing panel announced.

"Status of tubes, Shayne," Mako said into the headset at the second man in the torpedo room. Again, only silence at the other end.

He moved to the MFD screen and switched to video. The view of the torpedo room was blank.

"Fuck," Mako growled, stepping down from the

starboard side of the conn and moving past the attack-center consoles to the open door of the sonar room.

"Out," he snapped at Cavallaro, who was standing at one of the sonar stations, monitoring any movement around them. "Take the conn."

The young officer jumped at Mako's command and quickly moved into the control room.

Mako shut the door behind him and switched the channel on his headset. "Kilo, where are you?"

There was a three-second delay before his right-hand man answered.

"Second level, forward, sir."

"The shit has hit the fan in the torpedo room. It has to be McCann. Send a couple of your men down there." Mako's voice was loud and razor-sharp.

"I'll go after him myself."

"No, I need you for Code Brown. Read me? Code Brown."

"Time of engagement?" Kilo asked.

"Fourteen hundred. You have a lot to do."

"Consider it done, sir."

Thirty-Three

USS Hartford
12:06 p.m.

Amy Russell helped build nuclear submarines, but not because she believed in war. She wasn't a person who saw world domination through military superiority as a way of winning security for Americans. She hated the idea of superpowers, of the West dominating the East, and of the Third World resenting the industrial powers. She believed in diplomacy and in tolerance. It was true that she loved building these sleek, efficient machines, but Amy didn't work at Electric Boat because she loved ship construction. The yard was a dangerous, tough and dirty environment to work in. You were wet and freezing cold in the winter, and fighting for breath in the stifling heat of the summer. Amy was there night after night because she had two mouths to feed and it provided the best paying position around.

Amy had never seen anyone die violently before. She'd seen the bodies of three welders taken out of a tank on one of the subs, asphyxiated by a gas leak. She'd seen a painter fall off the top of a section of a hull cylinder, hitting every metal bar and bit of scaffolding on his drop to the concrete pier.

She didn't think she'd ever known anyone who was capable of ending someone else's life. That included her ex-husband. Regardless of his career in the military, Ryan Murray could never take a life. But locked inside the tiny engineering office where McCann had left her, Amy had watched on screen two men shot dead in quick succession. Commander McCann had taken those lives without any hesitation.

And she'd silently cheered him on for doing it.

A bubble burst inside her. Watching him aim the gun at the camera, Amy realized she no longer hovered somewhere in a dreamland of idealism. At that moment, life and death became reality. And at that moment, she understood that she could do whatever needed to be done. There were lives out there that depended on them.

Then, just before the screen went blank, Amy saw a sailor coming up behind McCann.

She stared at the screen, trying to comprehend all that she'd just witnessed, and then leaped out of the chair. The promise she'd made to McCann about staying where she was evaporated, forgotten in an instant. She tightened her grip around the handle of the gun, slipped the safety and opened the door.

There was no one waiting on the outside. She looked each way before running toward the ladder leading to the reactor tunnel.

Amy paid no mind to the warning signs posted in the tunnel. In a moment she'd cleared the forward end of it and passed under the forward escape trunk.

She didn't want to think about what she'd do if Mc-Cann was hurt. When she saw the man approaching McCann, she was certain he had a gun aimed at the commander's head.

"Please be there," she said under her breath, running past the crew's mess.

When Amy heard the noise ahead of her, she instinctively ducked into the officers' stateroom. She heard a couple of quick exchanges. A muffled gunshot. She shuddered, hoping McCann wasn't the recipient of the bullet. She heard footsteps coming her way. Closing the door would draw attention. She looked into the room.

Three built-in bunks lined the far wall. A curtain closed off each one. To her right, two desks offered no place to hide. To the left, cabinets and lockers. They were useless to her. The bunks were her only choice.

The footsteps grew louder. She ran across the cabin and pulled open the bottom curtain.

Her hand involuntarily covered her mouth and she gasped. Her stomach constricted as she fought back nausea.

She could not take her eyes off the body in the bunk. The dead man's eyes stared up at her. Beneath the chalky face, the man's throat had been cut. She looked at the machine-embroidered name on his one-piece coveralls. Gibbs.

She had no time to be sick. There were men nearing the doorway. She pushed herself up against the wall beside a small built-in desk.

"They don't come up those stairs alive. You hear me?" The commands were sharp.

"Aye, sir."

"I have to clean up," the same man ordered. "We engage at fourteen hundred."

Amy pressed her body closer to the wall, hoping to go unseen. The men paused right outside.

"What's going on, Kilo?" a new voice asked.

Amy jumped when two consecutive shots were fired. She tried to crawl on top of the desk as she heard the sound of bodies hitting the deck. A forearm of one of the victims flopped across the threshold.

She looked in horror at the door, waiting for whoever killed the two to step in and finish her, too.

Thirty-Four

Newport, Rhode Island
12:10 p.m.

John Penn had to cut short his plan to visit two New Bedford and Fall River shelters and take a helicopter back to Newport. It was absolutely critical, he was told, that he sit in on the teleconference that his campaign manager, Anthony McCarthy, had set up with the Department of Justice's Office of Legal Counsel and President Hawkins's national security adviser.

On the approach to landing at his mansion in Newport, he saw that the number of reporters behind the high gates had multiplied exponentially. McCarthy had done his best to get some of these people to chase Penn to the two neighboring cities in Massachusetts. But the reporters had set up camp here, and they weren't going anywhere. There were different crews waiting for him in Fall River and New Bedford. Penn had a feeling that was McCarthy's doing.

Although he'd tried to put them off, the reporters had been persistent. They wanted him to talk war. They wanted him to take back everything he'd said during his months of the campaign.

He wasn't talking. That was the president's job, and he wasn't going to undermine any ongoing efforts. Period.

As the chopper touched down on the lawn, Greg Moore and two additional Secret Service agents met Senator Penn.

"McCarthy had to pull out all the stops to set up this call," Greg told him as they moved toward the house. "They're just getting started."

Penn knew what his campaign manager was trying to do. It was risky, but McCarthy wanted to delay the election.

Yesterday, Penn was told with confidence that he was going to win by a landslide. Now, less than twenty-four hours later, the outcome of the election was anyone's guess. He figured that this suggestion would make Hawkins's campaign people happy, too. They had to agree. With the eastern half of the country trying to evacuate to safer areas, an election would be pointless.

He was greeted at the door by his wife, Anna, who kissed him and took his arm. "How is everything out there?" she asked. "As bad as it looks on TV?"

This was one of the million reasons he was still so crazy about his wife after all these years of marriage. She couldn't care less about the election tomorrow. Her only concern was people. Despite Greg's prodding, John took two minutes and told Anna about where he'd been and about the spirit of the people he'd seen at each shelter.

She gave him an affectionate hug before he had to go and whispered in his ear, "Don't forget. It doesn't matter. If they don't elect you, it's *their* fucking loss."

Penn was still chuckling when he entered the dining room, which was now set up for the teleconference. Two of his aides were sitting at the table, and McCarthy was already lecturing into the conference phone. He stopped midsentence to inform those on the other end that the senator had joined them.

John Penn exchanged pleasantries with the people on the phone before motioning to his campaign manager to continue what he was saying. He knew Jane Atwood, the national security adviser, very well, and Ned Harris from the Department of Justice even better. He'd gone to law school with Harris, and he'd been a pompous jerk back then. These two were nothing if not devoted watchdogs for President Hawkins.

"What I was saying, Ned," McCarthy started again, "is that there was a possible precedent set for this during the 2004 elections. After September 11, Homeland Security recommended that the country be prepared to postpone the election in the event of a terrorist attack on or about the actual day."

"I remember," Ned Harris said. "And have you contacted Homeland Security?"

From the bastard's arrogant tone, Penn figured the paper pusher already had his answer.

"Yes, we have contacted them," McCarthy said, rolling his eyes at Penn.

"And what did they say?"

"They pushed off all questions regarding the matter to your office. And that's why we're on the phone right now," McCarthy's tone took on a cutting edge. "We're not asking you to do us a favor, Ned. There are logistical issues about tomorrow that make voting impossible. Perhaps you've heard that the country is facing the possibility of a nuclear holocaust."

"I believe I heard the president say this morning that the U.S. government is open for business."

"I think the shops in Hiroshima were open for business when—"

"Gentlemen," Jane Atwood interrupted, "if we could just cut to the chase. I'm rather busy this morning."

"Sorry, Jane," McCarthy replied. "Go ahead."

"There is not enough time to get Congress involved in putting off the election."

"We don't need legislation," the campaign manager argued. "We feel that a legal memo from the Justice Department is all we need. Consider the circumstances. We're faced with a possible doomsday scenario. Who would even think to challenge it? It's the only reasonable course of action."

John Penn watched Greg Moore scribble a note and slide it to McCarthy. McCarthy looked down at it. "If you need some kind of actual precedent, New York officials postponed their September 11, 2001, primary elections after those planes flew into the World Trade Center. It has been done before," McCarthy said.

"We're discussing federal elections here," Ned Harris interrupted. "Not some local primary."

All of them knew this. But that wasn't the point.

John sat forward in his chair. "Jane?"

"Yes, Senator?"

"I also want to cut to the chase." He waved off his

campaign manager. "Has this issue come up with the president?"

There was a long pause before she replied.

"Yes, Senator," she said in an emotionless voice. "President Hawkins has discussed this matter with members of the Intelligence Committee, Homeland Security and select members of his cabinet. The election stands as scheduled for tomorrow."

McCarthy started to argue, but the National Security Adviser stopped him.

"The administration has taken the position that, in spite of being far behind in many of the polls, the correct course of action is to hold the elections as scheduled."

"Dr. Atwood—"

"Let me finish, Mr. McCarthy. We've held elections in this country during natural disasters like earthquakes and hurricanes. We've held elections while we were at war, and even during the Civil War. We will hold to that precedent, gentlemen. Tomorrow is a statutory election. It will go ahead, on schedule, and no one will change it."

"Thank you, Jane. Ned," Penn said, his attention drawn to the images on the muted TV that had been set up in the corner of the room.

There'd been another missile launch by *Hartford.*

They were done fighting this point. It was up to the American people to decide if Will Hawkins or John Penn was the best man to handle the country's future. Even if they were under attack at this very moment.

He was willing to wait and see where the chips fell.

Thirty-Five

"Brody, put the gun down," McCann ordered a second time, speaking in a low voice. But the young man's aim didn't change.

McCann looked intently at the man standing three steps away. The petty officer's pistol was pointed directly at his face. A quick glance told him that the firearm had been Rivera's.

Brody didn't seem too steady on his feet. One look at his face and McCann could see that the young man hadn't completely come around.

"You killed Rivera, sir." His speech was slurred, but the note of accusation in his tone was unmistakable.

Brody must have been unconscious for some time. He clearly had no clue what was happening on the boat. At least, McCann thought, he wasn't one of them.

"You killed…him," he said, not taking his eyes off McCann.

McCann could take him out right now. He held his own pistol at his side. But he couldn't do it. Brody was the only member of the crew left on the submarine that he could trust right now. And he needed the sonar man.

Still, time was running short. McCann was certain that whoever was running this operation must know by now that the loading of torpedoes had stopped. From the orders being barked into the headset, he also figured that there would be someone down here in a hurry. He didn't want to hazard a guess how many would be coming.

"Listen to me, Brody," McCann told the younger man with some urgency. "You've been out cold for hours. I'm the one who cut the tape binding you."

"You—"

"Listen. *Hartford* has been hijacked. I don't know by whom. But with the exception of you and me, I suspect everyone else who was left on board last night is either dead or cooperating with the hijackers."

"You killed Rivera," Brody repeated.

"Yes, Brody. I had to. He was helping to load and fire torpedoes at American targets. They shot their way out of New London harbor!"

The young man blinked a couple of times. McCann hoped this meant that the words were registering.

"Look at this man, Brody." Slowly, he reached down and lifted the head of the hijacker who'd been operating the small crane. "Do you know him? Is he a member of our crew?"

Brody stared at the gun still in McCann's hand before looking at the dead man. His confusion was obvious. He shook his head.

"He's not one of ours," McCann said.

"Who is he?"

"I don't know. And I don't know who's behind the hijacking. One thing I *do* know is that a few of them will be coming down those steps any minute."

Brody didn't move. The gears in his head were not operating at full capacity.

"We can't let them kill us, Brody."

The hand wavered a bit. He still didn't appear to comprehend what he was hearing.

"Petty Officer Brody," McCann snapped in an official tone.

There was an immediate straightening to attention by the young man. His face cleared somewhat. The hand holding the weapon actually dropped to his side.

"Shit," McCann cursed as he heard footsteps on the top of the stairs on the deck above them. "They're here."

He pushed Brody to the side just as the first shot was fired down at them, ricocheting off the torpedo rack near to where they were standing. They came down the stairs, guns blasting.

"They're shooting at us," Brody said in disbelief.

"Yes, they are. And they're planning to kill us," McCann asserted, moving along the end of the racks as he checked the weapon and what little ammunition he had.

"What are we gonna do?"

"We're going to finish what I started. Kill them before they kill us."

"How many are there?"

Brody's brain was starting to work. McCann peered

around one of the torpedoes. Two hijackers fired at him, the bullets striking the VLS panels behind him and causing the electronics to short out in an explosion of sparks.

"I only see three. There might be more," he told Brody. "They don't have a full crew. I think there's only a handful of them trying to pull this thing off."

"Tell me what you want me to do, sir," Brody demanded.

"Distract them so I can get around the outside of the rack."

Trust had once again been restored between them. There was no questioning, no doubt. The young man followed the orders as McCann slid around the rack.

The gunfire continued as he worked his way back from frame to frame until he reached the aft end of the torpedo rack. He could see the three hijackers spread along the racks.

This is it, he thought, taking a deep breath.

Aiming at the one closest, he fired at the man's temple and then fired repeatedly at the two gunmen further along.

The first two went down, but he had no time to take any satisfaction in it. The third hijacker's shot nicked McCann's left shoulder, and he immediately felt the burn of the bullet and the numbing of his arm.

Brody fired a series of shots from his position as the hijacker ducked behind the corner of the rack. The firing stopped for a moment, and then the man broke for the stairs, shooting at Brody and McCann as he went.

McCann fired back, and at the base of the stairs,

the hijacker ducked behind two large bottles of compressed air.

McCann could hear Brody uttering a string of curses. "Brody, are you hit?"

"It's only my leg, Skipper," Brody called back through gritted teeth.

The hijacker fired off a round in McCann's direction.

Thirty-Six

To Amy, it sounded as if the shooting was still happening right in the passageway. No, she decided, it had to be down one level.

As scary and nerve-racking as that was, at least it meant McCann had to be alive. The hijackers must have been shooting at someone in the torpedo room.

She stood against the wall beside the open door, holding the heavy pistol in her hand. She would use it. But she had no illusions about her ability to shoot. Before today, she'd never held a gun. She didn't know if she'd be a help or a hindrance if she were to enter the fray.

The shooting continued. Finally, Amy just couldn't wait any longer. She crept toward the door. Crouching down, she felt for a pulse on the man who lay slumped in the doorway. There was nothing. She noticed that he was wearing the same coveralls as Gibbs. He was probably one of McCann's crew, as well.

She angled her head into the passageway. A second body, again in *Hartford* coveralls, lay in a twisted pose a few feet away. Amy couldn't help but cringe at the sight of the blood that covered the man's face.

Something was happening. It was obvious that they'd started killing the crew members of *Hartford*. Whoever had killed these two men—they'd called him Kilo—had done so in cold blood. There had been no provocation. Amy wondered what had suddenly changed? She remembered what Kilo had said. *Clean up*.

Clean up seemed to mean death. The end. *Fourteen hundred*. Military time for 2:00 p.m. Engagement in less than two hours.

Amy took a couple of deep breaths and made sure she was holding the gun correctly, the way McCann had instructed her to. She jumped as more shots echoed in the passageway. The shots were definitely coming from below.

She moved to the top of the stairs and looked down just as McCann called out below. At the bottom of the stairs, crouching behind a pair of pressurized bottles, a man began to shoot in the direction of the commander's voice.

Raising her pistol with both hands, Amy squeezed the trigger.

The pistol almost bucked out of her grasp, but the man at the bottom of the stairs looked up in surprise, raised his gun and fired a shot at her. She pulled back, feeling the buzzing heat of the bullet an inch from her ear before it buried itself in the wiring above, showering her with sparks.

Stumbling over the bodies behind her, she backed away from the stairs.

Shots continued to ring out below, and then everything fell completely silent. She didn't know if she'd even hit her mark.

Thirty-Seven

White House
12:40 p.m.

With the exception of the vice president, who had to be relocated under the present crisis, the rest of President Hawkins's war cabinet were assembled at the White House when the executive order was issued.

"They're clearly targeting our energy resources," Hawkins told his group. "This time they hit that exploration facility in Long Island Sound. The next missiles will be headed for nuclear power plants. We won't let that happen. We've waited long enough."

"All the pieces are in place, sir," the deputy secretary of defense announced.

"That's correct, Mr. President," the head of the joint chiefs concurred. "USS *Pittsburgh* is in Long Island Sound and in hot pursuit. The navy has two frigates following and a destroyer standing by in New York harbor. Air support is ongoing. We're waiting for your order, sir."

"Good. We've discussed your tactical options, General. I want you to blow them out of the water."

The head of the joint chiefs and the secretary of defense both looked at Admiral Norman Pottinger and nodded.

He'd been waiting for this all morning. It was finally time to go to work.

Thirty-Eight

In the control room, Mako watched his crew as he tugged a Yankees cap out of his back pocket and pulled it on. He was ready for action.

Three of the men glanced over their shoulders at him, waiting for his orders. Paul Cavallaro, unaware of Mako's intentions, continued to plot their course on the charts.

Mako marked the time on his watch before beginning to bark out orders faster than they could be acknowledged.

"Officer of the Deck, all ahead one third. Helm, turn for fifteen knots, right ten degrees rudder, steady course. Prepare to dive, depth six hundred feet. Officer of the Deck, give me tube status. Dive, helm."

The deck inclined downward as the helmsman pushed the control yoke for the stern planes forward.

As the depth was called out, he eased back on the yoke. The deck leveled off, and several in the control room moved quickly to monitor the additional stations that they were manning.

Mako stalked to the firing panel, where one of his men was trying to program the torpedoes.

"Nothing down there, sir. We're shut down," he said under his breath.

"The VLS?"

The man checked the monitor at the next station. "Also down, sir."

"We don't need it," Mako said, stepping back onto the conn platform. He looked down at his watch again and saw Cavallaro as he moved into the sonar room.

"Conn? Sonar," the officer called out the door. "Captain, we have company. There's an approaching object. A small object."

"Can you identify it? Is it a torpedo?"

"Negative on the torpedo, sir. But I can run it through the computer."

"Negative, Lieutenant. That won't be necessary."

Mako smiled. They were right on schedule for their appointment.

Thirty-Nine

USS Hartford
12:55 p.m.

Brody was pressing a rag against the wound to stanch the bleeding, but McCann was not ready to leave him like that. A medical kit was bolted to the bulkhead by the stairs, and he went running for it. He was back in seconds.

"How are you holding up, Brody?"

"Real good, Skip."

McCann knew he was lying through his teeth.

"Let me look at that."

He peeled back the rag to examine the wound. He couldn't find it, so he went into the kit and removed a pair of surgical scissors. It only took a moment to slit the pant leg to the thigh. He carefully inspected the wound. There was no exit hole from the bullet, so he knew it was still lodged somewhere above the knee. The blood was flowing freely, so McCann quickly tore open the packet of antibiotic pads and held it firmly against the bullet hole.

"Sorry, sir," the young man said.

"Shut up, sailor."

McCann waited as long as he could, but he knew the bleeding wasn't going to stop while that bullet was in there. Using his teeth, he tore open a second packet. He had to replace the first pad because it was already soaked.

"No, I mean it, Skipper. I'm sorry."

"For what?" McCann reached into the kit and took out a roll of wide surgical tape.

"For questioning you. I shouldn't have. I wasn't really thinking straight, sir, but I should have remembered that Rivera and Dunbar were the only ones who could have knocked me out. They were in the galley when I left. They must have come out right behind me."

"Forget about it," McCann said, winding the tape tightly around Brody's leg. "That's the best we'll be able to do right now. How are you feeling?"

"Fine, sir. If you could just help me get to my feet."

"That's the last thing you should be doing."

Even so, he helped Brody up. The sonar man balanced on his good leg and leaned back against the torpedo rack.

McCann glanced toward the stairs. He didn't know who shot at the third gunman. The shot definitely came from the middle level. When the hijacker had responded, firing up the stairs, McCann had then been able to take the man down. He wondered if someone else, like Brody, had just been able to get free. If that was the case, why hadn't he come down when the shooting stopped?

It couldn't have been Amy, he told himself. She'd promised to stay where he'd left her.

"They've taken the sub deeper, sir," Brody said, trying to put a little weight on his leg. The blood was soaking through the man's pant leg.

"Yes, I felt it," McCann said, suddenly worried for Amy. "Okay, this is the plan. I'm ordering you to stay here and shoot anyone who tries to come down those stairs. I don't want them loading the tubes."

"That ain't gonna happen, sir."

"There's a woman on board. An EB ship super. She was in charge of fixing our system, but she got caught in the boat during hijacking. Don't shoot her."

"Where is she now?"

"She's supposed to be waiting in the engineering office, back aft. But she's not too good at following orders."

"Got it, Skipper," Brody assured him.

"We've got enough weapons now, so I'm going to make my way back to the engine room. I've got to take out the man in Maneuvering if I'm going to shut down the reactor. Then I'm coming back here, and we're going to take our ship back."

"I can be more help than just guarding the tubes, sir. Seriously."

"I know you can. But for now, I want you here." He reached over and tore the headset off the dead hijacker. He handed it to Brody. "Don't say anything into this until you hear my voice."

"Hold on, Skipper. You're gonna blast your way like Rambo all the way to the engine room and back and take on all of them yourself, is that it?"

"We can't let them do this, Brody. You drag yourself up to the control room as quick as you can when I tell you."

McCann collected all the pistols that had been dropped and left an extra gun with Brody. He took a quick look at the face of the man at the bottom of the stairs. The dead hijacker wasn't anyone he knew, and it occurred to McCann that he definitely looked more Scandinavian than Middle Eastern. He stepped over him and started cautiously up the stairs.

Two bodies were lying in the passageway, but there was no one else in sight. He moved quietly to the first of the two. There was little left of the face of the first one, but he was sure it was Kevin Barclay. The second corpse lay outside the officers' cabin, part of his upper body lying across the threshold. McCann took a step in that direction, and then whirled when he saw a movement in the cabin. He raised his pistol.

Amy gasped and backed up against the paneled wall.

"What are you doing here?" he asked sharply, immediately rushing toward her. He took hold of her hand—the one with the gun pointing at him—and lowered it to her side.

"I saw the gun pointed at your head, so I came up to save you. But there were these people in the passageway and I tried to hide in here…and…and…I saw *him,*" she said brokenly, pointing at the bunk.

McCann saw Gibbs's body. He looked back at Amy. Her breathing was unsteady. She dropped the gun on the desk next to her and leaned against it. He pulled her into his arms and she held him, pressing her face against his chest. There was no restraint with her. She was all emotion, up or down.

He wished they had met at a different time, a different place, under better circumstances. The fact that she could have been shot, that she could have been one of the bodies that was lying at their feet, mortified him. He took her hair with one hand and pulled her face away from his chest so he could look into her eyes.

"Why can't you follow orders?"

She ignored his question and her gaze moved to his shoulder.

"You're bleeding. Oh, my God…you're shot!" she said urgently, trying to open the front of his shirt.

He trapped her hands against his chest. "Only a scratch. There's nothing to it, really."

"Then let me see."

She tried to push his hands away, but he stopped her again. "We don't have time right now."

He looked around the room, forcing himself to see past the dead young men who were members of his crew only twenty-four hours ago. He had to figure out what the hell went wrong and what made them act the way they did.

McCann turned back to Amy. "How am I going to get it in your head that I need you to stay in one place?"

"No. No way. I refuse to stay in a room with all these dead bodies."

He knew she wouldn't stay in any other room, either. Showing up here had proved that much.

"Okay, you follow me," he told her. "But I expect you to obey orders. Got it?"

"Aye-aye, sir," she muttered, picking up her gun again.

He pushed the muzzle to the side, so it wasn't pointing at his chest. "I'm the good guy. Try to remember that."

As he leaned out the doorway, looking up and down the passageway, he could hear her mumbling under her breath, repeating what he'd said, but twisting the words. He thought that was a very good sign.

There was no one in sight.

"Where are we going?" she whispered.

"Back through the reactor tunnel to the engine room. First, I want to make sure Brody, my sonar man, is still conscious. I left him down in the torpedo room."

"He's not with them?"

"Definitely not," McCann said. "He was knocked cold. He was a little confused at first, but he's on our side, so don't shoot him. Understood?"

Her head butted him lightly on the back. He took that as a yes.

McCann looked both ways again before stepping over the sailor's body. She was right behind him. As they went, he touched his chest, feeling for the key he'd need to get into Maneuvering. It was still there.

In a moment, they were looking down the stairs into the torpedo room. He peered down through the entry. There was no sign of Brody.

"There's something important that you should know," she whispered. "There was a man they called Kilo who shot your two men by the officer's stateroom."

He stared at her. "You were there when they were shot?"

"Yes, but that's not the point," she told him. "I heard this Kilo guy say something to one of the men going down into the torpedo room. He said he was doing a *cleanup*. There was a mention of fourteen hundred, too, but I don't know what the context was."

McCann didn't know any Kilo, but most submariners went by one nickname or another. He looked down at his watch. It was already 1:25 p.m.

Little more than half an hour until 1400 hours.

He wasn't about to wait around wondering what the hijackers intended to do in another thirty-five minutes. The torpedo tubes were shut down, but the vertical launch system might be operational if they were to go back up to the periscope depth again. Why had they gone deeper?

It didn't really matter, he supposed. The nuclear reactor could be a disaster at any depth.

"I'm going to do what I planned to do from the beginning. I have to shut the reactor down before they can use that as a weapon, too."

Just as Darius stopped talking, he heard footsteps behind them, and then the shooting began again.

Forty

There were no new aerial shots of the pursuit of the *Hartford*. The media had been banned from the area, along with all private boats. All nonmilitary aircraft in a five-hundred-mile radius had been grounded. The camera crews from the local affiliates, however, were staying busy, filming from the shore with the most powerful lenses they had. Across the water, the smoke and flames rising from the oil rig made for dramatic footage.

Sarah stood in front of the television in the conference room. The room buzzed with faxes and phone calls coming and going and agents walking in and out. She was in her own world, enclosed in a bubble that blocked out the noise, the people, and everything else.

Her thoughts were on Darius. She was determined to think of him still alive, fighting the hijackers. He had a warrior streak in him, something he'd entered the navy with. She liked to think that it was in his blood, a fighting spirit that came to him through his ancestors. It was in the name his mother had given him. Darius the Great, of the royal family of Achemenides. King of Persia from 521 to 486 B.C.

Over the years, Sarah had studied Persian history, its culture, its customs. The curiosity had begun with her interest in Darius McCann, in an effort to understand him. But soon the civilization itself had won her over, the centuries of history and the evolution of the region had fascinated her. It was through this knowledge that she believed she was now better able to understand the conflicts in the Middle East.

Persia encompassed many countries, cultures and various religions. It had always been a bomb with a slow-burning fuse. The centuries-old conflicts had roots running back to the days of the Persian Empire, long before a prophet named Mohammed rode in from the desert. More recently, it has been an area rich in oil, where poverty-stricken people seethe at the excesses of the rich puppets who are kept in power by the West in general, and by American oil companies in particular. To many in the Middle East, America and the oil companies mean the same thing—brutality and decadence. What America called democracy and capitalism were simply terms for a Judeo-Christian coalition bent on taking all they could from those living in the region. They saw no evidence to make them think otherwise. They saw no reason to temper their resentment.

Sarah believed that the lack of understanding of all parties involved perpetrated the flaring violence. There seemed to be no end in sight. Fear and distrust were the breeding ground of war.

And terror was the weapon of those without weapons.

She tried to shake off thoughts of politics now. She had a job to do, and she focused on the running script at the bottom of the television screen. Most of the images were a continuous loop showing the damage to the lighthouse and the Coast Guard cutter in New London Harbor and to the oil rig on Long Island Sound. There were two known fatalities on the rig, but they expected the numbers to grow. The fire was nowhere under control.

"Anything new?" Bruce asked, moving next to her.

He handed her a cup of coffee. She didn't have to look. She knew it'd be perfect and just the way she liked it. She took a sip. "The networks are already announcing that President Hawkins is planning another press conference at three o'clock," she told him. "What do you think is left for him to say?"

"That they've attacked *Hartford*."

Her heart twisted. She looked at Dunn. "Have they?"

"My sources say engagement is imminent," he said quietly.

Sarah's breath caught in her chest. She forced herself to swallow the painful lump forming in her throat. Fighting to control her emotions, she took a long sip from the cup.

"It's okay to be upset," he said softly. "No one is going to think less of you because of it. For God's sake, I didn't even know most of those people, and I'm upset."

Sarah appreciated what he was trying to do. She looked past the brim of the cup at the television screen again, hoping the unshed tears would hurry up and dissolve.

They were now showing footage of the White House again. The president and some of his cabinet members were leaving the Oval Office.

"They must think that if they show President Hawkins enough times at the White House, then people might believe that he's really there holding the fort," Bruce commented.

"He *is* there, isn't he?" she asked.

Bruce nodded, taking a step closer to the screen. "But have you noticed that there are a couple of people who should be there, but aren't?"

Sarah focused on the faces, recognizing everyone she saw. The cameramen were catching every attendee.

"This is a submarine hijacking." Dunn said. "Who do you see from the military?"

Sarah understood that he wasn't necessarily asking her, but just questioning aloud.

"The members of the joint chiefs, the secretary of defense. There's the secretary of the navy," she said as the men appeared.

"And from the submarine service?"

"That's Admiral Pottinger, Commander of Submarine Force of Atlantic Fleet."

"He hasn't commanded a sub in fifteen years," he told her, staring at the television screen. "Where are the sub drivers? Not at the White House, and not here helping us." Bruce turned to her. "This is exactly what you were talking about before."

"You were the one who said we should attack."

"That's true, but they should have done it hours ago, before these people got their legs under them, before they got too far into this."

"Back to the experts." Sarah took the pad of paper she had tucked under her arm and flipped the pages until she found what she was looking for. "I've done a little research since we came back."

"About experts?"

"Right. For the past ten years or so, under the last three administrations, the exact same sub commanders have been called upon by the president and the media for advice and commentary whenever emergencies came up having to do with submarines. They're the same experts that General Dynamics Electric Boat Division and Newport News use as consultants to sit in on engineering-design reviews. They're supposedly sought after by people like Admiral Pottinger and Admiral Gerry for practical advice. I haven't heard even one of their names mentioned today."

"Let me guess." Bruce gave her a sideways glance. "You're talking about Whiting, Erensen and Barnhardt."

"Very good."

"Between them," Bruce continued, "they've commanded or supervised the sea trials of every sub that has been built for the navy since the late seventies. Since Admiral Rickover died, those three are considered more knowledgeable about subs than anyone on the planet."

Sarah looked down at her list. "I'm impressed, Commander Dunn."

"Don't be," he told her. "Our minds are in sync. I dug up the names ten minutes ago."

"If you and I could come up with the same list, then why isn't the Atlantic Fleet using these people? Why doesn't the media have them on television?"

"Maybe they *are* using them. Maybe they have them on the sub that's chasing *Hartford*. Maybe they're working behind the scenes in tactical positions."

"In that case, it would be nice to have them available to us, too," Sarah commented. "Some of the questions that are taking us hours to research, these people might have answered in seconds."

"You're talking about the overhaul *Hartford* went through this past year. Four months ago," he said specifically.

She wasn't surprised that he'd picked up on that. One of the items on their agenda this morning was to find everything that might be new and different about *Hartford.*

"There were some system changeovers that were unique to that SRA," Sarah added. "And the crew of *Hartford* had to go through some training for it. I'd like to know how practical it'd be for someone lacking this training to operate that submarine. And depending on what the answer might be, I have more questions that could narrow down our search of who could be qualified and trained to head this hijacking."

Before Bruce could say anything, Sarah continued. "Of course, my questions are based on the assumption that Commander McCann has no hand in the hijacking."

"Whether he's involved or not, we could use the help of one of these guys." Bruce nodded thoughtfully. "I think just because Meisner and company haven't assigned any of them to our team, it doesn't mean we can't go out and get them. Meisner said we have access to every resource and investigative unit of the U.S. government. And from what I found, Whiting, Erensen and Barnhardt are kept on retainer all the time."

"And if they're too busy with the tactical side of things?"

"I'll take care of that part," Bruce assured her. "There's three of them. We should be able to get at least one to lend his expertise for an hour or two."

Forty-One

Shoved back around a bend in the passageway, Amy held her pistol where she could hand it to McCann if he ran out of bullets.

She'd fired down at the hijacker standing at the bottom of the stairs to the torpedo room, but she wasn't about to risk shooting McCann in the back. Luckily, the firefight didn't last long. She didn't see it happen, but she knew their attacker was killed by one of the commander's bullets.

"Follow me," he told her.

She didn't have to be asked twice. McCann was a lifeline and she wasn't going to let more than a couple of steps come between them. At the top of the stairs to the torpedo room, he paused.

"How are you holding up, Brody?"

"I'm fine, Skipper. Is the bastard dead?"

"Yeah."

"Do you want me up there yet?"

"Not yet."

"I'm ready, Skip."

Amy could only make out the top of Brody's head from the angle she was looking. His voice sounded very weak.

"This is the ship super, Amy Russell," McCann said quickly to his man. "I told you about her before. She's been watching my back."

Amy could have laughed, but she was afraid that her laugh might sound a little hysterical at the moment. Brody moved enough to the side just until he and Amy each saw the other. The young man saluted. She returned the gesture. He looked very pale and there was a bloody footprint on the deck where he'd stepped.

"Stay alert, Brody." McCann turned and looked past the bodies down the passageway.

"How badly is he hurt?" she whispered.

"He's got a bullet in the knee."

"How's your shoulder?" she asked him, glancing at his blood-soaked shirt.

"What shoulder?" he asked, still looking down the passageway, ready to go again.

"Listen…" she started. She wanted to stay with Mc-Cann, but her common sense was nagging at her.

"What's the matter?"

"Could I do anything for Brody if I stayed with him?" She shook her head. "What I mean is, tell me where I can be the most help to you."

"How squeamish are you about blood?"

"I have two active kids, and I've seen plenty of shipyard accidents." She looked at his shirt again. "I've been watching you bleed to death, and I haven't passed out yet, have I?"

"No." He started to tell her where the closest first aid kit was. "I've got one down there, but you might want more gauze and tape to bind the wound tighter. I'll be needing both you and Brody before we're done."

"Aye-aye, sir," she told him as she headed forward to find the first aid kit.

As he disappeared toward the engine room, she had a moment's regret. She'd just cut the lifeline, and now she was roaming around *Hartford* alone. She could run into a hijacker anywhere and get her brains blown out.

Amy focused on what she was doing. She'd stayed alive this long.

Forty-Two

"Conn, Sonar. Contact has slowed. He's on a course parallel to ours," Cav announced loudly.

Mako smiled and looked at his watch before starting to bark out more orders.

"Helm, all back two-thirds!" he shouted. "Mark speed two knots."

The deck trembled violently as the two men in the engine room opened the astern turbine throttles and reversed the direction of the propeller. The submarine shuddered as it slowed. Orders continued to be passed until the submarine was again traveling ahead, but now at a crawl.

"Two knots, Captain," one of the men reported.

Mako stepped off the platform and looked into the sonar room. Cavallaro was carefully monitoring the contact on his screen. The hijacker turned back to the conn before speaking into his headset. "What's the progress, Kilo?"

The security man's response came back in seconds. "McCann is still alive, but I'm finished in the engine room. I'm on my way up."

"Eight minutes to the rendezvous. McCann is finished. You have more work here."

"Aye, sir."

Mako turned to the men in the control room.

"Helm, all stop. Diving officer, prepare to hover."

Paul Cavallaro came out of Sonar and approached the conn, looking perplexed.

"You're preparing to hover at this depth, Captain?" Cavallaro asked, looking over his shoulder at the instrumentation doubtfully.

Mako ignored him.

"Ready to hover, Captain."

"Commence automated hovering." Mako looked at Cavallaro. "Return to your station, Lieutenant."

As the officer moved back to Sonar, Mako signaled for his men to get ready. They immediately began picking up their equipment and gear.

"Conn? Sonar. Captain, contact is getting ready to connect to the sub," Cav announced questioningly. "It looks like a DSRV, sir."

Mako glanced at his watch once more and saw Kilo come into the control room. The captain motioned with his head toward the sonar room as the others started filing out.

Paul Cavallaro turned as Kilo entered the room. As

he looked up, he was surprised to see a pistol pointed at his head.

It was the last thing he saw.

Forty-Three

As McCann passed through the reactor tunnel into the engine room, he considered the possible reasons for bringing the submarine to a complete stop.

One reason was to hide. As silent as *Hartford* was, if the hijackers wanted to completely disappear from the sonar of a pursuing submarine, they may have decided to go "all quiet." But the engine room had not been completely shut down yet.

The second reason could have been that they were carrying out their escape. Too much to hope for, McCann thought, moving cautiously up the ladder toward Maneuvering.

He wouldn't have to break down the door, for he had a key that would give him access. The only thing he worried about was facing any resistance from the operator.

"It doesn't matter," he muttered to himself. "You'll do what you have to do."

Arriving at the door to Maneuvering, he found it partially open. He moved in quickly.

The sight of two dead bodies immediately stopped him. One of them belonged to his petty officer. He had slumped forward on his face at his station. Blood was spattered across the screen and there was a bullet hole in the panel holding the monitor. On the floor beside the reactor operator, McCann found the machinist mate. His life had ended execution-style. He leaned down and checked the pulse on the young man's neck. The body was still warm, but he was dead.

No one else was in the room. He had a feeling there was another dead machinist somewhere around.

He checked the displays. The reactor was in hot standby mode. Doing what he came to do, McCann went to work. In two minutes, he'd scrammed the reactor, taking it to noncritical.

Immediately, the lights dimmed as the batteries took over.

McCann left Maneuvering and made his way to the reactor tunnel. As he went through, he pulled the watertight door shut and secured it. If there was anyone left in there, that's where they were staying.

He stood for a moment by the closed door, trying to understand what the hell these people had up their sleeve. Brody was on McCann's side. With the exception of Cav and Dunbar, the rest of his crew appeared to be dead. He remembered what Amy had heard. Was this the end of their operation and they were cleaning house?

He looked at his watch. It was 1400 hours. Two o'clock.

There was only one place left on the sub to check. McCann ran toward the control room.

Forty-Four

USS Hartford
2:00 p.m.

"How does this feel?" Amy asked after she'd finished putting a new dressing on the wound. As she said it, the lights dimmed perceptibly.

"Much better, ma'am."

She knew Brody was trying to be tough, but she wasn't taken in. The bullet wound looked like raw meat above his knee. There was no distinguishing between the cartilage, bone or flesh. The loss of blood had to be a serious concern. Amy did the best she could, but he might as well have been bandaged up by a blind woman. Nursing was definitely not one of her gifts, and this was a little different than slapping a Band-Aid on a playground scrape.

She actually felt a sense of pride for the young man and his courage. And she'd told him that many times while she'd been working on the leg. She'd needed to say those words for her own sake as much as his. She couldn't even imagine the pain he was enduring—or how much she was making it worse with her poking and prodding.

Amy sat back against the heavy steel supports and looked across at Brody. The racks of torpedoes loomed above them, protection on many levels. She tried not to look at the dead bodies on either end of the aisle. She was certain she'd never be able to work on the construction of another submarine and not remember what they'd gone through here. She closed her eyes for a second and tried to clear her head. She was assuming that she'd survive. That they'd get out of here.

She wondered where McCann was. Everything was too quiet. "What do you think is going on?"

"We've stopped and the reactor is shut down," he said. "The skipper could have done it."

He fiddled with the earpiece of his headset.

She knew McCann's survival meant living or dying for both of them. But how could he handle so many of the hijackers alone? The name Kilo flashed into her mind. Amy remembered how brutally he'd shot the two men in the passageway upstairs. And they were supposedly on the same side of the fence as he was. There had been no argument. No word of warning. Just sudden death.

"Silent waters run deep," she murmured.

"Pardon, ma'am?"

"Nothing." She picked the gun off the floor, stood and peered around one of the torpedoes toward the stairwell. All was quiet. "Maybe we should go up."

"The skipper's orders were to stay down here until he calls for us."

Amy would never understand the military's culture of following orders. But they all lived by it. It was ingrained in them from their first days of training. They were brainwashed to accept it, to live by it.

She crouched and looked at Brody again. "How come you aren't one of them?"

He looked at her questioningly.

Amy remembered that he'd been knocked out for most of the morning. "The crew who stayed aboard *Hartford* are…or were…cooperating with the hijackers. Why not you?"

He bristled, and she watched him look at the body of Rivera before answering. Finally, he shrugged.

"I'm not a traitor," he said. "I don't understand them, but I'll tell you something else. I wouldn't have betrayed the skipper for any amount of money. They all knew that. Probably figured I'd give them away."

Brody's kind of loyalty tended to propagate itself. At least, this was the way things worked in the shipyard. Crews either hated their bosses or liked them. There weren't too many mixed bags. Amy didn't know any of the other men on *Hartford.* The little she'd seen of how McCann treated his crew before the hijacking and how he'd refused to believe that they'd have anything to do with it made her think of him as the type who would be liked.

Something crackled in Brody's headset. The young man adjusted the earpiece again. "I'm here, Skipper."

Amy couldn't hear what was said by McCann, but she saw Brody immediately sit forward, trying to push himself up. She tried to help him.

"I'm on my way. Yes, sir. I can handle it."

There was no way he could put any weight on the leg, Amy was sure of it. She didn't know how he'd be able to handle the stairs. Still, she was amazed by Brody's determination as he did stand up.

"What's going on?" she asked when Brody finished listening to the commander's instructions.

"They're all gone. The C.O. thinks it might have been a DSRV that took them away. We seem to have the boat to ourselves."

Amy couldn't believe it. *Did this mean that it was over?*

"He wants to talk to you."

She took the headset from him, and saw him quickly bend down and tape his bad leg to his good one.

"Amy, how familiar are you with Clyde?" McCann asked.

"I know Clyde very well," she answered as she walked up the aisle between the racks. She stopped at the doorway leading into the large space aft of the torpedo room. It was the same room where McCann said he found Brody tied and gagged. "It's the auxiliary diesel engine. The backup power source for the reactor."

She saw Brody start hopping toward the stairs and hurried back to help him.

"Do you know where it is?"

"Of course. It's twenty feet from where I'm standing." Amy was torn about staying where she was or helping Brody up the stairs. He'd tucked his pistols into his pockets and was hoisting himself up the stairs with his arms.

"Good. I need you to go there now. I'll walk you through the procedure to start Clyde up. We need our auxiliary power."

She had her answer. She was staying down here. "What's going on?"

"The reactor is shut down. We're running on batteries now, but that won't help us for what we need to do."

She rushed back to where the hulking diesel engine sat half buried beneath the deck.

"Tell me, McCann," she ordered quietly. "I'm ready."

"I'm sending out four SLOT buoys as we speak. That might help, but I can't guarantee they'll get any messages on time."

Amy knew SLOT buoys were one-way transmitters launched from the submarine. They could send a digitally encoded message, but—because of their depth— they were still unable to receive any responses.

"I swear to God, Commander, if you don't tell me what's going on, I'll wrap my fingers around your throat and choke you the next time I see you."

"I like that. But before you incapacitate me, you should know something." His voice turned serious. "I have one of our own subs on the sonar, and it's close to getting within strike range. It may be a matter of seconds before they start firing torpedoes at us."

Forty-Five

Pentagon
2:05 p.m.

Bruce Dunn respected Sarah's privacy.

He walked away from the conference table where she'd just received a phone call from Commander McCann's father. He'd never admit it to her, but Bruce had actually arranged for the phone call as soon as he'd learned through one of their field agents that Mina McCann's condition had stabilized. The older woman had suffered a minor stroke that morning upon hearing the news about McCann. Bruce thought it would be much more meaningful to hear the good news from the family than from a stranger like him.

Seth McDermott entered the conference room at that moment. Perfect timing.

"Did you get any answers for me?" Bruce asked.

"Admiral Meisner says he'll see you in two minutes."

Not exactly what he wanted to hear, but Dunn knew

the director of naval intelligence would be able to cut through the red tape and get answers, if anyone could.

"Where?"

"Outside the large conference room," McDermott said, grinning. "Things are about to get critical in the command center, but he had to go to the head. He said he'd give you some answers on his way back."

"I guess we should be grateful that admirals are human enough to take bathroom breaks." Dunn looked at his watch. It had to be two minutes by now. He stepped out and spotted Meisner walking back.

"Seth told me you've been trying to get some help but have run into some brick walls." Meisner talked as he continued to walk. There were no formalities between the two. No ceremony. They'd known each other for about ten years, and Bruce had investigated at least twenty cases for him. He fell in beside the older man.

"More like some paper walls, but considering the ticking clock, I don't want to waste time. What can you tell me about them? Where can I find them?"

Meisner stopped a step away from his destination. "Let's see. Whiting happened to be on USS *Pittsburgh*, the sub chasing *Hartford*. They've been testing two new systems. Which means the chance of contacting him is zilch."

"How about Erensen?"

"The miserable son of a bitch had a quadruple bypass surgery on Friday."

"Sorry about that," Dunn said.

"I tell you, it's the damn retirement." Meisner shrugged. "I don't think he'll be any good to us, at least not today. He's still in intensive care."

That explained why they hadn't seen those two faces beside the president or on the Fox talk shows. "How about Captain Barnhardt?"

"Canada. On one of his back-to-nature survival jaunts up there. This time it's bow hunting or some other crap like that. He left last week. He won't surface until Wednesday or so."

Bruce had heard about Barnhardt's fascination with hunting. He regularly led excursions to an island on Hudson Bay. A group of them would get dropped off on an island or in the woods in the middle of nowhere for so many days at a time.

"Can't we send some marines or park rangers after him?"

"The bastard would probably shoot them," Meisner answered.

Bruce recollected that there was no love lost between Meisner and Barnhardt.

"Work with Erensen if you have to. His wife says he's started talking. He's at Johns Hopkins."

Bruce nodded. "By the way, anything from *Hartford?*"

Meisner shook his head. "All the communication is shut down. *Pittsburgh* is getting ready to blast them into million pieces."

"That's a shame."

Meisner looked at him oddly. "You think so?"

"I sure as hell do. From what I can see, McCann deserved better than to go out like this."

Forty-Six

USS Pittsburgh
2:12 p.m.

"Torpedoes away."

The second pair of torpedoes sped off into the dark waters of the Sound.

"Close outer doors three and four. Drain tubes and reload."

The orders from the commander of *Pittsburgh* continued, and Captain Whiting, supervising the action, saw the effects of good training. It was a shame they were about to take out one of their own subs.

"Fire Control, I want a new solution on target."

Whiting knew it was difficult for the skipper of the sub, too. He couldn't bring himself to refer to *Hartford* by name. The deck officer approached the conn and handed the C.O. a message board.

The commander read it, looked at Captain Whiting and handed the board to him.

Looking at the message, Whiting felt as if he'd been punched in the gut. One minute would have made all the difference. Now it was too late. It would take less than ten minutes for the fish to reach *Hartford*. If only this message had come in a minute earlier.

"It's from Commander McCann, sir," the young deck officer said, as if Whiting couldn't read the damn thing himself.

"The authenticity code?" the commander barked.

"It matches, sir. It's from *Hartford*. From McCann."

Whiting read the short message again. McCann had regained control of the ship. The hijackers had left by way of what he suspected was a DSRV. The reactor plant was scrammed, and he was working on auxiliary to bring them to the surface. Three people were trying to run that goddamn sub—one of them a civilian.

They'd never make it.

The skipper was shouting orders. Radio was messaging the surface. Search for the DSRV would go to units in the air. Washington and Norfolk had to be immediately notified of the situation.

Whiting watched him turn to his combat. "Status of torpedoes?"

"At their cruising speed on the intercept course to the target," the young petty officer told him.

"With his power shut down, he has no chance to outrun them," Whiting commented. "He's going to take the hit."

One minute would have saved those three people's lives. The commander had another communication sent, this time ordering the deep-water-rescue equipment.

"You might try the electronics, Skipper," Whiting
suggested.

"The fish are too far out," the C.O. replied. "They're
out of range."

Forty-Seven

USS Hartford
2:18 p.m.

The battery charge was getting very low because of the life support systems and the sonar. Sonar by itself was a power hog. McCann had to keep it operating at full capacity, and the system's seawater pumps, required to cool its computers, were an awful power drain.

He looked at the display that showed the power on the grid from the ship's turbine generators.

"Come on, Amy. Fire that baby up."

Another few minutes and they'd be dead in the water.

"Come on…"

The display started to come alive.

"You're doing it, Amy," he said into the mouthpiece.

She had the auxiliary engine running. McCann watched the battery charge gauge jump.

"Yeah, baby," Brody shouted. "She's real good, sir.

We've got to get us one like her on board for the next patrol."

"Where are you, Amy? Get up here," McCann said into the mike.

"I'm coming. I'm coming," she shot back. "Will you please stop being so bossy?"

"Conn? Sonar," Brody shouted. "Multiple torpedoes in the water. Bearing on us. I read four fish, Skipper."

"What's the range gate?"

"Prolonged pinging, sir. Lead torpedo is maybe six thousand yards."

He'd known it was just a matter of time. They hadn't gotten their message off soon enough. McCann left the conn and ducked into Sonar, looking briefly over Brody's shoulder and checking the speed and coordinates.

They had only minutes.

Amy burst into the control room as McCann stepped back onto the conn. She was greasy and dirty and had bloodstains on her clothing, and McCann thought he'd never seen a more beautiful woman. He watched her come to a halt and stare at the bodies of Cav and Dunbar, lying by the navigation panels where he'd dragged them.

Considering what was going on right now, McCann shouldn't have felt so defensive. But he felt the urgent need to explain everything to her. An urge brought on by the stark uncertainty of whether or not they'd get out of here alive.

He went to her. "Here's the 'cleanup' you heard about. They were dead when I got up here."

Amy looked away, obviously accepting his words.

"I'm reporting for duty, Skipper. What else do you want me to do?"

He smiled. "I'm going to put you at the helm."

"Driving the sub?" she asked, her eyes rounding. "I can't do that."

"It's not much different than driving a car. I'll show you." He took her by the arm and seated her, starting to show her some of the controls.

"Conn? Sonar. Range gate dropping," Brody told him.

McCann knew he had no ability to fire off counter-measures that would draw the fire of the torpedoes. There was no running away from these fish, either. Not with the reactor shut down.

"How far do you figure, Brody?" The sonar man could judge the distance of the torpedo by the time between active sonar pings. The shorter the intervals between pings, the closer the torpedo.

"Range is about three thousand yards," Brody responded.

They were a sitting duck, fat and passive while a death blow drew nearer.

"No," McCann muttered. "There is one thing we can do."

He leaned over Amy.

"Heads up, Brody," he shouted. "You, too, Amy. Emergency blow, fore and aft. We're taking her up. Amy, pull back on the yoke and try to keep it at a twenty-degree up bubble."

Amy looked over her shoulder at him, nervously. He gave her a reassuring nod. If this worked, he might get up above the ceiling setting of the weapons…if they had them programmed for it. And even if they were hit, if they could make it to surface, McCann thought he could somehow save Amy's and Brody's lives. A very big somehow.

McCann slammed two steel levers into their cradles above his head, and the sound of high-pressure air displacing the water in the ballast tanks blasted in their ears. As the water was forced out of the tanks, the submarine immediately became lighter and began to rise with rapidly increasing speed. As the deck tilted upward, McCann put his hand over Amy's and helped her keep the ship's ascent at twenty degrees.

The numbers on the depth indicator flickered as the ship shot up from the depths. The speed indicator read fifteen knots. Eighteen knots. Twenty-one knots.

Over the roar of the emergency blow, McCann could hear Brody calling out the distance of the lead torpedo on their tail. The depth indicator showed three hundred feet to the surface. Two-fifty. Two hundred. He hoped there were no surface vessels above. They were going to burst up through the surface like a rocket.

"Continuous ramp wave on the lead fish."

The torpedo now had a precise fix on the sub's location. McCann glanced once more at the depth indicator. One hundred feet.

They weren't going to make it, he thought, and then three successive explosions rocked *Hartford*.

Forty-Eight

Captain Whiting and the C.O. of *Pittsburgh* stood on the bridge and waited. The C.O.'s headset crackled.

"Bridge? Combat," the voice came through. "Only three of our fish detonated, sir. One torpedo is still on target and closing."

"Shit," Whiting muttered. Using their sophisticated electronics, they'd tried to reprogram the torpedoes speeding toward *Hartford*. It was a miracle they'd been able to get three of them to self-destruct. The problem was that only one MK-48 torpedo was enough to annihilate the submarine.

"Shit," he said again.

Pittsburgh had surfaced only moments before. Cruising at only one-hundred fifty feet below the surface, the sub had risen to the surface after attempting to short-circuit their torpedoes.

"There she is," the C.O. said to Whiting, but the older man's binoculars were already locked on the sight.

The bow of *Hartford* shot up out of the water, her tremendous speed driving her upward until the sail cleared the surface. More of the sleek black hull followed, like the body of a great whale about to breach, until the massive weight of the vessel once again became the dominant force, plummeting the bow of the submarine back to the surface. As she reentered the waters of the Sound, a huge wall of water rose up around her.

At that precise moment, the single remaining torpedo struck the underside of *Hartford* and exploded, the powerful blast lifting the bow of the submarine out of the water.

With the eye of a seasoned veteran, Whiting judged that the fish must have struck the hull just aft of the torpedo tubes.

Forty-Nine

They'd been hit, and Amy's ears were ringing from the blast of the torpedo.

She looked around. It appeared that there was little damage to the control room. Even the lights, which had flickered several times, still lit the interior of the sub.

Amy leaned to the side and looked at Brody. He had his head back and was looking up into the overhead. Amy didn't know if he was saying a prayer or meditating, but it didn't matter. Somehow, they'd gone through hell and survived. She swung around in her seat to look for Mc-Cann. He was flipping switches and pressing buttons. He finished what he was doing and their gazes locked.

"Is it over?" she asked in a whisper, afraid she might be dreaming. She was terrified that they weren't really on the surface, but dead.

He nodded.

Amy got up from the chair and closed the distance between them. Throwing her arms around McCann, she pressed her face against his blood-soaked shirt. He wrapped his arms around her.

"Thank you," she said brokenly, overwhelmed with emotion and gratitude. "Thank you. Thank you for saving our lives."

He raised her chin, and she felt her heart skip a beat. There was no time to say or do anything before McCann's lips closed over hers. She kissed back hard. It was the hungry kiss of two people who'd just been given a second chance at life.

"We couldn't have done this without you," he whispered in her ear as he ended the kiss. But he didn't let her go.

They both turned and looked at Brody. He was staring at the sonar screen.

"Good work, Brody," McCann told him.

He turned in his chair. The loss of blood seemed to have caught up to him. His face was very pale and his eyes lacked focus.

"Skipper, I know why they didn't ask me to go in with—"

Before he could finish, an explosion ripped through the upper deck, tearing the deck plates and blasting a twenty-foot hole in *Hartford*'s hull. Amy found herself on the deck inside the communications center, one of the operator's chairs on top of her. Her ears felt as if they were blocked. But she was still alive.

She tried to sit up and looked around frantically, trying to find McCann and Brody. What she could see of the control room through the radio room door was a disaster area. The main lighting was out, but the emergency lights were somehow still working.

Daylight was pouring in along with the sea. As the green water rushed in, Amy thought that they couldn't have been hit by another torpedo. There'd been nothing else on the sonar.

It was either the navy bombarding them from above, she decided, or it was a present that the hijackers had left behind.

At that moment, the vessel pitched, and she looked up in time to see one of the radio panels directly above her tip precariously, right before it crashed down on her.

Fifty

"**M**y fellow Americans. Once again, good has triumphed over evil. Once again, in the face of danger, the best of America has showed itself." President Hawkins paused and looked into the cameras. "The crisis is over. As I speak to you, the men and women of our military forces are preparing to board the disabled submarine *Hartford.* The hijackers that have survived are on the run. Our nation, our way of life, is safe."

He smiled and then grew serious again. "This has been a trying day for every one of us. Today the very foundations of America came under attack. But our belief in freedom and our ability to resist evil never faded. Our light never dimmed. We went out there and fought the terrorists who brought this fight to our door. We stood our ground and proved to those nations who support such actions that we are not weak or unprepared or lacking in our determination to stand up for our beliefs. America is strong. We have showed the world that we stand together and that we will never be defeated."

The president continued to read the speech on the teleprompter in front of him. As always, Bob Fortier was prepared with the message they wanted to convey at just the right moment. And this was their moment. Every voter west of the Mississippi was glued to their television, and those on the East Coast who were not in front of their TVs were listening to him on the radio. All programming was preempted. This was his time. His show.

Tomorrow, they would go to their polling places and vote. And who would they be voting for? William Hawkins.

The president read on, smiling occasionally, sounding confident and showing his pride in being an American. The speech touched on what he'd accomplished in the past four years in preparing America's defenses for this kind of assault. He referred to the course of action he planned to keep the nation on for the next four. He talked about the hijacking and made it clear that his foreign policies must be credited for their ability to quash this threat and force these terrorists to abort their plans. Strength was the only way to answer terror, he told the nation. American strength.

Hawkins knew John Penn must be squirming in his small mansion in Rhode Island. There would be no rebuttal this time about the need for "balancing the interests of America with our responsibilities to the people on whose backs we've grown wealthy." This was no moderated debate. Will Hawkins, President William Hawkins, had the platform all to himself.

He folded his hands in a prayerful attitude. Looking straight into the camera, he finished the speech with his own words.

"Tomorrow, as a nation, we will go and exercise the right that Americans have fought and died for. No terrorist will ever jeopardize that freedom while I stand watch. Go, my fellow Americans, with the secure knowledge that the future is safe for you and your children. You, my brothers and sisters, who are on the road, return to your homes. Here in the White House, we have kept the light burning for you."

The director motioned for the camera crew to stop filming as those in the Oval Office started to cheer.

Hawkins moved from behind his desk and circulated among the crew and his staff and the members of his party's congressional leadership that had come to share in his glory. Now he could do what he was even better at—shaking hands and making small talk.

Fifty-One

The wall of seawater rushing in with each rise and fall of the vessel was washing away everything, including equipment that had been bolted in place.

The blast had separated McCann from Amy, and he remembered that his head had smashed against something. Now he was lying on top of the fire-control panel and seawater was slapping against his face.

McCann had no idea what time it was, or if he'd been knocked out or not. He could see light coming in from somewhere beyond the periscope platform and the cascading water. The battle lanterns above him were still burning. Beneath him, he could hear the banging bass sound of deep water. The forward compartment was filling quickly, and that meant the lower levels must be full.

If the ship went down now, they'd all go with it. He

looked around madly but he could see no sign of Amy or Brody. He remembered holding on to her until the blow.

He rolled off the panel and was nearly swept under by the turbulence of the seawater in the compartment. The water came almost to his chest. Wading through the control room, he clung to anything he could get a grip on.

It seemed like forever before he made it to where he'd last seen Amy. Filling his lungs with air, he went under. Darkness was all around him. He searched where she'd been standing before. He came up for air and looked around, shouting her name, before diving again.

The water was rising even higher. He could see where the light was seeping in. Back near the escape trunk, the explosion had torn open a gaping hole in the hull. Everything surrounding it was demolished.

He went under again and pulled himself toward Sonar. There was still no sign of Amy.

Surfacing, he pulled open the door to the sonar room. Brody was unconscious and still in his chair at the sonar station. His face was barely above water, and there was blood on his forehead. From the spiderweb breaks in what was still visible of the monitor screen, McCann guessed the young man's head had been driven into it by the force of either the explosion or the rushing water. He grabbed his man by the collar of his shirt and tried to lift him from the chair. No luck. Brody's leg was caught on something.

McCann didn't know if Brody was alive or already dead, but he had to try to get him out of there. The water was continuing to wash in around them. He reached down, yanking at the table that trapped Brody's legs. Brody's body started moving away from the chair. He was free.

McCann put an arm across the man's chest and began towing him through the control room toward the bridge-access ladder. The forward escape hatch was wrecked. He'd have to carry Brody up through the sail to the bridge. It was going to be a tough climb.

As he went, he continued to look for Amy. By the periscope platform, he lost his footing and went under, dragging Brody with him. Regaining his feet, he came up and heard Brody coughing and sputtering. At least he was still alive, McCann thought.

But what about Amy.

"Amy! *Amy!*"

It took some effort to lift Brody's body over his shoulder. It took even more to climb the ladder up through the narrow trunk that led to the bridge. At the top, he felt himself getting weak as he tried to open the hatch with one hand. The shoulder he'd been shot in was starting to go numb, and he was losing feeling in his hand and arm.

Finally, the hatch opened, and as McCann pushed it up, light streamed in.

Time was of the essence. Wherever Amy was, he had to find her soon. McCann carried Brody's body up until the young man was clear of the hatch, and then he rolled him onto the decking topside.

Leaving him there, McCann slid back down the ladder, entering the water again. The light from above improved visibility, but not the scene itself. The water had risen so high that he now had to swim. He saw no sign of Amy in what was left of the control room. He considered the direction of the blast and where the water might have carried her. He turned and looked past the helm. The communication shack was just forward of the control room. He took a deep breath and swam in that direction.

The door to the radio room was hanging at an angle, half torn from its hinge, and one of the helmsman's chairs was against it. The room was filling with water. He inhaled and dove, entering the radio room where the bottom of the door allowed him access.

Coming to the surface inside, McCann saw her.

She had a terrible cut on her forehead, and her mouth was barely above the water. He shouted to her but he didn't think she heard him. She seemed to be in a daze, but still conscious enough to keep fighting for her life. She was a scrapper.

McCann tried to get past the communications panels, but he had little success. Taking in another gulp of air and going down, he braced himself between a bulkhead and a panel and shoved. Slowly, the panel began to move, and then righted itself. He came up gasping, and pulled himself toward her. He was able to get in far enough to take hold of her hand.

"Amy!" he shouted. "We have to go under to get out."

She looked at him blankly.

"Trust me."

She didn't understand him, and she fought him as he pulled her around one of the panels. She went under once and then she was beside him in the cramped space. The water was rising quickly now. There were barely two or three inches of air left near the overhead. McCann's face was right next to hers.

"Amy," he said as he wrapped an arm tightly around her waist.

She stared ahead, her chin starting to drop into the water. Her eyes were closing.

"Hold your breath," he ordered before taking her under.

She fought him, but it was a halfhearted attempt. He held on to her, pulling her behind him through the door and then up. They both broke the surface, sputtering. They were between two frames in the overhead.

They'd have to swim underwater again to reach the ladder to the bridge, where he'd left Brody at the open hatch. He took her face in his hand.

"Amy!"

Her eyes flickered open, but she was slipping away.

"Take another deep breath. Do you hear me? Do it *now!*"

Pulling her down, McCann kicked hard to move the two of them. His lungs burned. Amy was limp as a rag doll in his grip.

He pushed up past the periscope tower and found the ladder. Driving himself with the last of his strength, he pulled them both up into the trunk to where the water ended. He was able to take his first gulp of air and looked at her. She wasn't breathing.

He pressed her back against the side of the trunk, expelling water from her stomach and lungs. Wedging her body with his, he tipped her head back and sealed her mouth with his. He breathed air into her lungs.

"Please, Amy," he told her when he stopped for air. "Don't give up now."

He repeated the action, over and over. Nothing.

Then suddenly, she sputtered and coughed. She was breathing.

McCann had never felt relief of this magnitude. She continued to cough. She was still not totally conscious, but he was happy to have her breathing.

"We're getting you out of here," he whispered in her ear.

Using his good arm, he held her against his side. He tried to manage the ladder with the other one. He looked up toward the opening at the top.

"Dammit." Brody's foot had been visible when Mc-Cann went back for Amy. It was gone.

Just as McCann was debating what to do, a shadow moved over the hatch. He looked up.

"Let me give you a hand with her, Commander."

McCann had never been so happy to see a navy SEAL.

"Be very careful with her," he ordered as he lifted Amy up.

Fifty-Two

The only place Sarah wanted to be right now was on a helicopter heading toward Long Island Sound, where they were in the process of rescuing any survivors on the damaged sub. She hoped and prayed that Darius had made it through alive.

The last communication with *Hartford* had been through the message that Darius had sent. He'd mentioned a deep-sea rescue vehicle that he thought had been used to spirit the hijackers away from the sub. Right now, she and Dunn had to collect and analyze all the new data flooding in, in addition to overseeing the teams of investigators that were being sent to every inlet, every boat, every rickety dock along the coastline of Connecticut and New York that could harbor such a vehicle.

The map grids that sectioned off the coast were

being studied and analyzed. The federal, state and local law enforcement agencies had been called and assigned to search specific locations. Satellite photos of the area were continuously being piped to the command center at the Pentagon. The movement of all nonmilitary vessels, be they ships or boats or trucks along the coast roads, continued to be restricted and monitored. Every government and research facility on the East Coast that had possession of a submersible vessel was contacted for its status.

She wanted to be there at the site. More than anything they could find on shore, Sarah believed the forensic evidence gathered from *Hartford* would provide the keys to the identities of the hijackers.

First thing, the submarine had to be kept afloat and eventually towed ashore. She didn't know when that would happening.

Dunn got off the phone, and Sarah went to him. Admiral Meisner entered the conference room and joined them.

"Did you get word of the action?" the admiral asked Bruce.

"Just now," he replied, turning to Sarah. "Four torpedoes were fired at *Hartford* by USS *Pittsburgh*. Immediately after launching the weapons, they received a communication from McCann via a SLOT buoy that he and two others were still aboard and that the hijackers had escaped. We received the same information. The C.O. of *Pittsburgh* immediately began electronic-detonation efforts on the torpedoes. Three of them were successfully destroyed before they made contact. McCann initiated emergency blow procedures in an effort to escape the torpedoes. The last one hit *Hartford* beneath the torpedo racks in the forward compartment, breaching the hull just as the submarine reached the surface."

"We don't know yet what caused the last explosion," Meisner said to her.

"I was just talking to Captain Whiting, aboard *Pittsburgh*," Dunn cut in.

"What did he say?" Sarah asked.

"He says the SEALs just boarding *Hartford* have communicated to them that the explosive may have been triggered by a timed device left by the hijackers. The rescue crews are about to go in, but the forward end is flooded, so the going is slow. And there's the additional concern that there may be more explosives planted on board."

"Any sign of survivors?" she asked.

Bruce shook his head. "Not yet, but they're not giving up hope."

"How is the sub staying afloat?" she asked.

Meisner answered. "*Pittsburgh* reported that they believe the forward and aft ballast tanks, as well as the engine room and the reactor compartment, are still intact. The air inside them is keeping the vessel afloat, though it's riding very low in the water."

Bruce concurred. "Whiting says that from what he can tell, the breech in the hull is by the forward escape truck, where the DSRV, or whatever it was they used, must have hooked up. His guess is that the explosive was planted to make sure nothing would remain of the control room."

"Or anyone aboard," Sarah added.

"If McCann hadn't gotten that sub to the surface," the admiral said grimly, "*Hartford* would have taken the blast at six hundred feet below the surface."

"With the added pressure down there, the sub would have broken in two and sunk to the bottom."

"So much for collecting any evidence," Sarah said.

"Well, we might still be able to gather evidence now. They may have left something down there that they didn't think we'd get our hands on," Meisner said. "I don't believe they ever counted on McCann being able to pull off what he did."

Sarah was greatly relieved that Admiral Meisner was referring to Darius as a hero and not as the one who engineered the hijacking. She hoped this sentiment was held throughout the Pentagon. If he could now just pull himself through this last hurdle…and survive.

Bruce turned to Meisner. "To bring you up to date on what we spoke about before, I've already sent a plane to bring Captain Barnhardt back from his trip. Two operatives have gone to Johns Hopkins to speak to Captain Erensen."

"Good. We need to follow up on every avenue." The admiral nodded. "When you talked to Captain Whiting, did you discuss possible perpetrators?"

"I did, sir."

"And?"

"His initial remarks were, and I quote, 'no fucking foreign terrorist could have pulled a job like this.'"

"Why?"

"It's his position that no living terrorist sub driver has *ever* had a sub in Long Island Sound. There is no way anyone but one of our own could have maneuvered that sub through those waters the way he did."

"We've been building a case that argues some of the crew members might have cooperated with the hijackers," Sarah reminded them.

Bruce lowered his voice. "But no one aboard besides McCann had that kind of know-how."

"If it wasn't McCann, then it had to be a foreigner working with the crew still on board."

"The ranking officer was Lieutenant Paul Cavallaro, and Whiting is certain he could not have handled the sub like that." Dunn shook his head. "Whiting also believes that the probability that the crew was working with the hijackers adds to the argument that those behind it are home-grown. It's almost an impossibility that any sailor in the submarine service would sell his soul to any foreign terrorist. According to Whiting, it's completely absurd to think that nine members of the same crew would."

"That puts a new twist on things." Meisner sat on the corner of the conference table, crossing his arms as he contemplated everything he'd been told. "From now on, **you**'ll keep all your findings between us. Access to anything you learn is hereby restricted to me and the half-dozen people going up the ladder from me to the president. This includes whatever you discover on *Hartford*. Is that clear?"

"What if there are survivors?" Bruce asked.

The admiral considered that. "Including information about them. No one is to know. Not even their families. An extra night won't kill anyone. There's no telling what they might have seen. And if someone expected them to be dead, they might just come after them to finish the job."

Sarah thought of Darius's parents and Amy Russell's children and how much difference a night would make. But she kept it to herself. There was no point in arguing when they didn't even know if any of them had survived the two explosions.

"What's next on your agenda?" Meisner asked them.

Bruce looked at Sarah. "We need to fly to Connecticut. If there are any survivors, we need to be there for the debriefing. Otherwise, we should be there for the recovery of *Hartford*."

"Are you okay with that, Lieutenant?" Meisner asked Sarah.

Once again, Bruce Dunn had known exactly what she'd been looking for.

"Absolutely," she said.

Fifty-Three

John Penn pushed his son's wheelchair along the paved path toward the lawns that overlooked the Cliff Walk and Atlantic Ocean. Three secret service agents trailed them.

"Nice to have the rain finally stop, don't you think?" he asked Owen.

The young man gave him a thumbs-up response.

"Tell me if you get cold."

The nineteen-year-old tapped the arm of his wheelchair. John knew that meant "Okay."

Owen's speech was still indistinct. He wasn't able to pronounce certain vowels, and words tended to run into one another. He hadn't regained the complete use of his vocal cords after the accident and the tracheotomy, but he *could* talk. Yet he only chose to exercise that ability with his family.

They were at the end of the campaign, and John now realized how much he missed his privacy. He regretted the discomfort he caused his son, his wife and his daughter by putting them in the public eye, twenty-four/seven.

Owen, though, was the one he felt sorry for most. Anna and Aileen were outspoken and could hand out two jabs for every one that came their way, but Owen had fewer resources to defend himself. He'd been limited to the bed and his wheelchair since he was sixteen. Two weeks after his birthday, he'd been a passenger in a car driven by one of his friends. Speeding, poor road conditions, lack of experience. They could have blamed it on a dozen things. The end result was that the driver had been killed instantly, and Aileen and John had to wait months before knowing if their child was going to make it through.

And Owen had made it. But the extent of his progress continued to be a big unknown. He had the use of both hands, although he lacked many motor skills. He could eat and drink and breathe without any apparatus. John was certain that Owen's mind was sharper than the rest of the Penn family combined.

As a family, they had come to peace with Owen's condition. He was alive and that was the most important thing to all of them.

John had been too caught up in the whirlwind of the campaign and how far ahead he was in the polls to take the time to reassess the pros and cons of what he was doing to his family. Today had been an eye-opener. He wasn't sure anymore which would be the worse fate, losing this election or winning it.

Owen made a motion with his hand, and John looked to their right.

Anthony McCarthy was coming their way, and from the look on the man's face and the length of his strides and distressed facial expression, John decided his campaign manager must be pissed off. The senator shook his head. He could only imagine what this was about.

McCarthy joined them where the two paths merged some twenty yards ahead. McCarthy and Owen exchanged a handshake.

"I've arranged a news conference for six o'clock. You should be inside, Senator, preparing."

"I don't have to prepare anything, because there isn't going to be a news conference."

"I knew it," McCarthy said with a heavy sigh. "John, don't do this to me."

The senator was getting to know this routine. Temper followed by the laying on of guilt. The second tactic always worked better on him than the first.

He didn't even look at his manager. "We agreed about this yesterday, Anthony. No. In fact, I think it was last week. No more campaigning. I'm spending the evening with my family. That's all there is to it."

"A week ago, even yesterday, you were light years ahead of Hawkins in the polls. Right now, with what's happened, it's suddenly a dead heat. He's had ample opportunities to be in front of television screens today, tooting his own horn."

"He's been doing his job as the president," Penn corrected.

"He's been taking credit for it, too. Now it's time for you to go out there and remind the American people that the end results wouldn't have been any different if you were the one in office. The armed forces were the ones who got the job done. No personal glory belongs to Hawkins."

Penn moved Owen's chair next to a bench so that his son was facing them. "I would never stand at a podium and tell the American people a blatant lie. And that would be a lie. The end result *would* have been different if I were the one calling the shots."

McCarthy brought a hand to his forehead. "You would never admit that you were planning to meet the hijackers' demands."

"I wouldn't say that because it isn't true," Penn said, bristling. "What I wouldn't have done was go in front of everyone and say that the crisis was over when those hijackers are still running free somewhere. This thing is far from over, but Hawkins is using the retaking of the submarine to swing votes. The problem is that he has jumped the gun. How can he know that the hijacking wasn't the first step in a multipronged-attack strategy? That a runaway oil tanker in the Midwest won't barrel into a government building. Or that some kind of missile isn't being aimed this minute at the Golden Gate Bridge. Or any of a dozen other possible disasters. He can't know, and he's irresponsible for telling Americans that they are safe."

"These are the concerns he'll bring up on Wednesday, the day *after* the election," McCarthy reminded him. "Right now, there's only one thing on Hawkins's mind and that is winning votes."

"Well, that's wrong," Penn said passionately. "We're no safer than we were three hours ago. That submarine is still sitting in the Sound, and he can't know that it won't be blown to pieces at any moment, poisoning the most densely populated area in the country with radiation that will render it uninhabitable for the next ten thousand years. He doesn't have a clue what's become of the people responsible for that hijacking. This job isn't even half done."

"Why don't you go to that press conference at six and tell the reporters what you just said?" McCarthy persisted.

Penn shrugged and sat on the bench next to Owen. "I can't. I hate back-seat drivers. That's never been my style."

"I can't fucking believe it," McCarthy cursed. "You're getting cold feet. You're turning your back on everything you've done so far."

"It's not that," Penn said, planting his elbows on his knees, looking down at the grass growing between blocks of stone.

"Then what is it?"

There were plenty of reasons, but the most important one was the young man sitting in the wheelchair next to him. John looked up, shaking his head, unable to respond.

Owen's hand reached for his father's. John took it and looked over at his son.

"You owe it to people, Dad," Owen said in his slow, labored way. "Hawkins is an asshole. We need you to tell truth. Go out…tell them. Please, Dad. Do it for me. For Mom. For all of us."

Fifty-Four

Yale–New Haven Hospital
8:30 p.m.

Under orders from Naval Intelligence, the survivors were not to be taken to any military hospital or installation. Instead, one floor of a wing of Yale–New Haven Hospital was evacuated of patients and made ready to accept the injured.

Following the rescue on USS *Hartford*, Amy Russell and Lee Brody were immediately flown to Yale–New Haven. But McCann had stayed with Captain Whiting and the two of them had boarded one of the support crafts that arrived to aid in the operation.

Whiting was supervising the preliminary efforts to secure what was left of the submarine. Several hours later, and after four navy tugs from Groton were successfully harnessed to the submarine, McCann had begun to feel comfortable enough in the knowledge that his ship would be saved. Only then was Whiting able to force him to follow the others to Yale–New Haven and have his shoulder tended to.

All three were at the hospital when Bruce Dunn and Sarah Connelly arrived from Washington. After asking Sarah to talk to Amy Russell, Dunn went in to see McCann.

The submarine commander was undergoing a number of tests on his shoulder. As soon as the wound was bandaged and he'd been moved into a private room, McCann had promptly kicked the doctors and nurses out so he could talk to the investigator.

If there was the slightest doubt left in Bruce Dunn's mind about Commander McCann's direct or indirect involvement with the hijacking, the information that he was hearing completely erased it.

McCann was precise in giving Dunn every detail of what happened, from the moment he'd been phoned in the middle of the night to go in for his X.O., to the moment the hijackers' bomb had exploded.

He recited specifics about which of his crew members he'd seen directly involved, assisting the hijackers, and told Bruce about the others that he'd found dead or injured like Brody.

"The rescue team has recovered some of the bodies. They're working hard to ID everyone," Bruce told him.

"With the exception of Brody, who's here at the hospital, and Juan Rivera, who I shot while he was loading weapons in the torpedo room, everyone else on my crew was killed by the hijackers before they escaped. Amy overheard one of them making a reference to 'cleaning out.'"

"Do you have any idea why they would do that, considering these same people had joined their ranks and were cooperating?"

"Fear of recognition," McCann said. "One of the first things the person running the show did was disable the cameras in the control room that fed the MFD video displays. He knew he could be recognized. At the end, he had to make sure there were no witnesses."

Bruce studied McCann for a minute. The commander had refused to stay in bed where the nurses had left him. He had also changed out of the hospital gown and into the borrowed uniform they'd given him on USS *Pittsburgh*.

"Is there a possibility that he thinks you or Ms. Russell or Petty Officer Brody might have seen him or any of those who got away?"

"Definitely," McCann said. "I assume that's why you've brought us here, isn't it? You're trying to lay a trap for them."

"No," Bruce said, surprised at the response. There wasn't a hint of anger in the commander's tone. In fact, he looked like he was hoping to get another whack at these guys. "We won't endanger your lives, not after what you've been through. We brought you here for your own protection."

"Who knows about it?"

"Only a handful of people. Admiral Meisner created a very restricted list."

McCann sat down in the faux-leather chair across from him. "What does your press release say about what's going on?"

"Only that the rescue operation is still under way, and it's too early to tell if there are any survivors."

Bruce watched McCann stare into space. He figured he was thinking of his family's reaction to this news. No one had mentioned a word to McCann about his mother's stroke yet. Actually, Bruce had been the only one in a position to say something, but he'd decided it might be better for Sarah to tell him. She'd spoken to them last.

One thing that had fascinated Bruce was McCann's complete lack of response to hearing Sarah Connelly was part of the investigating team. With the exception of a nod of recognition, he'd said nothing more about her. He didn't ask to see her, and he hadn't requested to have her debrief him.

Bruce didn't know if this was a hopeful sign that everything *was* finished between McCann and Sarah or not.

"Identifying some of the other bodies on board might give you more clues," McCann finally said, turning his attention back on Dunn.

"That's what we're hoping."

McCann got up from the chair and poured himself a cup of water, downing it in one gulp. "How has the public been taking the situation?"

"This morning, there was mass hysteria to get out of New York City. Actually, it was fairly chaotic everywhere else along the coast. After President Hawkins's speech this afternoon about *Hartford* being disabled, there was more chaos as everyone tried to get back home. But it isn't over."

"The hijackers are still free," McCann said.

Bruce nodded. "Those were the exact words Senator Penn used at his press conference a couple of hours ago. He reminded everyone that the country *isn't* safe until the perpetrators are all found."

"That should have caused some backtracking in the White House."

"I'm sure, though I haven't heard anything. I would guess that since Penn's speech, the president has even the Boy Scouts out searching for the DSRV."

McCann looked up at the clock on the wall. "That won't do anyone any good. Those sons of bitches are already out of the water."

Fifty-Five

Branford, Connecticut
8:35 p.m.

A grove of pines hid the farmhouse from neighboring properties. They couldn't have chosen a more ideal location for a transfer point, Mako thought. At this time of year, none of the nearby cottages were occupied. This deserted farm, with its flat acreage and close proximity to the interstate, was currently locked up in a drawn-out court battle.

Mako and his people only planned to use it for a couple of hours.

The small house sat within sight of an old pier with pilings deep enough to easily accommodate the eight-foot draft of the submersible. Behind the house and some sixty yards toward the woods was an airstrip, overrun with weeds and grass from disuse. Still, it was long enough to allow the landing and takeoff of a twin-engine turboprop. That was all they needed.

Everything moved according to plan. Everyone knew what they had to do.

Mako glanced at his watch and then looked up to see the fishing boat moving away from the dock. Her running lights flickered on the water in front of her. Behind her, she was towing the unmanned and submerged forty-foot DSRV that had brought them to shore from *Hartford*. The submersible was simply being returned to the vicinity of the oil rig on Long Island Sound, where it had originally been taken from.

The oil rig was still on fire. Mako's demolitions man had packed the rescue vehicle with explosives. Once the fishing boat's towline was cut and some distance was put between the two vessels, the submersible would self-destruct, joining the fate of its mother facility.

Mako turned around as one of the engines of the Beech 1900 aircraft came to life. The lights were on under the wings of the craft. A couple of the crew members closed the cargo bay on the plane. All the equipment was loaded. Mako turned around, looking for Kilo. He was standing in the spotlight of the plane, against an old station wagon by the garage. He had his back to Mako and appeared to be talking on his cell phone.

Mako motioned to his crew to board the plane. His sharp gaze swept over the moonlit property, checking for any mistakes, anything left behind. They'd stayed out of the farmhouse, so that wasn't a concern.

Kilo ended the call and headed in Mako's direction.

"We're ready to go," Mako said.

"I have to go separately."

"What's the matter?"

"The phone call." Kilo looked at the plane as the second engine started up. "Three survivors have been taken off *Hartford*."

"I didn't hear any of that. That information didn't come over our satellite channels." Mako had the de-encryption for all of *Pittsburgh*'s communications.

"They're already suspecting an inside job. That's why they've taken everything under. I've been directed to eliminate the three who survived. McCann is one of them. We don't know what they saw or heard."

"Where have they taken them?"

"Yale–New Haven. It should be easy to get in and out," Kilo told him. "You go on. I'll catch up to you at the last stop at 1600 hours tomorrow, before we go north."

Something didn't sit right with Mako. He didn't like the fact that they would hire *him* to do a job but would call Kilo to finish up the loose ends. He was tempted to tell the other man that he was coming with him to complete the assignment. But that was risky. Kilo operated on the edge. He could always have other directives. He was also too messy. The possibility of exposure wasn't worth it.

"All right," Mako said, giving the man a pat on the back before turning toward the plane. "I'll see you at 1600."

Fifty-Six

She was on dry land. In a hospital. Alive. But they weren't allowing her to call her children or Barbara or her parents.

Amy was becoming increasingly annoyed.

Still, she couldn't take it out on Lieutenant Connelly. The woman had been extremely pleasant to her while asking a thousand questions about each minute she'd been stuck on *Hartford*.

But Amy was starting to lose patience. She sent the other woman a narrow glare.

"You want to run that last question by me again?"

"Between your arrival on board before the hijacking and the moment Commander McCann summoned you and Brody back to the control room, *anyone* could have been in charge in the control room and you wouldn't have known."

"This isn't what you asked," Amy said shortly.

"I'm trying to break the question into smaller pieces."

"I'm not an infant. I can handle it."

What the hell, Amy thought. Her head pounded. She'd ended up with God knew how many stitches on her forehead. Her stomach still felt queasy as a result of what the emergency room doctor said was a concussion she suffered at the time of the explosion.

"Whatever your question was, my understanding of it is that you're accusing Commander McCann of being responsible for the hijacking. You're trying to get me to say he ordered his people to lock him in the ship's office. That he had them shoot at him. That he—"

"I'm not accusing him of anything," the lieutenant said quickly. "At the same time, I think it's important that we approach this from every possible angle. Neither you nor Brody saw who the leader was. What I'm trying to do is eliminate the possibility that Commander McCann could have been running the show when he wasn't in your company. I'm trying to head off any future investigation."

Amy sat up and swung her legs over the side of the bed. Her head pounded even worse when she sat up, and the stupid hospital gown probably offered a clear glimpse of her ass to anyone walking behind her, but she didn't care.

"You're bringing out the shipyard in me."

"What do you mean by that?"

"It means that I'm just about ready to start getting into your face." Amy stonily returned the startled look Connelly sent her. "And I mean right now."

"Amy, the last thing I want to do is upset you," Lieutenant Connelly said softly.

"The last thing you should be doing is accusing one of your own, a man who bravely stopped at least another dozen weapons from being launched. The same man who took the whole lot of those hijackers on almost single-handedly and succeeded in being such a pain in the ass to them that they ran with their tails between their legs. Commander McCann saved my life and Brody's life more than once while we were trapped in that sub." She threw both hands in the air, frustrated. "And the submarine itself. My God, I don't know what's left of it, but he brought it to surface, didn't he? You should celebrate him as a hero, not sit here questioning his honor."

The navy investigator started to speak, but Amy remembered something else and interrupted. Her mind was a total jumble. She wasn't willing to risk forgetting it.

"Wait a minute. In the ship's office on the second level, there's a laptop. It has one of those Electric Boat property stickers on it, so you won't miss it. I suppose that area got wet. But even if it did, get your computer guys to check the memory. Check the e-mail McCann tried to send your people right after we were locked up in there. You read that and tell me if it's from someone who's masterminding a hijacking operation."

Connelly nodded and wrote something on her pad of paper. "I appreciate your defense of him."

It may have been the quiet way that she said it, but the words seemed to sprout wings, and Amy found herself looking for their meaning as they took flight in her head.

The lieutenant's blue eyes shone with something that resembled affection when they looked up. "Ms. Russell. Like you, I believe he's innocent. I believe he's a hero."

Amy bit her tongue to keep from asking the question. She already knew the answer. It was woman's instinct. The sixth sense that told her there was something between Lieutenant Connelly and Commander McCann.

She was too tired, maybe even too doped up. Amy knew she wasn't herself as a tightness squeezed her throat. This was madness. She didn't know anything about McCann's personal life. She had no right to feel any ties, any connection. Her attraction to him was a surprise and totally inappropriate. She was becoming emotional over nothing.

"Are we done?" Amy asked in what she hoped was a clear voice.

"For now."

"Good. I want to call my son and daughter." She had to ask, even if it was for the umpteenth time.

"I'm sorry, but that's not possible yet. We'll let you know when it's safe."

Safe for who? Amy asked herself. What was safe about letting two seven-year-olds think their mother might be dead?

She felt herself really choking up now. "You can close the frigging door on your way out."

Amy lay back down and pulled the covers up to her chin. She closed her eyes, knowing sleep was hardly a possibility.

Fifty-Seven

Branford, Connecticut
8:38 p.m.

Mako closed the door to the airplane behind him. The
seat nearest to the door had been saved for him. He sat
down and buckled up. The lights in the cabin were off.
There were empty seats, and the others were scattered
throughout the small plane. Some of the men had died,
some lived. That was the nature of this line of business.
It was the risk they all took. Mako wasn't going to lose
any sleep over it.

He looked through the small window at Kilo, who
was now leaning against his car, cell phone again
held to his ear. Another phone call. Mako took his
own cell phone out of his pocket and looked at the display. No missed calls. He put the phone back in his
pocket.

One of the men sitting behind him was listening to
a news station on the radio. One specific word caught

Mako's attention. He peered over his shoulder. "What was it they just said?"

"Dead or alive. They're talking about the rescue on *Hartford*. They don't know how many are dead or how many are alive."

Mako turned around in his seat and looked out the window again. Kilo was getting into the station wagon.

There'd been too many screwups with this operation. *Hartford* was supposed to sink to the bottom of the Sound. There weren't supposed to be any survivors. A dead Darius McCann was supposed to take the rap for planning it. A few things had gone wrong and a few things had gone right.

The plane began rolling toward the end of the runway.

Mako tried to look at this entire operation through the eyes of those who'd hired him. The job was done. The three survivors were a problem, but they were being taken care of by Kilo. A bigger problem was that everyone knew they'd gotten away. That wasn't good. They'd be found. For the people that hired him, dead would be better than alive.

At the end of the runway, the pilot revved the engines. Mako looked out the small window. The taillights of the station wagon were disappearing down the dirt drive that led to the main road.

"Hold on," he said, tapping the pilot on the back. He unbuckled his seat belt and opened the door.

"I'm getting out."

Fifty-Eight

Yale–New Haven Hospital
8:39 p.m.

It was too hot, but they couldn't open the windows for safety reasons. McCann got up and looked for a thermostat. Finding it, he turned it down and opened the door. He was told they had the hospital wing to themselves. He scanned the empty hallway. He knew which room Brody was in, and wondered which one was Amy's.

Brody's condition wasn't too good. The bullets had been removed from his leg, but he was scheduled for another surgery tomorrow morning. There was a concern he might lose the leg. They had him drugged up for the night.

He hadn't seen Amy since they arrived here. He wanted to. Dunn had mentioned that Sarah was debriefing her. At least he'd been told the extent of her injuries and that she was okay.

He stepped back into the room. It didn't matter that the other man was a navy investigator. McCann felt comfortable enough with Dunn to cut through the bullshit and tell him what was on his mind.

"The fact that I'm half Middle Eastern was the sole reason they pushed Parker aside and arranged for me to be on board this morning. They were trying to pin this entire thing on me."

"Interestingly enough," Dunn said, "during the first briefing at the Pentagon, that little tidbit of information about your parentage was one of the first things to come up."

"Who brought it up?"

"Rear Admiral Smith."

"I thought he was dead," McCann said.

"He was, but he was resurrected this morning by President Hawkins himself."

"Did anyone pounce on that information?" McCann asked, angry that idiots like Smith would press that button in spite of his exemplary record.

"No one. In fact, Admiral Meisner worked hard to quash that discussion as a red herring."

"So did Commander Dunn."

Both of them turned toward the doorway. Sarah was leaning against the doorjamb, her arms crossed over her chest. She looked as beautiful as ever. Beautiful, polished and professional.

McCann felt a peculiar rush and realized that it wasn't for the woman standing in the doorway. This woman had been a friend and even a girlfriend at one time, but that wasn't it.

Because Sarah was standing here, it meant he could

go and check on Amy now, and that gave him a very pleasant sensation.

"It's good to see you, Sarah," he said.

He'd heard from Dunn that she didn't have to work on this case, but she'd wanted to. McCann knew her well enough to know she'd only put herself in this position because she believed in his innocence.

"Thank you for what you're doing," he told her. He then turned to Bruce. "And I appreciate you being a voice of reason on my behalf this morning."

Bruce nodded before getting to his feet. "I should leave you two alone for a couple of minutes to—"

"That won't be necessary," McCann interrupted. "Actually, I was hoping to visit with Amy for a bit."

The two investigators exchanged a look. "I don't see a problem with it," Sarah replied.

Dunn nodded.

Their response told McCann a lot about whether they considered him a suspect or not in this investigation. They clearly didn't, or they wouldn't allow him out of their sight.

He paused at the door. Sarah hadn't moved. He'd known her a long time. Long enough to understand what she needed. What he'd failed to give her. Closure.

"Thank you for being here," he said gently.

Her composure faltered slightly. He opened his arm, and she hugged him. He held her against his chest for a long time.

"I'm glad you're alive," she said, pulling back and smiling. "Happy birthday, you old man."

"The big 4-0," he said. She wasn't far behind him, but he didn't think she needed a reminder.

"How does it feel?"

"The mileage I've put on over the past twenty hours or so is catching up to me. I could probably fall asleep standing up."

"That goes for Amy, too," she told him. "You'd better hurry if you want to catch her awake. Second door down, across the hall."

That was all McCann needed to hear. He crossed to her door and knocked softly.

Fifty-Nine

Branford, Connecticut
8:40 p.m.

The Beech 1900 twin-engine aircraft never even cleared the line of trees. Mako figured the fuel tank would be blamed for the explosion that occurred immediately after takeoff. Later, the investigators wouldn't worry too much about the possibility of foul play, not after the evidence began to mount that the victims of the plane crash were the same hijackers who'd squeezed America's throat that very morning.

The headlines alone would be nearly enough to explain everything and close the case for the public, Mako thought. Eventually, they'd identify some of them. Home-grown terrorists. Mercenaries. All the bodies were found. No survivors. The explosion had guaranteed that.

He was just crossing the moonlit field toward the woods when he heard the sound of sirens in the distance.

He wasn't even pissed off. In fact, a great calm had settled over him. There was great comfort in knowing that he'd guessed right. He'd cheated death at the last minute. He could have saved the lives of the rest of his crew, he supposed. But in this line of work, everyone was on his own.

As he made his way to the main road, he had to hand it to the men that hired him. It was a truly brilliant move to wrap everything up so tidily.

But even brilliant plans could go wrong.

Darius McCann had ruined their plan by simply refusing to die. Mako planned to do some ruining himself.

He wasn't angry. But he was certainly going to get even.

Sixty

The nurses and doctors knocked and then just entered, so Amy knew it couldn't be one of them at the door. She grabbed a tissue out of a box on the bedside table, wiped her face and blew her nose. It had to be Lieutenant Connelly, who'd probably remembered more questions to ask. She sat up in the bed.

Or maybe the lieutenant had decided to let her use the phone, after all. Amy much preferred the second scenario.

She called to whoever it was to come in.

"For a minute I thought you were already asleep," McCann said, poking his head in.

Amy was mad as hell at herself for the way her pulse jumped at the sight of him. Something was fluttering inside of her as if she were twelve years old. What was wrong with her? She'd known he was in the hospital.

Lieutenant Connelly had mentioned that when Amy asked about him earlier. She'd never imagined he'd stop to see her.

"No," she said. "No sleep."

"Can I come in?"

She should have said no. "Yeah, sure."

He didn't have any right to look this good. Not after what they'd gone through. And especially not when she was looking like a dishrag.

Amy noticed that he closed the door. Nerves pushed to the surface. If she weren't in a hospital bed, Amy figured she'd be running away by now. She was horrible in situations like this. She didn't know what to say, what to do, how to avoid being nervous and acting like an idiot. That was why she'd refused to date after her divorce. It had been a miracle that her ex-husband, Ryan, had even lasted through their early dates. Maybe she should have thought of that jitteriness as a warning. No, thinking of Kaitlyn and Zack, Amy was thrilled that her life had taken the shape that it had.

"How's your shoulder?" she asked as he approached her.

He moved it. "It's still numb from whatever they injected in it. But it should be as good as new."

His dark gaze moved over her. She felt a charge pass through her, electrifying something at her very core. There was something very intimate happening now. He was interested and she couldn't figure how he could be, considering how horrible she looked.

"How's Brody?" she asked in a rush.

"Sleeping. He has another surgery in the morning."

Amy already knew that. She looked around her as he walked toward the bed. "How's your sub?"

"They're still working on her. I don't know if they'll be able to save her or not."

He reached the side of the bed.

"How did your debriefing go?"

"Good. Very good," he answered.

"How come they gave you a change of clothes and I'm still in a hospital gown with a turban wrapped around my head?"

"Maybe because you look better in it?"

"That's not an answer," she told him, shivering as he sat down on the edge of the bed. "How's—"

"Amy," he said, taking her hand.

She hadn't realized how cold her hands were until his touch warmed them.

"It's my turn to ask some questions," he said with a smile.

"This is not your ship. You're not in command…uh, Commander."

"Well, we aren't in a shipyard. So you're not in charge, either, Ms. Russell."

"Amy to you."

"Only if you call me Darius."

"Darius McCann. Persian and Irish," she said with a grin. "Do you have a horrible temper?"

"You're about to find out."

"Ooh, I'm almost frightened." Amy felt the most comfortable when they were kidding around. "What have I done now?"

"You were trying to control the conversation."

"You're mistaken, Commander…Darius," she said.

"I was being socially adept. Charming. Making sure there'd be no dead air in the room."

He caressed her hand. "There doesn't seem to be any dead air in any room while you and I are together in it."

"Are you bragging?"

"No. Only stating the fact, ma'am."

As far as Amy was concerned, his smile was the most dangerous part of him. It gave him a boyish and vulnerable look that was even more irresistible than his clean-cut, chiseled features. And it made her lose her head. She looked down at their joined hands, not knowing what to expect, or what she was expected to do. She was totally out of practice.

"You should know that I'm all talk," she murmured. "Nothing else."

He lifted her chin with his hand until she was looking into his eyes. "I don't know. I think I'd like to find that out for myself." His hand slipped around the nape of her neck, and he drew her mouth to his.

Darius McCann knew how to kiss. Well enough that Amy felt all of her inhibitions suddenly begin to slip away.

She didn't know who was more out of breath—or whose hands were straying more—when they broke the kiss.

"This is much better. You are *not* all talk," he told her, placing a kiss on the tip of her nose. He still wasn't letting her go. "Do you know the one thing I was wishing for on that submarine?"

"That we'd make it through alive?"

He laughed. "Okay. I was wishing for two things."

"That I'd occasionally follow your orders?"

"Three things."

"That—" She was silenced by another kiss. She liked his technique. This kiss was hotter than the last, and it took longer for them to surface for air. How long had it been since anyone had kissed her like that?

"I give up. What was the third thing?" she asked.

"That we'd meet again, have another chance at it, in a difference place, different time. Hopefully under less stressful conditions."

His words clutched her heart. But her conscience wouldn't let her enjoy the moment. Dammit.

"Please tell me you're not married, Commander McCann."

"I'm not. Never have been."

She considered that for a few seconds and shook her head. "I still think what we're doing here isn't fair to Lieutenant Connelly."

He stared at her for a moment and then smiled. "No more than what we're doing isn't fair to your ex-husband. Sarah and I broke off our relationship a while ago."

"What's a while?"

"More than a year."

"Does she know you're here with me?"

He nodded.

"Does she have any objection to it?"

He smiled, shaking his head.

"In that case…" Amy wrapped her arms around Darius's neck again and kissed him, this time with no guilt and no reserve.

Sixty-One

Yale–New Haven Hospital
9:25 p.m.

Kilo walked past two black sedans on the street and the black SUV parked along the circular driveway of the hospital entrance. Extra help was on hand, just in case he needed it. He tugged on the earpiece, testing its connection. They had a live one.

The combination of civilian clothes and NCIS badge always worked like a charm. The security guard at the front desk looked up at his face as he gave back the ID.

"Would you please sign in, sir?" He pushed a clipboard in front of Kilo.

He preferred not to, but the last thing he wanted was to bring any extra attention to himself. A healthy dose of foot traffic continued to stream out through the same door he'd entered. He scribbled the name on the page.

"Commander Dunn and Lieutenant Connelly are expecting me."

"So you know where you're going?"

Kilo contemplated telling the truth and saying he didn't. But the guard's hand was on the phone. He guessed the man was ready to call upstairs and announce his arrival. The hospital spread in a couple of different directions. He'd never been inside the building, but he knew his backup on the street could walk him through, once he got past the security desk.

"Yes, I do. I just got off the phone with Commander Dunn."

The man let him go, and Kilo spotted the elevators down the hallway to the left. He turned and headed straight toward them.

Sixty-Two

Bruce Dunn ended the call and pocketed his cell phone.

"Anything new?" Sarah asked.

"The group we sent to Canada looking for Captain Barnhardt was able to contact another hunter on the island. They don't believe Barnhardt is there this week. I guess they all keep an eye on one another in the wilderness."

"Does anyone know where he is, then?"

Bruce sat on one of the faux-leather chairs next to Sarah: "We're making some calls and visits. We should hear something soon."

The two of them had been using McCann's room as a place to compare notes since he'd gone to see Amy.

"Considering that we have access to Captain Whiting and now Darius, is it that critical to find Barnhardt?"

Bruce shrugged. "Maybe not. But considering his expertise and other things that Seth has dug up over the past couple of hours—things he just told me about—it might be good to get hold of him."

"What things?"

He paused. "Six of the nine people who were left on *Hartford* while docked at Electric Boat, including Paul Cavallaro, reported to Captain Barnhardt at some point earlier in their careers."

Sarah's head snapped up. "You're kidding."

"No, I'm not."

She thought for a moment. "Was Lee Brody ever on his crew?"

"No," Bruce told her. "Between talking to Barnhardt and McCann, we should be able to come up with some logical reason why these people decided to help the hijackers. They knew these sailors."

He looked at the direction of the doorway.

"Is McCann still across the hall?"

"I definitely think there's a romance blooming over there."

Bruce glanced over at Sarah, trying to gauge her mood. She'd been putting on a great charade of looking relaxed since McCann walked out.

"You really think so?" he asked.

She gave a long and knowing nod. Bruce had been conscious of giving Sarah her space. But she'd appeared focused on what they were doing. And even when he'd been on the phone, he'd watched her stay busy the entire time.

"Are you okay with it?"

She sat back and fiddled with the pen she was using.

"I'm very much okay with it. In fact, I believe this is what I needed."

"What's that?"

"Seeing Darius genuinely interested in someone else. It makes me feel…feel…"

"Like crap," he finished for her.

Her blue eyes rounded on him. "Why would you say something like that?"

He shrugged. "Because I've been there. I know what you're going through."

She seemed at a loss for words, so he decided to reveal a little more of himself for her. "My marriage broke up because my wife became 'genuinely interested' in someone else. Unfortunately, that was while we were still married."

"That's a problem."

"It was for me," he told her.

"Darius and I broke up over a year ago. There's no reason for me to feel like crap, as you so delicately put it."

"Have you gone out with anyone else since?"

"No," she admitted. "I hear rebound relationships are the pits."

"A year later no longer counts as a rebound."

She gave him a suspicious look. "Are you speaking from experience again?"

"No. I'm saying that so you'd agree to go out with me."

She had the most beautiful laugh. Bruce found himself laughing, too. "So what is it? Yes or no?"

"We're in the middle of a case, Commander Dunn. Don't you think this isn't the most appropriate time to plan social engagements?"

"I can wait," he said honestly. "So long as I know the answer is yes."

"How about a maybe?"

"I can live with that." Bruce pushed himself to his feet. "Now, before you change your mind, let me buy you a cup of coffee. I hear this hospital knows how to make the perfect brew. It only sits in the machine for a week at a time."

"I'm sold."

He pulled Sarah to her feet. They walked to the door. In the hallway, a shadow moved into one of the rooms some twenty yards down. Bruce looked to where a guard had been posted by the hall leading to the elevator. No one was there.

His cell phone rang in that very moment. He answered it on the first ring.

"Commander Dunn?" a voice said at the other end.

"Speaking."

"I hear you've been looking for me."

"Who am I speaking with?" Bruce asked, not taking his eyes off the hallway.

"Ramsey Barnhardt."

It took a split second to stifle his surprise.

"Captain Barnhardt," he repeated, looking at Sarah. Her interest was immediately piqued, too. "Yes, we have been looking for you, Captain. I don't know if you've heard anything that has been going on with USS *Hartford*."

"Yes, I'm very familiar with what's happening."

"We need a few minutes of your time, Captain, to sit down and go over some things. We need your expertise, sir."

"I thought you would. That's why I'm calling."

"What's a good time and place for you?" Bruce asked, knowing he had to jump on the opportunity. "Lieutenant Connelly and I would like to meet you in person, if that's at all possible."

"How about now?" the man said from the other end.

"Now?" Bruce repeated for the sake of Sarah knowing what was going on.

She mouthed to him that they should split up. One of them could stay here and the other go to meet Barnhardt.

"Where would you like to meet, sir?" Bruce asked.

"In the hospital parking lot."

Bruce turned and looked in the direction of the elevators. "You're here, Captain? Why don't you come up?"

"I don't think that's a good idea. From what I hear, it's not too safe on your floor," Barnhardt told him. "But you and your friends might want to come down and join me. If you get away alive, that is."

Bruce looked up and down the hall. No security guards, no doctors or nurses. He and Sarah were the only people there.

"All the security guards on your floor have been dismissed or erased, Commander. And as we speak, a man who goes by the code name Kilo is on your floor. He's been assigned the task of eliminating the survivors taken off *Hartford,* along with you and Lieutenant Connelly, if it becomes necessary."

Both McCann and Amy had mentioned the name Kilo in referring to the one who was doing the "cleanup" on *Hartford.* Apparently, he wasn't done. But how would Barnhardt know any of this?

"Captain Barnhardt—"

"Get out now." The phone went dead.

"What's wrong?" Sarah asked.

"We're part of what's left to be cleaned up. Get Mc-Cann and Amy. We have to get them out of here. I'll get Brody."

Neither he nor Sarah were carrying guns.

Bruce spotted the fire alarm across the hall.

He immediately went to it and pulled the lever.

The hospital wing filled with the blaring buzz of the alarm.

Sixty-Three

Lee Brody never had a chance.

He died in his sleep from a single bullet to the brain. As far as Kilo was concerned, he was on borrowed time, anyway. The instructions to Rivera and Dunbar this morning had been to put the kid out of commission. Leave it to them to figure a bang on the head was good enough. Of course, the instructions Kilo received with regard to the hijacking were very different from theirs. They thought it was all a big exercise. A drill.

And they didn't know that before it was over, they'd all be eliminated. It was no drill.

Kilo looked around the hospital room one last time before reaching for the door. The suddenness of the fire alarm made him stop.

Between the regular blasts of the alarm, he heard the sound of running feet coming his way. He moved behind the door, his weapon drawn. The door opened with one sharp kick, and only Kilo's boot stopped it from smashing against his face. He had no target. He couldn't see anyone through the slit at the edge of the door.

"Christ!" a voice muttered from the outside of the room.

The lights from the hall illuminated the room. The dead man's face was turned toward the door, the bullet hole visible even from a distance.

He saw a figure move outside the door. He fired, and the door slammed into him again, harder this time. He'd missed. He shoved the door back with his shoulder. He didn't think they'd be armed, but he couldn't be sure.

His earpiece buzzed. He ignored the voices and jerked the door open. A fire extinguisher smashed into his chest, knocking him off balance. Kilo never lost his grip on the gun, and he fired again as he stumbled backward.

Someone was running down the hall. He rushed out in time to see the emergency fire-exit doors swinging shut.

"They're heading down the stairs," he said into the microphone. "Pick them up."

Sixty-Four

The White House
9:43 p.m.

"The news of the plane crash and the explosion is all over the networks," Bob Fortier said to the president, flipping through the channels on the muted television. "What they don't know yet is that there were no survivors."

William Hawkins filled his glass with more Scotch and drank it down. The liquor produced the same warm feeling in his throat as the last three glasses. He and Bob were alone in the sitting room on the residential side of the White House.

"How are they going to make the connection with *Hartford?*" the president asked.

"Give our boys a little more credit. There'll be so many clues that the investigators have to be blind not to stumble over them."

"How soon?" Hawkins asked, starting to pace the

room. "We can't have people going to the polls tomorrow morning without knowing these results. We have to get some factual stuff to the press before the eleven o'clock news."

"Relax, Mr. President. Everything is moving just like clockwork," Fortier assured him.

Hawkins didn't like clockwork. Clocks were too damn complicated. He liked things simple. He poured himself another Scotch and downed half of the glass in one swallow. He'd been against this plot from the moment he heard about it, but Fortier had assured him that he had the right people lined up. The entire operation would be completed in less than twenty-four hours, and campaign-soft money would finance the deal. Fatalities would be minimal. His campaign manager had argued that it'd be a hell of a lot cheaper and easier to do this than invade some little piss-pot country.

He should have put his foot down and refused. Penn was too smart to let anything slide by. For the past year, the pompous ass jumped at every opportunity to get his face on television, always accusing Hawkins of lying or exaggerating the facts. The simplest plan for this election would have been to send a single person to take Penn out. It'd been done before. It could have been done this time, too. Penn's running mate, Peter Gresham, was a nothing. He was no threat.

But what was happening now *was* a threat. To William Hawkins.

"What about the three they took to the hospital? Is there any reason to go after them?"

"We already talked about that, Mr. President. Everything is being taken care of," Fortier said.

Hawkins found his tone condescending. He wanted specifics. He wanted an end to this. Preelection jitters were bad enough. This was too much.

The phone rang and Hawkins almost dropped his drink. It was his private line.

Fortier reached for the phone, but Hawkins snapped it up. He was tired of hearing everything second- and thirdhand. Fortier was starting to tell him only the short versions. Only what he wanted the president to know.

"Mr. President," someone from the other end said.

Hawkins looked at Bob Fortier. He was picking up the other phone in the room without asking his permission.

"Speaking."

"Mako here," the voice said.

He and Fortier looked at each other. Barnhardt and the rest of his crew were supposed to be dead. He should have been in that airplane. Hawkins knew that much.

"Are you there, Mr. President?"

"I'm here."

"I thought we had a deal."

Fortier motioned to him to stretch the conversation as he pulled out his cell to dial another number. Hawkins watched him talk into it quietly.

"Of course we did. We do. What's wrong, Ramsey?" Hawkins asked, hoping the use of the man's first name would breed confidence.

"I'm done playing games, sir. You gave us specific instructions to do a job. My crew and I accomplished that goal. Now, instead of transferring the funds to my account as we agreed in your office, you blew up the plane that was taking us home. Does that sound like someone operating in good faith to you, Mr. President? Does that sound like an appropriate reward for loyalty, sir?"

"That was an accident. You can't think that we're responsible for that. I truly appreciate your loyalty, Ramsey, your personal loyalty to me and to your country. I cannot believe that—"

"A very convenient accident," Barnhardt said sarcastically. "But I have no time to listen to any excuses or lies, so here's the deal. You'll triple the amount of the payment and the transfer has to take place by—"

"Now, wait a minute, Ramsey," Hawkins blasted, standing up. Fortier started motioning something, but Hawkins turned his back on the campaign manager. "I don't see why I have to pay for your mistakes. Your job was to hijack and sink *Hartford,* making everyone think it was the work of foreign terrorists. Instead, you left a huge mess behind that we're still trying to clean up. If anything, we should be cutting—"

Fortier's hand slammed down on the phone, disconnecting the call.

"What the hell are you doing?" Hawkins turned angrily to his man.

"We know where he is, Mr. President."

"Where?"

"New Haven. At the hospital. We'll get him."

Sixty-Five

"They expect us to go downstairs," Sarah said.

"Then we should go up," McCann suggested.

A line of patients and hospital workers were moving down the stairs in an orderly fashion. The fire alarm continued to buzz in the halls. They welcomed the alarm. It was a way to get people around them. There was safety in numbers. Bruce Dunn broke through the door near them.

"Where's Brody?" McCann asked.

"Dead," Bruce said with a sigh. "Whoever this Kilo is, he was in Brody's room. He's armed."

"I'm going back there."

Amy reached around to grab McCann's arm while Bruce blocked his path.

"You can't. He's got other help in the building," Dunn said. "You would only be making his job easier.

You must know something that you don't even realize. That's why they're after you."

"Please," Amy added quietly, tugging on his arm again. "You'll get them, but you have do it on your own terms."

"They could be coming through that door any minute. We should hurry," Sarah's urging got them going again.

Amy tightened the blanket around her shoulder and followed Sarah's path as she cut through the descending crowd. She glanced over her shoulder and was relieved to see Darius was right behind her.

"Let's get out on the next floor," Bruce suggested. "We can use a different staircase."

At the landing, Sarah led the way into the hall. They followed her. The corridor was deserted.

"Does anyone know their way around this hospital?" Bruce asked.

"I know it a little. My father was hospitalized here for a week last year," Amy offered. "What do you want to do?"

"I need to call for help," Bruce said.

"Is there anyone out there that you can trust?" Darius asked.

"Good question," Bruce said under his breath.

"I think we should get out of here first before deciding who to call," Sarah told them.

"We have no car," Darius said as he looked down the hallway.

Amy read the signs on the wall, trying to find her bearings. "I can get us to the emergency room. There's a chance someone might have left their car at the entrance with the keys in it."

"Lead the way," McCann said.

A few steps away, through the small windows of a double door, Amy saw two security guards heading their way. They were opening doors and looking inside the rooms. Fear gripped her. A spike of adrenaline rushed through her body. She was back on the submarine again. People looking for her. Trying to kill her.

"Over here." Bruce held a door open on their right. All four of them pushed into the small supply room. He turned a latch on the inside. With the door closed, total darkness surrounded them.

They waited, listening for any noise. Amy felt McCann's hand on her shoulder. She took hold of it, needing his strength.

Footsteps approached. Someone tested the door. They all stared at the sliver of light under the door. McCann pushed Amy behind him. The door was tested one more time before they moved on.

Amy searched the shelves behind her. One of the stacks felt like scrubs. She took one and after a little struggle was able to pull it up her legs. She found the top on the same shelf.

"Those two guards could have been harmless," Sarah said quietly.

"We can't be sure." McCann said.

"Only a handful of people were told about you three being brought here," Bruce informed them. "One of them must have leaked the information."

Amy was able to pull the shirt over her head, but some of the bandages caught and came loose. She tugged at them, ripping the rest off.

"What's the story with Barnhardt?" McCann asked. "Sarah said he was the one that called to warn you."

"I can't tell you. But he seems to know quite a bit about what's going on."

"Maybe he's the one we should call," Sarah suggested.

"Let's get out of here first," Bruce told them, opening the door. He looked down the hall before motioning them to follow.

"You changed," Darius said to Amy as the light poured in. "But what did you do to your head?"

Amy touched the stitches and pulled some of her hair over it. "They heal much faster exposed to the air."

"With the scrubs on, you actually look official," Sarah remarked as Amy led them through the labyrinthine hallways and down several flights into a different section of the hospital.

"Please don't let anyone pull me into a surgery."

The double doors that led to the emergency room were closed but not locked. No fire alarms were sounding in this section. Amy realized that Sarah was right—she did look official. A number of people they walked by completely dismissed her, but they definitely noticed Sarah, Bruce and McCann, dressed in their navy uniforms.

But no one stopped them, and they soon found themselves at the sliding glass doors where patients were wheeled in from ambulances.

"You wait here. I'll go outside and take a look," Bruce instructed.

"No. You wait here. I'll tell you when to come out," Amy said, going through the door before anyone could stop her.

Stepping out into the cold night, dressed only in the scrubs, she noticed that McCann was right beside her.

"I'm glad to know that I'm not the only one you don't listen to."

"No. I'm pretty even-handed when it comes to disobeying orders," she said.

An ambulance backed toward the door with its lights flashing. A police car following the ambulance parked along the curb.

"Pretend that you don't know me, will you?"

The ambulance came to a stop. Amy moved to the back door and opened it. An EMT stepped out of the ambulance and brushed past her. In seconds, he was pulling the gurney out of the back and another EMT followed, taking the head of the gurney. As it rolled out, the wheeled legs dropped into position. The patient already had an IV hooked up. There was blood all over his shirt. The two EMTs wheeled him in through the doors, and the two police officers followed them.

Amy looked over her shoulder at McCann and pointed to the police car with her head. He walked to the front of the ambulance. She took a couple of steps toward the ambulance's rear doors and saw Connelly and Dunn coming out.

Amy opened the ambulance doors. The two agents climbed in. She closed the doors and went around to the passenger side.

"That was easy," Dunn said as he got in. "Great job."

"I think you've missed your calling, Amy," Sarah said from the back as McCann steered around the police car and pulled out of the drive.

"Please don't encourage her," McCann said lightly.

Amy looked into the side-view mirror to see if anyone was following them. No one seemed to be. The fire
alarms were still blasting in other sections of the hospital. There was a crowd of people on the sidewalk and
fire trucks were pulling in by the front doors. Everyone
on the street focused their attention on what was going
on in the hospital.

"Where am I going?" McCann asked.

Bruce's cell phone rang. "Same number as the last
time. It's Barnhardt." He answered it on the second
ring.

"Yes, Captain." There was a pause. "You were correct about that. But how did you know?"

McCann made a turn and another turn. He was cir-
cling the block to give Bruce time to decide where they
should go. The hospital and attached medical school
took up about twelve blocks of downtown New Haven.

"You saw us leave?" Dunn asked, looking at Sarah.
Amy looked in the mirror again. "You want us to pick
you up?"

"It could be a trap," Sarah whispered.

"Captain Barnhardt, why don't I come and see you
alone. Maybe—"

McCann slammed on the brakes as a car pulled out of
a side street right in front of them. The passenger-side
window of the car was partially shattered and there were
holes along the side that had clearly been made by bullets. The driver stepped out, holding a cell phone to his
ear.

"Too late," McCann said under his breath.

The driver was short and squarely built. Under the
streetlight, a Yankees cap shadowed most of his face.

Amy saw him stare at the ambulance as he continued to talk into his phone.

"He says they know what Mako's driving. If we want accurate information on the hijacking, we have to take him." Bruce brought the phone down. "What do you think?"

"We can handle him," McCann answered.

Barnhardt didn't appear to have any doubts that they'd take him. He started for the passenger side, and Amy scrambled through between the seats into the back. Sarah motioned to her to sit low. She did.

Barnhardt opened the ambulance door, took a quick glance inside at all the faces and climbed in without any greeting. McCann glared at the older man, then gave him a cold nod of recognition.

"You might want to turn your cell phones off. They're using them like a homing device to track you," Barnhardt told them, following his own suggestion and turning off his phone.

Bruce and Sarah were the only ones who had cell phones on them. They both turned them off.

Darius backed up the ambulance and drove around the car Barnhardt had been driving. A moment later, they were racing down the street in the direction of New Haven's downtown. "Where to?"

"Where there are lots of people and hopefully tons of reporters with television cameras. I'd like to have a stage for my performance," Barnhardt said. He sounded ruffled.

"There was supposed to be a political rally on the green tonight," Amy said. "But that was before all the craziness happened today."

"Try it," Barnhardt told McCann. "It's worth a shot."

"You keep referring to *they*," Sarah said. "Who are you referring to, Captain?"

Barnhardt looked over his shoulder at them. "What I have to tell you will probably mean your death sentence. Are you sure you want to hear it?"

"They killed a sedated young man in his hospital bed ten minutes ago," Bruce challenged. "They were coming after Commander McCann or Ms. Russell. I'd say the death sentence has already been issued."

"You're right. In fact, the crew left behind on *Hartford* was condemned to death the moment we sailed the sub away from that pier. Ms. Russell was included in that because she was in the wrong place at the wrong time."

McCann pulled the ambulance to the side of the road next to a boarded-up mall and slammed on the brakes. All of them in the back were tossed around. Emergency apparatus and various supplies shifted and rattled. McCann lunged at Barnhardt, grabbing him by the throat and practically breaking the passenger-side window with the man's head.

"You commanded that operation," he barked. "You killed members of my crew."

The older man tried to reach for something at his belt, but McCann was faster. He took the gun and held it to Barnhardt's head, his other hand still wrapped around the old sub driver's throat.

"There's no reason to lose your temper, Commander McCann," Barnhardt rasped. "I called Commander Dunn. I climbed inside this ambulance of my own accord. I came to you to tell the absolute truth. I am voluntarily telling you everything I've done…and everything I know."

McCann's hold on the man's neck didn't ease a bit. "Nine of my crew members are dead. A billion dollar submarine is in danger of sinking to the bottom of Long Island Sound as we speak. A number of targets were hit using *Hartford*'s weapons. There are fatalities. How the hell can you say there's no reason to lose my temper?"

Barnhardt didn't flinch. He looked directly into McCann's eyes. "You're too emotional and loyal to be in this line of business, Commander. Sub drivers like us don't see people. Death has only one dimension, and that dimension doesn't touch us. We can't afford to have friends. We're given a job, and it's our responsibility to obey our overarching orders, sometimes ignoring the gutless calls of paper-pushers in a moment of crisis. We do what we have to do, no matter what the consequences."

"Under whose orders did you take *Hartford?*" McCann asked.

Barnhardt tried to look down at where McCann's hand squeezed his neck. "Commander Dunn, your friend is changing my mind about what I'd like to contribute to your investigation."

"Regardless of what Commander McCann does," Bruce told him, "you will contribute what you can, Captain Barnhardt. I believe you've been given the same death sentence and you're looking for a way to save your life."

"If my life was all that I was worried about, I'd be out of the country by now," Barnhardt said. "No. I'm looking for a way to get even. But if you don't get moving soon, none of us are going to live long enough to even any scores or solve any investigation. We're sitting ducks here, and they're going to spot us, sure as hell."

McCann let go of the man's throat and handed the gun to Bruce. The ambulance pulled back onto the road.

"Are we going to play games or are you going to start answering some of our questions?" Sarah asked.

"I want to make a deal first."

"What do you want?" Bruce asked.

"Protection."

Sarah and Bruce put their heads together for a couple of seconds, whispering to each other.

"There will have to be a guilty plea. We'll ask for a reduced sentence," Sarah told him.

"I'm not guilty. I was only following orders," Barnhardt explained.

"Following orders is not a reasonable defense," Sarah reminded him.

"I don't care what the plea is. I want a guarantee that I walk."

Bruce and Sarah spoke quietly among themselves again. Amy looked at McCann. She could see how he was struggling to stay neutral in this situation. Finally, he couldn't stay quiet.

"Following orders," McCann hissed at the man next to him. "Is that how you got the crew on *Hartford* to go along with the hijacking?"

"That's correct, Commander. The ones who helped us believe the entire operation was just an elaborate naval exercise. A terror-response drill. They were following specific orders."

"Given by you?"

"Yes. They knew me. But they knew the entire mission was also approved by someone above me."

"Who?" McCann asked.

Barnhardt looked over his shoulder at the two investigators. "Do we have a deal?"

Dunn was the one who spoke. "Whatever evidence you have better be good."

"It doesn't get any better," Barnhardt said.

"That depends on what you can offer the prosecution," Sarah told him. "It has to stand up in court."

"I have it."

Dunn nodded. "Then we have a deal."

A heavy silence fell inside the car. Barnhardt looked out the window first. They were approaching the green. There were people on the street, all walking in the same direction, some chanting, others carrying political campaign signs. Most of the signs were against the present administration. Everyone carried flashlights or glow sticks or what looked to be candles. The ambulance stopped at a stoplight, and pedestrians crossed in front of them.

"The hijacking was about this," the older man said.

Everyone's gaze turned to him.

"Politics. The election," he explained. "Today was supposed to be a shock to wake up the American voter. It was to be a sudden and stark affirmation of President Hawkins's military strengths."

The passengers were speechless. Amy looked at the protestors on the street, then back at the man sitting in the passenger seat. The country wanted Hawkins out. Staunch supporters admitted that his election had been a mistake. He'd barely gotten his own party's nomination for reelection, and even that had come with bitterness about his people's strong-arm techniques.

When it came to the internal affairs and the everyday life of Americans, nothing had been accomplished over the past four years. There was still a lack of decent health care for most of the country. Unemployment rates continued to climb. And many other important issues had been pushed aside while the president kept his focus on his bullying foreign policies. With the exception of a couple of countries who claimed to be U.S. allies, the rest of the world seemed to hate America.

It had been four painful years, but people seemed to be waking up. There'd been no doubt that Hawkins would be defeated by John Penn.

"Are you saying that the president of United States ordered this hijacking just to get reelected?" Amy asked.

"This is really nothing new. Everyone knows that during the Bush administration, they overrode the director of Homeland Security and used the terror-alert system to sway opinion polls before the election," Barnhardt told them. "Nervous voters stay the course."

"Answer the question, Captain," Sarah demanded. "Was the president of the United States involved in this?"

Barnhardt turned around and looked at her. "Yes."

"Can you prove it?" Bruce asked.

Amy saw the black SUV that pulled to their right. "I think you should drive," she urged McCann.

He pressed his foot on the gas.

"I left you a present. See what you can do with it," Barnhardt said before the passenger window exploded, spattering McCann with the captain's blood.

Sixty-Six

"He's dead," Bruce announced after reaching over the seat to check for Barnhardt's pulse.

Glancing at the body slumped over the center console, McCann had no doubt. Turning on the siren and lights, he gunned the ambulance along Church Street, swerving between cars. Checking the side-view mirror, he could see the black SUV was right on his tail.

"Check his pockets. He must have something on him. What did he mean by leaving you a present?"

"Whether he was lying or telling the truth," Sarah said from the back, "everything he told us is worthless without proof. There's no way we can repeat any of this to Admiral Meisner without having him hand our heads back to us."

"Can you trust this Admiral Meisner?" Amy asked.

Neither of the two working for the admiral answered the question.

Nearing the end of the city green, the SUV pulled beside them. Jerking the wheel of the ambulance to the right, McCann buffeted the car onto the far right lane and then cranked the wheel to the left, his vehicle bouncing up onto the sidewalk in front of the courthouse before racing along the north side of the green.

Thankfully, most of the foot traffic for the demonstration was in the center of the green. The only things McCann hit were a couple of newspaper boxes, a sign or two and a mailbox.

Bruce pulled a few things out of the dead man's pockets. "Wallet, cell phone, pocket knife, house keys. Damn it! There's nothing."

McCann took another look in the side mirror. Two cars were chasing after them now. Both unmarked SUVs. Very much government-type, he thought. A police car followed them.

"We can't get away from them in this thing," McCann warned them. "And it's only a matter of minutes before the hospital reports the ambulance stolen. Then every police car in the state will be after us, too."

"Remember what Barnhardt said about reporters and cameras?" Amy asked.

McCann spotted a Channel 8 News van in the center of the crowd.

"Police, reporters, cameras," he repeated. "I wonder how they're going to explain this chase to them."

As McCann cranked the wheel again to the left, the ambulance jerked up onto the sidewalk. McCann floored it across the green with his siren blaring.

"What are you going to do?" Sarah asked.

"You two better call someone you trust. You've got one minute," he ordered.

McCann steered around groups of pedestrians toward the parked news van. Behind them, the black SUVs were making their way more cautiously across the green.

Church Street was ahead, and on the far side, the steps of the newly renovated city hall were brightly lit.

"Hold on," he told them as the ambulance crashed through the wrought-iron fence bordering the green, tearing across the wide sidewalk.

McCann drove straight into traffic, narrowly missing cars coming from the right before smashing into two police cars that sat in a line of squad cars at the curb.

Cops came running from everywhere, swarming around the ambulance in seconds.

Bruce turned on his cell phone and started to make a call.

Sixty-Seven

Newport, Rhode Island
11:00 p.m.

John Penn threw his reading glasses on the desk and ran a tired hand down his face. "I'm done, boys."

"Five more minutes. Let me check out this last one," McCarthy pleaded, taking a fax from Greg and perusing the page.

John knew it wouldn't be five minutes. They were waiting for the results of the latest poll they were running, based on the unsubstantiated report that the plane crash in Branford, Connecticut, had *Hartford* hijackers on board.

This fax was from Oregon. Then they had to wait for Washington State. Then it'd be the big one, California. And it didn't matter that they thought they had California wrapped up last week.

The inner circle of staff members—and John—had stayed up to make sure the phone surveys matched their expectations. If they didn't, McCarthy wouldn't stop whining until John would agree to some last-minute television or radio interview.

So much for not campaigning today.

The phone rang. John looked at the display and recognized the number. It was the public line to his office. At this time on any other night, the answering machine would greet the caller. But tonight, one of the weary campaign aides answered the call.

John heard the young woman start her standard screening questions, but she quickly turned to him.

"It's for you, Senator," she told him, mouthing that it was important.

John considered letting either Moore or McCarthy handle the call. Whoever was on the phone couldn't be a family member or a member of any of the Senate committees. They would have called on his private line. But he changed his mind and decided to take it.

"Senator Penn." The voice was sharp, and John could hear sirens and shouting in the background.

"Speaking."

"Sir, this is Commander Bruce Dunn, one of the two naval intelligence officers put in charge of the investigation of the *Hartford* hijacking this morning. My colleague and I report to Admiral Meisner."

Penn knew Meisner and his job at the Pentagon. "What can I do for you, Commander?"

"Sir, we're presently getting picked up by the New Haven, Connecticut, police for questioning. In my company is the other investigator in charge of this case, Lieutenant Connelly, and the only two survivors from

Hartford, Commander McCann and the Electric Boat ship superintendent, Amy Russell."

Penn didn't know the two had survived. None of this had been released to the public.

"We also have with us the dead body of the individual who claimed responsibility for spearheading the hijacking. His name was Captain Ramsey Barnhardt."

Penn's mind reeled with all the information. He'd met Barnhardt, heard him speak at a number of Senate hearings a few years back. An arrogant bastard, but well qualified.

"Captain Barnhardt took responsibility for the hijacking?"

"Yes, sir."

"Why are you calling me, Commander, and not Admiral Meisner?"

"Because prior to being shot by those who've been pursuing us, sir, Captain Ramsey accused the president of the United States of being the one who ordered the hijacking."

"Shit." Penn wasn't aware that he'd sworn aloud. Everyone in the room was staring at him.

"Sir, at this point we don't know who's involved in the conspiracy. You're the only person we're contacting for assistance."

"Of course. Of course." Penn started pacing, motioning for his staff to stop what they were doing. "Are you in any present danger, Commander Dunn?"

"We've been requested to go to the New Haven Police Station for questioning. We're certain, however, that our pursuers are no farther away than the crowd's edge." Dunn paused. "Sorry, sir, they're telling me to cut the call and get in the car."

"That's a good idea, Commander. Stay safe. I'll take care of things from this end."

Penn hadn't even hung up before his shouts rang into the room. "Gibbs, I need a helicopter to take me to New Haven. And I want it escorted by military choppers." He whirled on the other aides. "We have to make some calls, and I don't care what time it is. Wake them up if you have to, but get all these people on the phone. Tell them it's a matter of national security, of life and death. I want calls to the vice president, the Speaker of the House, both Senate leaders, the secretary of state, secretary of defense, the attorney general—"

"What's this about?" McCarthy interrupted him.

"I was just told that Will Hawkins has committed the most reprehensible act that a sitting president could ever do. He ordered an act that has put more than ten million Americans' lives in danger."

"That's great," McCarthy replied. "I'll put a press conference together right away."

"Cut the crap, Anthony," Penn snapped. "All of that has to wait. We have to take care of this country and its people first."

"I have the vice president on line, Senator," one of the aides called from the other end of the room.

"Why are you calling so many of them?" McCarthy asked.

"Because one or two might be in on this. But all of them?" he shook his head. "My long-held faith in the system of checks and balances has just been reaffirmed."

Penn pressed the blinking light and picked up the phone. "Mr. Vice President. Before I give you a run-down of the disaster we have on our hands, you should know that this same phone call is being made to the attorney general and every member of the president's cabinet."

Sixty-Eight

New Haven, Connecticut
11:15 p.m.

Two police cruisers took them to the station. Another ambulance had arrived before they left the scene, and the two EMTs declared the fifth passenger dead.

Amy and McCann were in the first cruiser, and Sarah and Bruce followed in the second. All of them, with the exception of Amy, who was dressed in borrowed scrubs, had shown identification. But they'd refused to make a statement, insisting on being taken to the station. The shattered window of the ambulance made it clear that Barnhardt had been shot, but there were still many questions about the stolen vehicle, why they'd been driving in excess of eighty miles per hour around New Haven green, and who the gun that Bruce had belonged to.

Sarah was glad their identification had carried some clout, since they hadn't been searched or handcuffed. They were just asked to ride in the back seat.

The police cars struggled to cut through the crowds of curiosity seekers who'd forgotten their rally. As they crawled past, Sarah was blinded by the lights of the camera crews of the news station filming footage of the escapade.

"How far away do you think it is to the police station?" she asked Bruce as the officer driving their car blasted the siren intermittently to encourage people to step back.

"I don't know, but I doubt Kilo and his crew would be stupid enough to try to stop us before we get there," Bruce told her.

Sarah looked over her shoulder. People were closing the gap as the police car moved along. She couldn't see the SUVs that had been in pursuit of them earlier.

"Do you think we might have jumped the gun?" she asked quietly. The police car turned right and picked up speed.

"About Barnhardt's claim?"

She nodded. "What happens if we don't find anything? Or if there's no evidence as he promised?"

"Unless we're just part of an elaborate setup, which I don't think is likely, there has to be a money trail."

"True, but I would bet my life that it doesn't reach the president," Sarah said.

"That's true," Bruce admitted. "But we had no choice. Even on the surface, Penn is the only one who wouldn't benefit from this hijacking. But I can't honestly say who in the administration would go along with something this crazy."

"If we're wrong, then we're taking Senator Penn's career down with us," Sarah said.

Bruce sighed. "But I tend to believe Barnhardt was

telling the truth. Why else did they send those goons to kill him?"

Sarah looked out the window. The crowd was much larger now than it had been when McCann had been racing around in the ambulance. She wondered how it was that the rally could bring out so many after such a chaotic day. Perhaps it was exactly because of that. People wanted to be part of history.

Bruce broke into her thoughts. "Meisner is the only one who has me concerned. He should have been our first call, but in a situation like this, I have no take on him."

"He had ulterior motives for choosing me for this case," Sarah said. "He assumed I'd muddle the investigation. That doesn't inspire confidence."

"The same goes for choosing me."

"Why?"

"I asked to work with you. Maybe he figured I'd be so blinded by your charm and beauty that I'd forget what I was doing."

"Come on."

"Well, that's partly true."

"Were you blinded, Commander?"

"Of course," he deadpanned. "If I'd paid attention to what the heck I was doing, this case would have been wrapped up before lunchtime."

She smiled, shaking her head. "You sure know how to pick your moments, don't you?"

Bruce's phone beeped. He had a voice message. Sarah decided to turn on her cell phone, too, just in case Senator Penn wanted to contact them. She checked the display. She had three voice mails.

The police officer who was driving the car looked

in the rearview mirror at her. "Officer, is it okay to check my messages? They could be important."

The young man gave a halfhearted nod. He looked as if he didn't know whether to treat them as criminals or to salute them.

Bruce didn't bother to ask. He was already listening to his messages.

"First one, Meisner," he told her. "The hospital called him about Brody. He doesn't know where we are or what the hell is going on."

Sarah dialed her own voice mail. An identical message was left by the admiral on her phone, as well. She saw Bruce sit forward, adjusting the phone to his ear.

"I have a forwarded message from Barnhardt. It's also distributed to you, too."

She still had her phone on. The message Bruce was talking about started.

"Here's something for your investigations, Commander Dunn, Lieutenant Connelly."

Several clicks followed, and then the sound of a number being punched in. When the voices came on, Sarah realized she was listening to a taped conversation between the president and Barnhardt. The ability to record calls on cell phones had been available on some high-end models for some time, but privacy advocates had been trying to prevent them from being sold in the United States. Obviously, Barnhardt wasn't worried about something so irrelevant to him.

She listened to the conversation, hearing the president's voice as he implicated himself in the hijacking. Bruce and Sarah looked at each other when the conversation cut short.

"Everything is here," he said quietly as he glanced at the cop behind the wheel. "Barnhardt was Mako and the other guy spells out his involvement."

"Yes, but this won't stand up in court,'" Sarah challenged.

"Maybe it will and maybe it won't," he admitted. "But it will definitely start the ball rolling for impeachment."

She lowered her voice. "The election is tomorrow. A voluntary resignation might be the fastest way to get him out of the office."

"You'd let him walk after all this?" he asked.

"We'd be taking away his power." She shrugged. "But who knows, maybe the money trail will lead to him, anyway. Or perhaps we can find the man they call Kilo. He seems to be getting his orders right from the top. There's nothing like first-person testimony."

"That's assuming they let him…or any of us…live."

Sixty-Nine

New Haven, Connecticut
11:25 p.m.

"Thanks for the offer, but I really don't want anything to eat or drink," Amy told the female officer who had her sit and wait by one of the desks. Suddenly, she was so exhausted that she could hardly think straight. "I do need to use the phone, though."

"Sorry, ma'am, but I can only let you use it when I get the okay."

Amy tried to be patient, but she couldn't, not after all she'd been through today. She wanted to call home and see if Kaitlyn and Zack were all right. She didn't know who was looking after them. Back at the hospital, when she'd first introduced herself, Lieutenant Connelly had said that they were being cared for. But that was it. No more information.

At this hour, with the rally going after what had to be a law-enforcement day from hell, the police station was practically deserted. Darius, Sarah and Bruce were in one of the offices speaking to whoever was in charge. Everyone figured that Amy had nothing to do with anything.

Then why wouldn't they let her call her family?

She leaned forward, cradling her head in her hands. Somewhere along the way, she'd forgotten about the headache, but it was back, pounding away with a vengeance.

"I'm making a fresh pot of coffee. If you change your mind, let me know," the officer said, disappearing inside of what looked to be an employee lounge at the far end of the room.

Amy sat back in the chair, quite aware that she was the only person in the large open area, surrounded by clusters of desks and chairs. There were extra computer terminals on desks in the center of the room. The door to the office where Darius and the others had entered was closed. She heard a noise from the hall. It sounded like someone falling down.

Or maybe…someone getting shot.

Seventy

"**I** don't care how we do it, but we have to cut our losses," Hawkins bellowed at Bob Fortier.

"You're overreacting, Mr. President. This has to be a bluff. Let it ride. We must stay on course."

"Five phone calls isn't a bluff, you idiot." Hawkins held up his spread hand so the other man could count his fingers. "Five of my cabinet members have called me in the past ten minutes wondering what the hell is going on. And if I am really tied to the hijacking in some way. The attorney general hasn't, yet. But I know what the fuck he's doing. He's getting a warrant for my arrest."

"Mr. President." Fortier put both hands up in his patronizing style that was really starting to get under Hawkins's skin. "I think you and everyone else should just relax and get some sleep. There is nothing that can be traced back to you. An investigation like this takes months to conduct. And there are all kinds of legal loopholes. Meanwhile, tomorrow is the election. A lot of people have invested in you, all the way down the ladder to the local level."

Hawkins barked at him. "You're not hearing me. I don't give a fuck about local or party politics."

"No one—not John Penn or anyone else—can touch you. If this hits the news, we just laugh it off. Call it a slanderous hoax being foisted off on the public by an opponent desperate to win. They can't prove anything. You're going to be reelected, Mr. President, and then you're—"

"Are you fucking deaf?" Hawkins shouted. "Right now, I don't care about being reelected. I only care about one thing, and that is keeping my ass out of the fire. Understood?"

Wisely, Fortier didn't argue.

"We have to turn this thing around *tonight,* so that *we* are the good guys," Hawkins told him. "Blowing up the plane with the hijackers was a positive move. Killing that lunatic, Barnhardt, was another step in the right direction. Now we have to stop that maniac Kilo before he totally gets out of control."

"I agree that Nick Harmon can become somewhat overzealous at times. That's why he should always be kept on a short leash—the way Captain Barnhardt used him. Specific orders, short duration of time," Fortier explained.

"Then reel him in. I don't want him to burn down that whole damn city because of a couple of people who can't hurt us."

"I tried to do that. But he's, well, unavailable."

"What do you mean, *unavailable?*" Hawkins roared.

"Our men said Kilo is already inside the police station."

Seventy-One

Kilo tucked his pistol in his jacket and stepped over the dead body of the policeman. Down the hall, he could see the open space of an office area. His NCIS badge had once again helped him to gain clearance past the front entrance. The unsuspecting dispatcher had been completely unaware that he'd just sealed his own death warrant.

Several desks filled the large space, but no one seemed to be around. Kilo looked at the three closed doors along the right wall. He wondered which one of those offices his prey were hiding in. As he moved into the room, a noise to his left drew his attention. Beyond a partially open door, he could hear water running. He drew his weapon and silently approached.

A counter with cabinets, a couple of coffeepots. A kitchen table with chairs. With each step, he saw a little more of the employee lounge area. The water in the sink was running, but no one was standing by it.

He shoved the door all the way open. It banged against the wall and bounced back. He looked in. No one was there. He backed out quickly.

"NHPD," a woman's voice called out behind him. "Drop your weapon and put your hands behind your head. *Now!*"

He started to turn around.

"Drop your weapon *now!*" the woman shouted.

He heard a door open across the room. He looked over his shoulder and saw a plainclothes cop rush into the room with his weapon drawn. McCann was right beside him. And there was the EB bitch that had given him so much grief all day.

Kilo looked back at the female cop. She didn't want to shoot. He knew he could take both cops out before she even got off one round. He glanced at McCann. No threat there, either.

They'd already wasted too much time. He had to finish the job.

He spun and lifted his pistol with a speed that he knew was unmatched by anything these greenhorns ever faced. A gun fired. Kilo thought it was his, but suddenly he couldn't find enough strength to fire a second shot. His pistol dropped to the floor. A second shot fired.

That one wasn't his, either, he thought with surprise as the floor rose up to meet him.

Seventy-Two

Stonington, Connecticut
One month later,
Friday 8:10 a.m.

"The school bus will be here in fifteen minutes," Amy warned her rambunctious children.

This morning, Kaitlyn couldn't seem to decide between the white sneakers or the blue clogs.

Zack had been in the bathroom for more than five minutes, which meant there'd be some kind of disaster waiting for Amy in there. Yesterday, he'd created a mummy out of her bathroom magazine basket with toilet paper. The day before that, he'd poured an entire bottle of bath bubbles into the toilet. She didn't want to guess what would be waiting for her today.

As Amy finished packing the two lunches and put them in their school bags, she found herself thankful, as always, for the noise and the mess and the bickering. She also found herself dwelling on changes that were in store for them.

After the hijacking, she'd taken a week off. Upon going back to EB the following week, however, Amy had realized that she couldn't do it. She was ready for change. New hours. A different job. Something. She had to get out of the shipyard and away from the reminders of what she'd gone through.

These feelings were helped along by the fact that it was inevitable for another wave of layoffs to take place. The security problems associated with the *Hartford* hijacking was a smear on the shipyard's reputation that wouldn't be erased too easily. She was planning on putting a new résumé together next week.

Amy's gaze drifted for a second to the folded newspaper sitting on the counter. Darius smiled back at her from his photo in the Accent page, and she felt the now-familiar tug on her heart. Darius McCann's handsome face was worthy of a thousand articles, and he was a story that never got old. America loved its heroes, and he'd become even bigger news than John Penn's narrow defeat of Hawkins in the presidential election.

As far as the press and the public knew, the hijacking had been the work of a group of home-grown terrorists, although the details were still sketchy. Barnhardt's name had reached the press, but not the others. The rest of the culprits had died in the plane crash. The tabloid press was still fuming daily at the secrecy with which the "ongoing investigation" was being handled.

Interestingly enough, since the recovery of the submarine, there had not been one whisper about any possible involvement on the part of William Hawkins or anyone else in his administration.

Sarah Connelly had called Amy the week following the ordeal. With the election turning out as it had, she'd told Amy that there probably wouldn't be any immediate action to remove the president, but that the vice president would be assuming most of his duties, without fanfare, for the final days of the term. Still, she and Bruce were working with an elite group at the Justice Department to build the criminal case against the president, his campaign manager and a handful of their helpers and financial backers. Admiral Meisner had not been implicated, Sarah told her.

Criminal charges would be brought against Hawkins and the others once he left office in January. Of course, there was always the chance that John Penn would sign a pardon for his former rival, but Sarah doubted that would happen. Knowing what she knew, Amy couldn't help but agree.

Meanwhile, stories had leaked to the press about Commander Darius McCann's bravery. He'd granted very few interviews. He'd made a point of flying to Florida to visit his parents and make sure his mother was recovering well, but he had yet to show up on *Oprah* or *Good Morning America* or any of the other talk shows. The navy wanted to show him off, but he wasn't ready to step into the limelight.

Amy had also been approached by reporters wanting her to talk about her experience, but she'd refused all of them—even the movie people. She wanted no reminders and no attention. She wanted to forget that she had ever been there. Besides, she had someone much better than Tom Cruise in her life.

Due to the investigations, Darius had been needed in Washington while Amy and the kids were in Connecticut. But for the past month, he'd come every Saturday and Sunday to visit. There was something very right about the time they all spent together. The twins had accepted him right away. He was fun, and he showed genuine interest in them, in their activities, their interests, and in Amy.

At the same time, she continued to have the nagging fear that he'd soon realize she was no fun. She and the kids were a package deal. There had been no crazy weekends with just the two of them. Their romance had to wait until the twins were tucked in bed. And even after that, she couldn't let him stay the night.

Still, the sex was...

Amy let out a shaky sigh, wishing it was already Saturday. Then again, in spite of what he'd said, there was no guarantee that he'd even come this weekend.

"I want to wear the clogs, but I don't have any blue socks."

Kaitlyn's voice from the doorway drew Amy's attention back to reality. She fought back a moment of guilt at allowing herself to daydream like this, but she couldn't help but feel the heat on her face. She looked at the clock.

"Five minutes till the bus," she said, hurriedly zipping up the lunch bags. "Honey, you don't wear blue socks with blue shoes. White socks will look better." She knocked on the bathroom door. "Zack, did you fall in?"

"But I want to try blue socks."

"You don't have blue socks. Why don't you wear

white ones today, and I'll buy you blue socks over the weekend." She turned in the direction of the bathroom again. "Zack, it's time to go."

Kaitlyn disappeared inside her bedroom. Amy glanced at the kitchen and all the dirty dishes and cringed. She'd made chocolate-chip pancakes for breakfast.

She caught a glimpse of her daughter passing by the doorway. Kaitlyn was undressing. Amy rushed to the bedroom.

"Honey, what are you doing?"

"I'm changing my clothes."

"Why?"

"'Cuz I've decided to wear my black boots."

"Your black boots will go perfectly with the blue sweater and checkered skirt you have on."

Kaitlyn crinkled her nose as she looked at herself in the mirror. "No, it doesn't look good." She continued to undress.

The bathroom door opened at that moment and Zack stepped out. Amy gasped.

"How do you like my hair?"

Zack had rubbed about a quart of mousse into his hair. He had it spiked up with the ends standing three inches from his scalp.

"Do you like it?" he asked again.

Amy cracked up. The whole situation was just too ridiculous. Over this past month, she'd lost her rhythm. They all had. But she'd certainly lightened up in general, and Amy didn't think that was such a bad thing.

"I like it, but you might have used just a tad too much hair mousse."

He stepped back in the bathroom, looking in the mirror again. "I think you're right, Mommy. Maybe I could fix it."

"Just don't get close to any open flames, Zack."

There was a knock on the apartment door. She figured it had to be Barbara. Perhaps the older woman had forgotten something. Amy rushed to the door and opened it.

Darius was standing in the hallway.

"Crap." Her heart slammed in her chest, then she slammed the door.

She'd come home at the end of her shift at six-thirty this morning and hadn't bothered to take a shower or even look at herself in the mirror. Amy looked down at her bare feet and the old pair of jeans and T-shirt she was wearing.

Another knock. She opened the door.

"What did you say?"

"I said...uh, *glad*. I'm glad to see you." She wrinkled her nose and went into his arms. He kissed her deeply. She ended it as she gestured for him to go inside the apartment with a toss of her head. "The beasties are getting ready for school."

He looked amused. He also looked damn good in his khakis and a black sweater. He smelled good, too, she decided, breathing in his spicy cologne. His hair was still wet, and he had a close shave.

She kissed his neck, but she had to stop herself before she got carried away. "What are you doing here? We weren't expecting you until tomorrow."

"I think Zack and Kaitlyn missed the school bus." He pointed to the street.

"Shoot." She looked at her watch. "Yes, they did. We've been having a little trouble this morning. Zack? Kaitlyn?" She started to walk toward the bedrooms. Darius followed her in.

She peered into the living room. It was reasonably neat. On weekends, she tried to present the best of them to him, but Amy guessed a small dose of family reality wasn't a bad thing. And this wasn't too bad.

She knocked on the bathroom door again.

"Zack, you can't stay in there all day."

She had to change, too. Look in the mirror, at least. Do something to tame her wild hair.

Amy turned around. "I have to drive them to school." Darius was right behind her.

"Can I drive the three of you? Then maybe you'll let me take you out for breakfast."

The twins must have heard his voice because they both tumbled out to greet him. Feeling a rush of emotion, Amy took the chance to escape to her bedroom to hide it. It was terrifying how much he already meant to them. And to her.

She almost died at the sight of her reflection in the mirror. Her hair was flattened in places from the hard hat, while the rest of the curls stood out in every which way. Zack's hair looked normal compared to hers. She had pancake batter on her shirt. Her face was pale from working third shift and not getting enough sleep. She looked at the clock. There wasn't enough time to take a shower.

Amy grabbed a sweater out of her closet and pulled it over her head. She tried tying her hair back with a scrunchy, but the curls wouldn't be contained. She gave up that struggle, put on some lipstick, grabbed a pair of socks and walked out.

Kaitlyn had a clog on one foot and a black boot on the other, and she was asking Darius's opinion as to which looked better. He was standing and looking very seriously at the little girl.

Kaitlyn beamed up at seeing her mother. "Darius says the white socks and the blue clogs look good."

"That's 'Commander McCann' to you," Amy corrected. "And I think I told you the same thing, thank you."

"White socks it is, then." The seven-year-old smiled at Darius before going into her bedroom.

Amy turned to face Darius. "Where's Zack?"

"Back in the bathroom." He smiled.

"I'm sorry. You haven't seen us like this. This isn't really the norm. It's just that I got out of work a little early and tried to do a bit too much in the breakfast department this morning, and I think they're already on a sugar high with the chocolate-chip pancakes I fed them and—"

He leaned down and kissed her. It was just a gentle brush of the lips, but Amy felt a delicious twist of desire in her middle. She could have just melted against him, but her gaze shifted to the clock on the wall.

"Zack! You have to get out of there *now*."

The mother's voice worked. The bathroom door immediately opened and the boy stepped out. He'd brushed his hair straight down, and it now had formed itself around his small face like a helmet.

"What do you think?" he asked Darius, who discreetly cocked an eyebrow.

"You're getting a haircut this afternoon," Amy warned.

He started heading back into the bathroom, but Amy got there first. With a wet hand towel and some serious bribing, she had him fireproofed and ready for school in two minutes.

Zack, though, was too excited to tell Darius about the latest his friends were saying about WarioWare.

Another five minutes and she had everyone out of the apartment. The twins went down the stairs ahead of them, bickering the entire time.

"Are you sure you don't mind driving?" she asked again.

"I've been insisting on it," he reminded her, his hand lingering around her waist.

Amy felt a rush of sensations, already thinking that after dropping the twins off, they could go back to her apartment. Six hours. They'd have six hours to do whatever they wanted. She looked at Darius, and their eyes locked for a moment. Then Kaitlyn pushed the outside door open, and Amy welcomed the blast of cold air against her flushed skin.

"By the way, how did you get in the building?"

"Barbara let me in. She was going out when I was coming in."

They walked toward the parking lot and to his black Volvo sedan.

"Is Darius staying for dinner?" Kaitlyn asked in what was meant to be a hushed voice.

Amy looked at him and was thrilled to see the nod. "Yes, Commander McCann will stay for dinner."

"Can Darius sleep over?" Zack asked much less tactfully.

"We're not talking about this now."

The twins climbed in, but Amy saw Darius's face over the roof of the car. He was mouthing *Please*.

She was in serious trouble.

The elementary school was only five minutes away. Darius stayed in the car while Amy walked her children in.

"I'm so glad he came early," Zack announced when they were away from the car.

"Me, too," Kaitlyn said, turning around and giving another wave to Darius.

"I'm more glad," Zack insisted.

Thankfully, Kaitlyn wasn't feeling up to the challenge.

"But he's in the navy…like Daddy, isn't he?" the little girl asked.

"Yes, he is," Amy replied as they crossed the sidewalk.

"Does that mean he'll have to go away for a long, long time, like Daddy?"

The three of them had reached the main entrance to the school. The twins looked up at her expectantly. She wished she could answer them.

"I don't know, honey, but I'll find out."

They both gave her a hug, and she watched them enter the school. Their last words weighed heavy on her heart. Could she do this to them again?

Who was she fooling? Darius probably wasn't looking for a long-term relationship. She wasn't sure that she and her family even knew how to take a road halfway.

A bittersweet feeling dogged Amy as she made her way back to the car.

"Everything okay?" he asked when she got in.

Amy stared straight ahead. This was as good a time as any to do it. She could force herself to forget what they had between them. She had to.

"We need to talk," she said quietly.

"I agree," he answered. "Your apartment?"

"No." She shook her head. "Not your house, either. Someplace where we can *only* talk."

Darius nodded and drove out of the school parking lot. Neither said anything more until he pulled into the empty lot of a strip mall a couple of miles down the road. He parked by the edge of some trees.

"Amy?" he touched her cheek.

She turned to tell him the truth, but his mouth was right there. Before she knew it, she was kissing him. Then she broke off the kiss.

"I can't," she blurted out.

His fingers threaded into her hair, and he had to give the slightest nudge of his mouth against hers before she was back at it again, taking and giving, kissing him until she felt scorched by the heat between them.

The next time she pulled away, she immediately opened the car door and got out. The cold morning air slapped her with reality.

He got out of the car, too. She closed the door and leaned against it as he came around.

"What's wrong?" he said softly, wrapping an arm around her shoulder.

She couldn't step away from his touch. "We're wrong."

"Why?"

"Because you're sweeping me off my feet and I'm

not used to it. Because I can't resist you, don't want to resist you, but I know it'll be a mistake."

He kissed her temple. "We're not a mistake."

"Okay, we're not a mistake."

"That's better." He brushed a kiss across her lips.

She had to talk fast before she lost her courage. "But I'm trouble. You're the first man I've slept with since my divorce."

"That's a bad thing?" he asked with a smile.

She shook her head. "No, but listen to me. My life is my children. We're a package deal. But I know that when I fall for someone, I'm ready to jump in with both feet or not at all. There are no overnight stays. No halfway. And that scares the hell out of men."

He kept her in the circle of his arms. "It's not working. I found that out on my own the first weekend up. I'm not scared. You'd better come up with something better than that."

"Okay, then try this. Your job sucks, and so does mine. But I'm doing something about mine. Yours is worse. You're here today, gone tomorrow. You already know my first husband was in the navy. I don't do too well with part-time arrangements. My kids don't do well with it. I don't want to go through that again."

Darius's arms brought her closer. "That's not working, either."

"How can you say that?" she asked. "This is not a scare tactic. This is reality. I'm telling you what I can and can't live with."

"You're saying we can't be together because you can't live with my job."

"You got it. It's out. Now, go."

His arms tightened around her instead. "I'm changing my job."

"What do you mean you're changing your job?"

"I'm leaving the sub service," he told her. "Giving up my command."

Amy was speechless. "Is it because of the hijacking?"

He shrugged. "I've been thinking about it for a while. My part in the investigation should be wrapped up by the New Year. I have a standing offer to teach at the Naval War College in Newport. Permanent. That's only an hour away from here. I guess I've been waiting for the right moment. Or maybe I wanted to see a snapshot of what my life would be like if I were to do it."

"Do you have that snapshot?"

He smiled. "You brought it into clear focus for me this past month."

"I did?"

"You and your children," he repeated. "I love you, Amy. And anybody would love them."

Tears welled in her eyes, and her heart pounded as the significance of what he was telling her sank in.

"Even with all the mess and noise?" she finally got out.

"Even that." He smiled. "They're great kids."

"They love you, too."

"And how about their mother?"

Amy's hands inched up his chest. "She's crazy about you, Commander McCann. Absolutely nuts. She loves you very much—"

He pulled her closer to his chest. "Will you marry me, Amy?"

Once again, she was speechless. Looking up into his handsome face, she saw the love, the affection. "Are you sure you want this?"

"I've never wanted anything more in my life. So what do you say, Amy?"

"I say yes."

Their mouths sealed the promise. They kissed each other in the parking lot under the December sky, oblivious to the world until the horn of a car passing by brought them back to reality.

"Get a room!" the driver shouted out his window.

Amy smiled up at Darius. "Now, that's an order I can live with."

Author's Note

Thank you for allowing us to take you on this undersea journey. We hope it was a suspenseful ride.

Between the two of us, we have nearly fifteen years of experience building nuclear submarines, working at Electric Boat in Groton and Quonset Point in Rhode Island. Because of that background, writing this book wasn't entirely a product of our imaginations. At the same time, we had to take a few liberties with minor details of the submarine to make the story come together. But for the most part, the action and capabilities of the vessel are accurate.

We'd also like to thank the brave men of the United States Navy and the Submarine Force, as well as the men and women who continue to build these powerful and sophisticated machines at the Electric Boat and Newport News Shipyards. We'd also like to send our best wishes to all those skilled workers who have lost their jobs due to the various cuts in defense budgets over the past few years.

We live in a different world today, a world where diplomacy can hopefully be used more effectively than our most dangerous weapons of war. With any luck, our world leaders will rise to the rapidly changing challenges that face us in this new millennium.

Wishing you peace and health!

We love hearing from you:

Jan Coffey
c/o Nikoo & Jim McGoldrick
P.O. Box 665
Watertown, CT 06795
or
McGoldMay@aol.com
www.JanCoffey.com